AN IRISH VOLUNTEER

I can't keep you from yourself
You'll do what you will do,

AN IRISH VOLUNTEER

JULIET CARDINAL

Cover and Interior Design: Cyrus Wraith Walker
Cover Art: Jason Van Brumwell

ISBN: 978-0-9861170-0-8

Published in the United States by:
Salthill Press
PO Box 15097
Portland, OR 97293
salthillpress.com

To my grandparents,
Avis and Kenneth Nichols

Introduction

Tribe after tribe, the Celts arrived like waves. One generation after another ventured across the water to conquer and claim a portion of this land at the end of the world. In battle they were savage but incredibly skilled. The Celts were notorious throughout Europe and beyond, even terrorizing the indomitable Roman Empire for decades. Emerging from the darker side of Europe, they had long ago proven themselves to be an unpredictable and recurring nightmare to the confident, settled people of the Mediterranean.

The tribes spread north. The last and greatest of all of the Celts to come over the water from Europe were the Gaels, who made Ireland their own for hundreds of years, a claim virtually undisputed.

While not seriously challenged from the outside, warfare between the many Celtic chieftains raged on—a normal part of life for a people so accustomed to battle. The little island at the end of the world was divided into dozens of tribal kingdoms with boundaries that ebbed and flowed as fierce warrior clans alternately invaded and defended them. One great chieftain at a time was declared the High King of all of Ireland in ceremonies on the Hill of Tara on the east side of the island.

The Celts had many deities who lent assistance with the harvests and provided comfort and safety in the home. But the greatest gods of this land were fearsome and capricious warriors who could shape-shift and enter into frenzied, ecstatic fighting states that caused epic carnage. These beings were generally magnificent but also imperfect and almost human at times, according to the legends. They seduced and deceived. They coveted and raged. They tore down the communities of their foes and rebuilt their own atop the tattered foundations of the past.

People performed numerous sacrifices and ceremonies in order to appease the erratic will of their volatile gods, who were powerful but often unkind. These mighty deities would have served as an inspiration to the conqueror and the warrior but could not have inspired a sense of well-being in the vulnerable. While the priestess and druid might find comfort in their own esoteric knowledge of higher truths, for many ordinary citizens, it only made sense to place their faith in the biggest and most skilled of heroes, who protected their community and who most resembled their greatest gods.

The Celts were also prolific pirates and slave traders who cruised the surrounding coasts in search of vulnerable prey. Across the water in Roman Briton, between the rivers Clyde and Severn, lived a sixteen-year-old boy. He was captured by these Irish raiders, brought across the water with thousands of other prisoners, and forced into slavery around the year 400. He roamed the countryside alone, herding his captor's sheep. Having no one else to speak with, this teenager spoke to the god of his faraway home all day long and through the cold, hungry nights. His god was kind, and his prayers brought him comfort.

After several years the boy escaped, finally making his way back to Briton and joining his family, who begged him to never leave again. But over time, Patrick began to miss the wild land where he had been a slave for so many years. He felt drawn to go back to help the poor and oppressed. He wanted to inspire leaders to be more generous and kind, and to give up their slaves.

He became a priest and returned to Ireland, becoming loved and revered in the land in which he was formerly held captive. Saint Patrick baptized thousands and founded numerous churches, convents, and monasteries. Like the god of his prayers, he was kind and championed the downtrodden.

Isolated from the Roman Catholic Church, the Irish developed a faith that valued kindness and knowledge over power or the fierce eradication of sin at all costs. The Irish faith was a little wilder, warmer, and closer to the earth. Women were allowed to run churches. Confessions were given in private to a trusted spiritual leader instead of declared in public, as they were in Rome at the time.

Instead of rejecting the old ways, the Irish monks embraced and preserved the stories, legends, and ways of the pagans and their gods. They spent much of their days preserving culture and knowledge by teaching villagers and copying books by hand. They copied Christian, pagan, and secular books. They wrote out the stories of legend and history, known formerly only through oral tradition. Vast libraries were developed and schools were built.

During this time Rome's power began to wane. As the influence of the barbarian Germanic tribes spread and grew, Europe sank into the Dark Ages, and all over the former empire, much that had been written down was burned and forgotten. The world's Classical culture descended into shadow and ash.

A world away and almost totally isolated from all of this darkness and destruction, the Irish monks continued to teach, study, and gather and preserve knowledge. In addition to creating some of the most beautiful and ornate illuminated manuscripts in the world, the Irish monks and other craftspeople flourished in the arts of metalworking and sculpture, amassing large stores of jewelry and treasure.

The monasteries and surrounding towns continued to thrive, and their treasures eventually drew the attention of Viking raiders. Despite years of relatively few challenges from the outside, fighting had continued between the various Celtic chieftains, and the Irish were still formidable warriors. In the end, their people and civilization survived generations of persistent Viking attacks, although two hundred years of plunder and violence took their toll. Viking power was able to persist, and the invaders established major coastal settlements, like Dublin and Cork. Many Scandinavians stayed permanently, but they were absorbed into the enduring Irish culture.

More changes came in the early twelfth century, when foreign armies were invited ashore. After he was exiled from his domain for kidnapping another king's wife, the Irish chieftain Diarmait Mac Murchada convinced a Welsh earl under Henry II, known as Strongbow, to help him get his land back. Strongbow was successful; he helped retake the land and then married the chieftain's daughter. Eventually the earl inherited the kingdom, and his power continued to grow.

He was so successful, in fact, that Henry II stepped in to firmly secure his own power on the island, and the beginning of Anglo-Norman rule was established. This new influence continued to flow in, with its feudal laws replacing the old ways a little at a time. Soon began the English crown's attempts to force Protestantism upon a staunchly Catholic Ireland. This continued for hundreds of years, with England's rulers sometimes employing cruel and devious measures.

England's rule became official when Henry VIII declared himself the King of Ireland in 1541. Brutal conquests by Anglo-Norman monarchies continued and eventually broke down the will of the northern Gaelic chieftains, having greatly minimized their powers. England's rule was further secured on the day these chieftains fled their own lands. The chiefs assured their frightened people that they were only going to Spain to ask for help in fighting the English, but they brought along their families and valuables and seemed to be leaving for good.

On that day in September of 1607, the people of the northern Irish fishing village, Rathmullan, watched as their leaders set sail for the Continent in what would become their permanent exile. This was the end of the Gaelic Order and the final symbolic defeat of the old ways. These kings were descended from the original Celtic tribes that had ruled in Ireland's north for hundreds of years. They now abandoned their land, sailing to mainland Europe on a French ship, leaving their people vulnerable and virtually defenseless against the impending onslaught from England.

With the absence of the Gaelic chieftains came the perfect opportunity for English rulers to take control of Northern Ireland. Irish Catholics were banished from their own farms and homes, their lands handed over to Protestant settlers from England, Scotland, and Wales, changing forever the face of Ireland. Catholicism was diminished, along with Irish identity.

The establishment of a Protestant ruling class, with its sense of superiority over the native Irish, made peaceful assimilation impossible. These attempts to reassign land, power, faith, and culture continued relentlessly as the remaining descendants of the Gaelic tribes fought and rebelled at every opportunity.

In the 1600s also came the Penal Laws, which, along with the Protestant Ascendency, assured dominance over the huge Catholic majority for the next two hundred years. These laws forbade Catholics from carrying weapons, voting, obtaining a higher education, or running for public office. They could not send their children abroad to Catholic schools and were imprisoned if they tried to teach their children themselves. Catholics could not marry Protestants, own a horse worth more than five pounds, adopt a child, or build any church made of stone.

Meanwhile, there were many rewards for converting to the Protestant Church of England. When a Catholic landowner died, for instance, he was required to divide his property between all of his sons unless the eldest would convert to Protestantism, in which case he could inherit all the land. Most remained true to their faith, and over the years, Irish Catholic farms were divided into smaller and smaller plots, which were rarely able to succeed. This continued until most families lost their farms altogether and had to rent tiny pieces of their own land from new, largely absentee, English landowners.

These newly created Irish tenant laborers could be evicted for almost any reason at their landlords' whim, and upon eviction the land was divided into still smaller pieces to increase rent revenues. On the small rented plots of land, only the most barren corners were allotted for the laborers to grow their own food. Potatoes were often the only crop that could grow with any success in this poor, rocky soil, so this is what the families ate. As these former landowners sank into deeper poverty by the year, millions of pounds in profit were exported to the absentee landlords in England.

Within a relatively short period of time, the Catholic majority in Ireland had been transformed into one of the most desperate and destitute peasant classes in all of Europe. Conditions were dire even in the best of years, but there were many times when the potato crops failed, with catastrophic results. Since this was all there was to eat for many poor families living in rural Ireland, many starved.

In the mid-1840s came potato crop failures that led to The Great Hunger. Over three million Irish people were totally dependent on potatoes for food, and over one million died of starvation and related disease. Even more fled their homeland for survival, but setting sail for the Americas was often just as dangerous. Mortality rates of 30 percent were common aboard the "coffin ships" bound for lands of hope and greater opportunity. It is said that hungry sharks could be seen following these ships because so many dead bodies were thrown overboard. Meanwhile, the rulers in England paid little attention and did almost nothing to help their desperate Irish citizens—sometimes even blocking the aid that was offered from other countries.

In 1847, Ottoman sultan Abdul Medjid Khan announced that he would send 10,000 British pounds' worth of gold to the Irish farmers to help end the starvation, but Queen Victoria insisted that he give only 1,000. She herself had provided 2,000 pounds in aid—how would it look if he were to send more? The sultan appeared to acquiesce to her power, sending only 1,000 pounds in gold, but he also secretly sent three ships to Ireland packed full of food for the starving families. He was found out, and although the English courts tried to block the shipment, it arrived safely on Ireland's east coast.

Even the English politicians who were appointed to provide relief for their starving citizens to the north did almost nothing to help. Baronet Sir Charles Edward Trevelyan wrote in a letter to a colleague that the starvation was the Judgment of God upon the Irish, as well as an "effective mechanism for reducing surplus population."

This desperate time cannot rightfully be called a famine, because Ireland was still a fertile land, and far more than enough food was being consistently harvested to feed every starving family. The Protestant Anglo elites in Ireland were eating well while much of the rest of the food was exported for profit. At the docks, the Irish food was patrolled by armed guards as it awaited exportation, out of reach of the starving people who had produced it.

Just when poverty and starvation had weakened the resolve of the Catholic majority to the breaking point, the absentee landlords pushed even harder. Because the starving and dead cannot pay rent, many thousands of families were evicted from their tiny plots of rocky land, their pathetic makeshift cabins leveled.

Although many of the evicted begged to be taken into the prison-like workhouses, there was often no room. Many families were turned away to walk the country roads and build little shelters in the ditches. Some people committed crimes just to get into jail so they would have gruel to eat and a roof over their heads. Many people left the countryside and flocked to the city of Dublin in a desperate search for work and food.

Part One

1

The end was coming soon. He could feel it.

It followed his shadow like the seabirds trailed the wake of the ship.

The cold sea air whipped through his black hair and scoured the wide deck of the massive ship, *Leinster*, as it followed its daily route from Holyhead, Wales, to Dublin loaded with tourists, merchants, and families. He squinted up at the pale, icy blue of the sky for a moment or two before looking again at Ireland's east coast slowly emerging now from the haze of distance.

The familiar low, rolling hills of Ireland's coast came into view, opulent green in the sun's light as it descended in pale beams between banks of low clouds. Beyond these hills rose the high, dark Wicklow Mountains lining the expanse of the distant horizon, their indigo peaks beneath the shade of clouds.

Joe thought of the journey his ancestors had made when arriving in this new land. Looking at the ancient shore, green and rocky, it was easy to imagine how things might have looked at the time. It gave him comfort when he had doubts. He would think about the era of the proud Celtic tribes, which had been followed by centuries of struggles against a foreign occupation that had reduced many of the descendants of early Irish kings and queens to starving peasants.

He tried to fathom how many people had viewed these shores from the sea on their way to a new life. These thoughts quieted his fears and strengthened his determination that his would be the last generation to face this fight against England. They would finish the job, once and for all, seeing freedom before they saw death.

Athens? he thought. *Maybe all the way back to Algiers or Malta*? *Or maybe just to Marseille*. While sitting at the docks waiting to board in Holyhead a few hours before, he had felt a momentary, shameful impulse to just turn around and head the other way. He wanted to run like hell for the nearest train south and never stop until he reached the shores of the Mediterranean.

He hadn't been to Marseille in a long time, and that would be just far enough to disappear. With one hand holding tight to the cold, metal railing of the *Leinster* as it surged through the rough and choppy water of the Irish Sea, Joe wrapped his long wool coat tightly against the chilled sea wind and allowed himself a moment of escapist daydreaming, thinking of the last time he felt the overpowering sun of France's southern coast.

He had been on his way to Algiers about four years ago when he took some extra time with his father in the ancient southern port city of Marseille before setting off across the Mediterranean. The two of them spent days strolling along the port, sampling the city's famous seafood stew, bouillabaisse, and exploring the tiny fishing villages that trailed east along the Mediterranean coast, tucked into rocky coves. After his dad continued on to Italy, Joe sat near the fish market on the port waiting for his ship to Algiers.

Looking out past the hundreds of white sails toward the mouth of the port where it opened up to the Mediterranean, he had thought that it was nothing like the ocean he knew back home. The water in Marseille mirrored the clearest, sunny blue skies as it glided rhythmically up and down the warm sands of the arid coast. It was never shockingly cold and did not seem driven by angry winds; instead, it gently lapped against the ivory rocks of the cornices.

In Marseille, he could live a long life with his books and poetry and sports. In the anonymity of that city, there would be no nationalistic obligations or violent insurrection for him. Marseille was a place for thriving. The city vibrated with the constant bustle of carriages and vendors and the omnipotent sun that baked and bleached all things raised by human hands to match the pale shades of the surrounding crumbling, ragged, rocky shore.

The sky—and its mirror, the sea—seemed to have been painted from a pigment too vibrantly blue to exist in the real world. But everything solid in Marseille was the color of bones, dry grain, and almond shells. The Mediterranean breezes carried the scents of saffron, mint, and coriander from Algiers, along with the smell of the fishing boats and the salty air.

Sitting near the boats next to the fishermen's stands, Joe was able to see the two forts stationed on either side of the port, just before it opened to the Mediterranean—Fort Saint-Jean to the right and Fort Saint-Nicolas on the left. When King Louis XIV had them built in the mid-1600s, he claimed that it was to please the inhabitants of the city who, he said, "were extremely fond of nice fortresses." In fact, the two forts were built to defend the authorities from their own people after a recent uprising. All of the cannons of both forts faced in toward the city, not out to sea.

When Joe had heard the story of these two forts, it had reminded him of the statue of justice at Dublin Castle, the seat of Britain's power in Ireland. Previously a residence for representatives sent by the British monarchy to rule in Dublin, the castle had been converted mainly to offices and meeting rooms for the many politicians who worked for the British Empire.

Poised high above the front entrance to the castle was a statue of Lady Justice who had apparently turned her back on the Irish. She was facing not out to the streets, to greet the people of the city as they entered, but in, toward the offices of the British government. She also had no blindfold; she wore instead a knowing smile. Even worse, the constant rain in Ireland had filled one side of her scales more than the other, and they were now severely tipped. The scales of justice in Ireland had become quite uneven over the years.

Standing against the railing of the ship headed home to Dublin, Joe knew he could choose to run away if he wanted to. But he also knew that he could never run away from the looming fight for the freedom of his country. He had never spoken of the possibility of leaving and actually felt guilty for even allowing himself the momentary daydream of running away.

During the famine his own grandfather had been forced to flee the land of the High Kings in County Meath, moving to Dublin in search of a better life. He was one of the few Catholics who had recovered with great success, and now Joe's family was wealthy again. Joe's own father was a Papal Count for his service to the Vatican, and the family was firmly settled in Dublin. Joe would stay and fight.

If the rebellion was successful, he would help build the new government. If they lost this coming battle, then his death would come with unbroken oaths and gunfire. Either way, the end would come at home.

2

When Grace was a little girl, her favorite nanny was Bridget, from County Wexford. Bridget came into the Gifford household to take charge of Grace and her eleven siblings until they were old enough to move from the nursery, on the top floor of the house, into other bedrooms below.

Grace and the other children looked to Bridget for nearly all of their physical and emotional needs. Their own mother, Isabella, had no use whatsoever for babies or children and had made that quite clear for as long as Grace could remember. But Bridget was always there for them as their disciplinarian, defender, and comforter. Every day she dressed them, bathed them, corrected their manners, and taught them to keep the nursery spotless.

On Sundays Bridget had the afternoon off to stroll through the neighborhood with her British soldier boyfriend. Not too long after the nanny left the house, Grace could see the look of apprehension in her mother's eyes. When a quarrel broke out among the children or they became too loud in their games, Isabella's tense expression blossomed darkly. Grace would quickly quiet down and offer to go outside or read a story to her younger sister, Sydney. Grace hated it when her mother shouted at them, and almost anything could bring on her anger or contempt, even a moment of childish clumsiness or a silly question. By Sunday evening Bridget was back, and the children chattered and smiled again, full of stories to share and angling for room on her lap.

In the morning Bridget sometimes brought the children to Palmerston Park, just down the tree-lined street from their home in the upscale, Protestant neighborhood of Rathmines. Here they were set free to chase each other, climb trees, and forage for berries. Other times she took them up to Portobello Barracks so she could visit her Redcoat boyfriend. The soldiers gave the children candy and hoisted them onto their broad shoulders for rides and races.

In the evenings, after the children were tucked into their beds, Bridget would tell them stories and sing songs about the great Irish heroes. She had a little bed of her own, right in the nursery. Bridget was Catholic, of course, like most of the other staff, and once she thought all the kids were sleeping, she would quietly recite her rosary in her corner of the room.

Pretending to be asleep, Grace used to watch enthralled as her nanny gently fingered the little wooden beads and whispered unknown prayers. Grace recognized most of Our Father, but that was all. Having no knowledge of Catholicism whatsoever, she came to regard Bridget's late-night ceremony as something secret and mystical. When she was very little, she even thought the beads must have magical powers, like faery tale talismans.

Usually Bridget was loud and cheerful, and constantly bustling from place to place—cleaning and scolding and comforting as she went. But she seemed so different while she sat and whispered the mysterious prayers. She looked devout and calm and beautiful, like Grace imagined the Virgin Mary must have looked.

But Bridget was clearly no saint, so Grace thought it must have been those beads and prayers. She felt like she was missing out on something important and began to long for that mystical transformation herself.

One day, when Grace was still very young, her mother fired Bridget during a losing battle against her own naturally intolerant nature. Other nannies followed, but Grace never forgot about Bridget's secret prayers and magic beads.

Grace's own father Frederick was Catholic, but he kept it to himself. He didn't chase women or go to the track, but he did attend Mass. That was her dad's dirty little secret. The family never spoke of it—not to strangers and not to each other. Isabella hated the fact that her husband was Catholic and had apparently sworn to him that if he were to die before she did, she would allow no priest to go anywhere near his deathbed. He would be buried as a Protestant.

Frederick was helpless to do anything about it. He kept any worries about the eventual state of his soul to himself, along with his other thoughts and feelings. He went off alone to a church of his own somewhere unknown to the rest of the family every Sunday while they attended the protestant St. Philip's Church of Ireland.

Grace disliked her family church. As a child she thought that God must not have liked it there either, because she never felt a spiritual presence among the pews during services. Everyone behaved so coldly and properly at all times, and it seemed to Grace that they mainly came to show off their new dresses and hats and to catch up on the latest news about their neighbors.

When she was twenty-one years old, Grace went looking for Bridget's Catholic magic on her own. She couldn't try out any churches in her own neighborhood, because word might get back to her mother. She didn't know where her father attended services, but she guessed it was in a neighborhood where people were well off and lived much like her own family. She began to secretly attend Masses at various Catholic churches throughout the poorer neighborhoods in the city. After exploring a bit, she found St. Audoen's Church in one of the most impoverished of Dublin's parishes.

The first time Grace attended Mass at St. Audoen's was in the late spring, seven years earlier. She had watched her sisters and Isabella walk down the front steps on their way to St. Philip's that morning with parasols in their kid-glove-wrapped hands, jewel-toned satin skirts, and wide hats decked with velvet bows and artificial flowers. She then quickly put on her simplest dress, in charcoal gray linen with skirts long enough to hide her shiny new boots even when sitting or kneeling, and a plain, black shawl she had made years before, when she was learning to knit. She got her bike and rode to the city.

As she approached the church, the sky was blue, marbled with shallow wisps of white clouds that drifted in a cool breeze off the Irish Sea. The huge, dirt-gray, stony presence of the old church was like a chilled patch of winter placed in the street before her. She took a deep breath and walked up the steps. She paused inside the broad, arched doorway just behind a woman surrounded by a group of children of all ages. A girl around nine years old held a baby, and an older girl had two toddlers by the hands. Neither of the toddlers had any shoes, and their clothes hung on them as if they were playing dress up with older children's clothing.

Grace watched as the woman reached her fingers into a little bowl of water then traced the shape of the cross before her—from her forehead to her sternum, then from shoulder to shoulder.

When it was her turn, Grace reached her fingertips into the little bowl of water, imitated the woman's gesture, then made her way through the knots of families chattering in hushed voices as they found their seats and settled in. She picked a spot in the corner of the very last pew. The Mass was in Latin, and there were men in brightly colored robes in procession down the center row and little children lighting candles. At some points during the service, the parishioners knelt together or recited words she couldn't understand.

The stone cavern of a church was cold despite the fact that it was packed with people and there were many loudly distracting children present throughout the morning. Apparently there was no Sunday school, and she didn't see a single nanny. But there was also a solemnity in the midst of the chaos that she had not felt before. The large room was filled with a deep, almost desperate, devotion, along with an incense of earth, amber, and sweet spice that made her think of faraway places she would probably never see.

As the crowd began to file out after Mass, Grace watched a few people move toward an altar of Mary to light a candle. Some returned to a kneeling position in their pew, where they remained in prayer. She saw a woman shedding silent tears. The people she saw at Mass seemed to be more open in their devotion than those she had seen at her own family's church, and she longed more than ever to be a part of this world.

After church at St. Audoen's one Sunday, she saw a group of parishioners at the foot of the stone steps just outside the door. One woman was crying while another held her. Several people surrounded them; some offered kind words to the crying woman while the others spoke to each other in hissed whispers. Every once in a while, someone would erupt loudly in anger, but the others would calm the person down, motioning to the crying woman at the center of the group. Grace lingered nearby, listening, her curiosity distracting her from her usual role as the awkward outsider.

It appeared that the crying woman's sister and two nephews had been killed earlier in the week when their poorly and cheaply built tenement house collapsed. A brother-in-law and niece were terribly injured but alive. Grace heard a man near her muttering curses at the landlords in England while his wife gently touched his arm, her sad, dark eyes darting nervously toward the priest who stood near the door speaking with his parishioners.

"I don't give a damn what he thinks," her husband said aloud, shaking off her hand. "I don't give a damn what anyone thinks anymore." Louder now. "It's just too much! These British landlords get fatter and fatter while our people go without proper shelter."

"You've got that right," an old woman standing right next to Grace agreed. Her dark-green, rough, woolen shawl was wrapped tightly around her narrow shoulders, which looked brittle as the wings of a tiny, old bird. She went on in a voice that seemed impossibly strong and fierce, given the source. "The poor don't matter to Westminster Abbey as long as they stay here in Dublin! Y'know more are dying right here from disease and starvation than in Calcutta!" No one was surprised; it sounded about right.

Angry waves surged through the crowd with increasing force as voices grew louder. England was doing nothing to help. When London passed the bill to feed the impoverished children in their own schools, no such law was passed for Dublin's children, despite the fact that things were much worse here. England had ignored Dubliners' problems for years while taking their taxes, and now, with conscription likely, Dublin's young men would soon be forced to fight England's war.

As Grace absorbed the electricity of their defiance, she became angry too. She no longer worried that she would be noticed and judged as an outsider—worse yet, a Protestant from a wealthy family. She realized that, while she had been attending dances and art classes, many people in Dublin were truly in danger and going hungry. The inner city's rat-infested slums were packed far beyond capacity, with entire families living in single rooms. The sewage systems were hopelessly inadequate, and clean water was in short supply, resulting in unlivable conditions.

On her ride home from church, Grace found that the smell in many of the side streets was unbearable. She saw sad-eyed, hollow-cheeked children wandering alone. They seemed to be all dirty, bony knees and elbows, so cold and wet in their tattered, oversized, hand-me-down clothing that their tiny hands and bare feet were blue.

She needed to do something.

Grace talked to her sisters about it, and they joined groups that provided food and clothing for the hundreds of poor, hungry children of Dublin. Their involvement introduced them to many people in the nationalist and labor movements. More recently Grace had been pulled right into the middle of the political action by her new friend Joe, the editor of *The Irish Review.*

3

As Ireland's coast drew nearer, Joe gripped the railing of the deck, staring at the funnels and peaks in the cold, wild water below and thinking about his friend Grace. He had been gone for months now, and he missed her.

Joe had gone to Germany in secret for the Irish Republican Brotherhood—IRB—the secret organization planning a rebellion in the coming spring. He was sent to secure support in the form of guns and ammunition for the fight. The Germans were busy at war with England, but the IRB leaders hoped they might be able to convince leaders in Berlin to help anyway. Previous attempts to do so by others in the movement had not convinced German leaders that the Irish rebels were established or organized enough to take seriously. Joe had made this trip in a final attempt to rectify this problem and had been able to do so, as far as he could tell.

Having convinced the Germans that the rebels were well-prepared soldiers and not just a bunch of overzealous poets with a dream, Joe had left Germany with a promise of a large shipment of weapons and ammunition, which would improve their chances tremendously.

He then traveled south from Berlin and across the Mediterranean to Spain. He sailed out of Cadiz, Andalucía's major seaport, to England and was now finishing his trip home to Dublin aboard the *Leinster*. He felt satisfied in completing his mission, but he had needed to share many of the IRB's plans for the coming insurrection with the Germans, creating a greater risk of either betrayal or an intercepted message. The fewer people who knew what the IRB was up to, the better. IRB members involved in the planning were therefore sworn to secrecy. This oath had been easy for Joe to keep in all but one case.

He had not been able to tell his friend Grace anything at all—not even where he was going when he left for Germany. He had told everyone that he was headed south to Jersey because of illness. It was a great cover—getting out of the cold, damp Irish air at the doctor's orders. But he didn't like deceiving Grace.

There was something about the innate innocence and openness in her dark eyes that made him feel like a Machiavellian wretch for telling her lies. He often felt like this around Grace. It wasn't because she was judgmental—she was not. It was because she seemed so honest and good. His expressions and thoughts always felt dark and complicated in comparison, as if they were filtered through layers of translation from feeling to thought to conceptualization to metaphor, and then finally to communication.

He felt that Grace, on the other hand, was all brilliant simplicity. She felt and thought and said what she meant in one honest and breezy step, as if she were opening a door and letting out a blue sky from within. Her smile and presence could part his occasional sullen storm clouds like a penetrating beam of sunlight. He felt calmer around her, and he smiled more easily—even with no wine or whisky in sight and no music playing.

It was as if God had named Grace personally. The clarity of her faith and the generosity of her spirit seemed to come naturally, whereas Joe felt like he had chopped though a jungle of over-intellectualized concepts, doubts, and fears to finally find the relief of his faith. He sometimes felt like he had spent years trying to discover, define, and achieve what she had always known instinctually, as clearly as a sense or a feeling, like hunger or joy.

In his mind Joe had started calling her "Babbaly," a word he had learned while living in Algiers that meant "gate of God." He could not tell her that, of course. She thought of him as only a friend, as far as he could tell, and he was happy with what they had. But despite his intense love of God and country, when Joe was with Grace, he felt more devoted to her than to anything else. He wanted to protect her, learn from her, and do things for her. He wanted to fight for her. Her worries became his own, and if he could make her smile, it felt like a personal victory.

Joe thought once again about the first time he had ever met Grace, years before. He had attended an event at Patrick Pearse's school. Pearse was still a bit of a hero to Joe back then. He was a great speaker, a devoted patriot, and the person who had convinced Joe that a violent insurrection would be necessary to win freedom for Ireland.

Joe was standing on the front steps of the school when he first saw Grace. He was sometimes painfully shy around strangers—especially women—and he could still remember how his mind raced, searching for something clever to say to her. But when he met her dark eyes, their depth rendered him more tongue-tied than before, and he gave up on trying to be witty at all for the moment. He had thought he might try to speak with her after a drink or two but never got up the courage.

In 1913, two years after that first encounter, Joe was able to get to know Grace better when she joined the staff of *The Irish*

Review, the nationalist newspaper he was editing at the time. They spent many hours alone together talking while working on the paper's layout. Grace had admitted to him one night that she wanted to learn about Catholicism and asked if he would teach her. She thought she might like to convert one day. She knew that this would most likely mean being rejected by much of her family and community, and yet she had still confided in him, telling him that she knew of no one else she could trust who could adequately explain the faith to her.

After the paper was shut down by Dublin Castle, Joe and Grace started meeting at a little restaurant called Sibley's, spending hours together over tea discussing faith, the Church's history, and the conversion process. They had met often ever since.

But Joe could not let himself fall in love with Grace. Despite being the son of a count, he had nothing of value to offer her; he had no profession, and he needed to focus on the insurrection, which was just months away now. It was very possible that he wouldn't live through it anyway. He would be no good for anyone now, and Grace deserved all the happiness in the world.

If he were to fall in love now, just before the rising, it would make the thought of facing death and leaving Grace behind too excruciating. If he were to be executed or killed in battle, it was important that he face death bravely and without regret. He knew that history would be watching. All of his faith and love of country might not be enough to get him through an execution with any dignity at all if he were losing the love of his life.

Besides, Joe thought, staring vacantly at the churning water below, *if I were trying to get Grace to love me, I might not be able to talk to her at all.* Her dark eyes seemed to see right through him, understanding him in ways he had never known before. She was also quite pretty and had many admirers. He felt fortunate and content just to enjoy her friendship and didn't let himself think of anything more—most of the time.

Sometimes, however, he felt that Grace looked at him with admiration while he explained some Catholic mystery or enthusiastically espoused the need for the Irish to rise up in revolution against their invaders. They talked about these two things a lot—Catholicism and Irish independence, his two passions in life. Even though she was raised in a unionist family, Grace and her sisters had moved over to the nationalist side, supporting the work of the various rebel groups like the Irish Volunteers.

Catholicism and rebellion must have been what Grace was thinking about when she looked at him that way—as if he were somehow admirable. Joe's whole life was centered on the two subjects to which she was most drawn. He was helping her to connect with these things, and he doubted that her apparent admiration could be anything more than this.

As the ship approached Kingstown Port, Joe looked beyond the rocky shoreline to the gently rolling grassy fields spread like a crumpled piece of green velvet. A feeling of delight shot through his chest at the sight of home, like the rush of the pale, liquid gold of sparkling wine as the cork pops. "My cup runneth over," he quoted beneath his breath. Ireland's fierce beauty now gathered his wandering thoughts to order. Joe focused once more on the many things that needed to be done before the rebellion.

4

Grace looked out the drawing room window at the sound of her father making his way slowly up the front stairs. Frederick was late getting home from his solicitor's office in Dawson Street. His shoulders and head stooped slightly, and his right palm pressed against his forehead, thumb and fingers massaging each of his temples. It appeared that he had spent a long and thankless day reviewing contracts and Land Acts.

A moment later he entered the room, his posture and features rearranged in an impressive attempt to appear cheerful as he greeted his daughters, Grace and Nellie. The two young women were settled in opposite corners of the wide, ivory-colored sofa surrounded by books and papers and pillows of peach and vanilla satin.

"Is anything wrong? Are you girls ill?" Frederick asked with exaggerated concern, since he almost never saw them home in the evening.

"Very funny!" Grace laughed, looking up from her drawing.

"You know we're fine, but it seems like we've been going out all the time lately. We thought we'd have a night in," Nellie explained. She put down her book and went to hug him in greeting.

Nellie and Father were right, Grace knew. It did seem like she had been out almost every afternoon or night for weeks now. There was just so much to do these days. Besides her classes at the Dublin Metropolitan School of Art and her work at the soup kitchen, there were now free Irish language classes being given regularly in the city. In order to encourage attendance at classes, they would even put on dances afterward with live music and ceili set dancing that sometimes lasted until early in the morning. On nights with no dances, there was generally something on at the Abbey Theatre. If Grace was not designing and painting sets, she was going over lines with the actors or attending a show. Afterward, a group usually went out for a late dinner nearby, often with more music and dancing. She was also secretly studying Catholicism with her friend Joe.

"What about your mother?" Frederick asked, his eyes darting toward the staircase. "Is Isabella at home as well?"

"She's upstairs," Nellie told him, and Grace watched her father's cheerful expression wilt just a little, although he was still trying. "She came in about an hour ago, complaining that she had a headache and went right upstairs. We haven't seen her since."

He tried not to show it, but Frederick had clearly been hoping that his wife would be out, or too busy to pay him any attention for a while. He just needed some time to relax a bit before he could sit and listen with patience and sympathy to her daily recitation of grievances. Grace couldn't blame her father. Isabella was generally angry about something, and she tended to take it out on him more than any of the others.

Even when she wasn't angry, Isabella was almost always complaining about something. It seemed as if she gathered each petty injustice—and all of the little outrages from throughout her day—into a neat bundle, which she would bring home and unwrap for her family every evening, one item at a time.

She complained about the quality of the dealer women's produce and the guests who had stayed too long at her open house—or worse, not come at all. She complained about how the poor families had let the city neighborhoods get so bad. This was especially frustrating to her daughters, who spent so much time dealing with the cruel realities of poverty in Dublin. Their mother knew nothing about real life. Nothing at all.

"Girls, is that Frederick? Are you home, Frederick?" Isabella was descending the stairs in a crisp, gliding trot, brows furrowed, her head snapping back and forth, surveying the ground floor like an angry parrot. She spoke as if she were scolding a classroom of unruly seven-year-olds.

"Oh, thank God, Frederick! Where have you been? I've been waiting for ages."

Grace watched as her father's chest swelled slightly with a deep breath. The cheer drained from his eyes, but his lips remained in a frozen smile.

"You've got to stop those Home Rule lunatics, Frederick. You're a solicitor. You know lots of important people. Surely you can do something! Oh, look at the time! We need to change for dinner." Isabella scolded as she took him by the arm and tried to pull him from the room. "Come on, come on, you're so late already.

"You know I had to go see about your suit today. Well, one of those Home Rulers handed me a nationalist flyer as I was leaving the shop," Isabella continued as she and Frederick started up the long, curved staircase. "He kept talking to me. All sorts of nonsense. I tried to tell him I wasn't interested, and what good do you think that did? Frederick? Frederick, are you listening to me? I tell you, the man simply wouldn't stop! Kept going on and on about Irish independence. Independence from what?" she demanded as they walked down the hall to their room. "Can't those nationalists appreciate that we're . . . we're a part of the greatest empire in the world? Why would we want a government here in Dublin when we're already represented in London?"

"Politics is bad enough, but at least she wasn't complaining about us tonight," Grace said after her mother's voice finally drifted away into silence. She took a deep breath and let it out with a weary sigh. "I know we're not always easy for her to take. She's convinced we've all turned on her, but you'd think she'd be used to it by now."

"Poor Mother," Nellie said with a smile that showed no sympathy at all. "She's like a hen who's hatched out ducklings."

"Did you hear her shouting at Father about Sydney last night? Like it was his fault that her baby's run off to America."

Grace was second from the youngest in the family. The youngest was their sister Sydney, who had gone to live in the United States the previous summer. A journalist, Sydney supported the nationalists and their fight for independence—not just the Home Rulers, who were working within the political system, but the Irish Volunteers and the IRB—radical nationalists who spoke of all-out rebellion. Sometimes Grace felt that Sydney must not have any fears at all. She showed no concern over being arrested for her controversial views, and it seemed so easy for her to disregard their parents' criticisms. Grace had to admit that Sydney was a good journalist, and she envied her little sister's brash courage.

"Mom's still not over Muriel's conversion, and it's been almost four years now!" Grace reminded her sister.

"She's upset about the conversion but not so much about the marriage," Nellie said. "Thomas finally managed to win Mother over. It's because he's always so sweet and funny, and he treats Muriel like a queen." Here Nellie paused and smiled at Grace, eyes narrowed. "But what about his friend Joe? He's been coming around to see you an awful lot these days. What's going on there?"

"He's just a friend, Nellie. Don't start any trouble!" Grace insisted, suddenly embarrassed.

"I don't know, Grace. I hope you're right, or you could give Mother the biggest shock of all of us," Nellie cautioned, though she obviously loved the thought of it. "Joe is the son of that Count Plunkett—a papal count, no less. That family is as Catholic as you can get, and they've been rebelling against England for generations. Everybody knows about them." Nellie paused, smiled conspiratorially at her sister, then added, "Grace, I think you should marry him!"

"Nellie, stop it. Please don't even say that," Grace pleaded.

"C'mon, it'd be wonderful! Can you imagine? I really don't think it could get much worse!" Nellie was laughing like a little girl.

"Stop it, Nellie!" Grace tried to sound stern, but she could feel her cheeks burning. She hoped Nellie wouldn't notice.

"I'm sorry, little sister," Nellie relented. "I understand! He's just a friend. So tell me when you met your *friend* Joe."

Grace ignored her overemphasis on the word *friend*. "About four years ago, I think—well, it was the same night Muriel met Thomas," Grace said. "Nora Dryhurst brought me and Muriel and Sydney to the opening night party at Patrick Pearse's boarding school, St. Edna's—at the new building."

"Did you meet Patrick Pearse? What's he like?"

"Well, I was a little nervous to meet him, since he's such a big deal in the movement. But I guess he's a good friend of Nora's. He was polite. Friendly, but also kind of formal and... I don't know, a little aloof, maybe? His little brother,

Willie, was there too, and he seemed sweet—easier to talk to. We were just going up the front steps when we came across the two of them, and they were with Thomas and Joe. So Nora introduced us all, and then—you know how she is—she said something dreadful to the young men about how she wanted them to all fall in love with us and get married."

"What?" Nellie laughed and got more comfortable on the couch, folding her legs under her and hugging a cream-colored satin pillow. "What did you do? You must have been so embarrassed."

"Oh, it was Nora. You know how she's always teasing and matchmaking. We just kind of ignored it. But Willie and Joe seemed kind of embarrassed—'cause they don't know her at all, I don't think. But Thomas said something charming and funny and everything was fine." Grace thought for a moment. "You know, I could tell even then that Tom liked Muriel—the way he was looking at her. And she was talking about him after—how pretty his smile was, and his gray eyes and everything. So funny!"

"Then he started showing up at the house to see Muriel all the time," Nellie added. "But he'd always show up in all that Gaelic dress—the kilt and everything! I thought Mother would die, always talking about how he was scandalizing the family in our good, Anglo-Irish neighborhood!"

"But she couldn't stop it. After that they were married in no time."

"So, what about Joe?" Nellie insisted.

"Well, he was younger than the other men. He's just a year older than me—so about twenty-four at the time. And . . . well, you know Joe." Grace thought about the first time she saw him. He was the tallest of the four men, and his black hair was tousled, as if he had just been walking in a windstorm. His clothes looked expensive, but he wore them with a careless ease that implied they were what he wore daily—not that he was dressed up for the evening. He wore a long, cape-like woolen coat and rings and other jewelry—quite uncommon for men in Dublin.

"Even at the time," Grace continued, "I remember thinking that Mother would have an attack if he ever came over. Besides all of the nationalist stuff, there was just something a little ... I don't know ... eccentric or foreign about him. I know he's spent a lot of time abroad."

"So, did you like him right away?" Nellie wasn't going to let it go.

"No, I told you, we're just friends! And he was too skinny for me, and ... well, he didn't seem to like me much anyway, so it didn't matter." He had seemed friendly enough with everyone else but never even spoke to Grace at all—hardly looked at her.

Nellie looked disappointed, but Grace continued, "I remember thinking that he might be like Sydney, and maybe that's why he didn't talk to me—like he didn't think I was serious enough. You how Sydney always seems to be judging us for spending time on art or, you know, reading novels and going to dances."

"Oh, I know!" Nellie agreed. "To her everything's a waste of time if it's not in support of the nationalist cause."

"I don't know why I let it get to me, but it does. People like that always make me feel insecure," Grace said. "But then, a couple of years later, I started working with Joe at *The Irish Review*, and it turns out, he's actually very sweet—maybe just a little shy at first." Grace couldn't help smiling a little when she thought about Joe; she decided not to tell Nellie what she thought of his dark eyes.

5

Joe got back to Dublin in late July. The underlying tension in the city had increased noticeably during the few months he had been in Europe. The Irish Volunteers had staged a number of exercises and drills that had shut down large sections of the city at times and led to serious confrontations between the nationalist group and the Dublin Metropolitan Police. Detectives from the Castle were scurrying around like rats in the corners, following the more prominent rebel leaders from their homes to meetings and drills.

The Volunteers were exhilarated and inspired; this small taste of insurrection had stimulated their appetites for more. For tactical reasons Joe was forced to stay in most of the time, but he felt swept up in the wave of enthusiasm, and it was difficult for him to stay away from the frequent rallies and drills. He attended only rarely, when he thought he could do so without being recognized by too many.

More than ever, it seemed that the majority of the Dublin public were resentful of the frequent intrusions into their lives—loudly jeering and criticizing when they saw the Irish Volunteers marching and practicing their maneuvers. There was a war going on in Europe now, and many saw the rebels as nothing more than tiresome, stubborn little boys who refused to grow up and had traded in their toy guns for secondhand rifles smuggled in on fishing boats. Now they were running around the city causing chaos and risking the lives of civilians who had a hard enough time just keeping a roof over their families' heads and putting food on the table.

Even among staunch nationalists, there was no overwhelming call for immediate action. While support for a violent uprising against England was strong among a few, the majority of Irish nationalists—who also claimed to desire freedom—were content to continue to wait for Westminster to hand it over to them.

Home Rule—in which England would allow the Irish to form their own government while still holding them firmly within the British Empire—was the golden promise that had been held out temptingly to the Irish people for many generations. Yet it was always just out of reach. Generations had been forced to fight and die to help expand the British Empire while receiving almost nothing in return for their citizenship and sacrifice. This recurring promise of Home Rule had been offered again very recently, and it had pacified the more moderate nationalists.

But when the war broke out the previous summer, in 1914, the politicians at Westminster Abbey once again put the whole idea of Home Rule on hold and asked the Irish to fight with the British Army once again. This is when the Irish Volunteers had split into two uneven parts: the much larger and more moderate group of about 90,000 men followed John Redmond. They changed their name to the National Volunteers and agreed to fight with England, hoping that this time their loyalty would convince the Empire to grant them Home Rule.

A group of about 10,000 kept the name Irish Volunteers and vowed not to wait any longer for British politicians to keep their promises. They refused to fight in the war in Europe, concentrating instead on pushing harder for Irish independence at home on their own terms. Joe had sided with this smaller group. Why, he wondered, should they trust England now after hundreds of years of oppression, starvation, and broken promises?

Then there were the unionists who celebrated their place in the British Empire. In the case of English immigrants, this stance came as no surprise. But there were also many Irish who were content to continue to live under British occupation. Maybe they thought it was their only chance for something better; things were bad in Dublin, and Joe could understand that. But it was not long ago that Ireland had lost most of her own to starvation, emigration, and disease, and so much of that was due to the negligence and greed of British rulers.

The fact that they weren't currently being starved by the thousands was apparently enough for some to forget about the past. But Joe wondered what the English would impose on the Irish next. As it was, conditions were deplorable in Dublin, with poverty and infant death rates much worse than in London, and still the great British Empire did next to nothing. Now that the war was on, still more Irish men—unionists and nationalists alike—were being killed every day while fighting with the British Army. Despite all of this, Joe knew that few of the people he passed in the streets of Dublin would support his revolution.

He sometimes struggled with the idea of fighting and dying for the independence of his people when so many of them wished he would do nothing. Even more, he struggled with the thought of killing for this largely unpopular cause. But he never struggled for long, and he never gave voice to his uncertainty. He wanted more than anything to help win freedom for Ireland in the coming spring.

He also believed with all his heart that they would find eventual victory even if they lost this coming battle. Win or lose, if they fought hard enough, they could win over the loyalty of the whole country. Even if he and his friends were defeated and killed, they believed their passion and devotion to the cause would awaken the nationalism of the population, who could then rise to victory in the next wave.

Soon Joe would be sent to the United States on another job for the IRB. It was crucial that the British authorities at Dublin Castle remain unaware of this trip. To minimize the risk of being found out and followed, he tried not to be seen too often in Dublin before he left. Most of the time, he remained at his family's large estate, Larkfield, in Kimmage, just south of Dublin. This is where he hosted meetings of the IRB.

Thankfully, he was still able to meet regularly with Grace. Since their meetings were unrelated to the rebellion, it didn't matter if he was followed. The Castle's detectives were often waiting for him when he left home, but if they wanted to spend their time following him into the city to meet with a pretty girl, Joe had no problem with that. If nothing else, it distracted them from their task.

There was one nationalist event that Joe could not miss, however. This was the funeral of the Old Fenian, O'Donovan Rossa.

6

Jeremiah O'Donovan Rossa was said to be "the last of the old Fenians." The Fenians were the previous generation's radical rebels for the cause of Irish freedom and were therefore heroes to any nationalist who believed that violent insurrection was necessary.

Many years before, O'Donovan Rossa had been charged with plotting an uprising against the British government and sentenced to a lifetime of penal servitude. After serving time in various prisons in England, he was eventually released in exile and lived the rest of his life in the United States, where he joined the US-based Irish nationalist groups the Fenian Brotherhood and Clan na Gael. He became an increasingly controversial figure after organizing a series of bombings in England in the 1880s.

Not long after word of Rossa's death reached Ireland, Joe received a request from Pearse to report to Volunteer headquarters in Dawson Street for an urgent meeting. When he made it to Pearse's office, Tom Clarke was already there.

Clarke was a fiercely dedicated nationalist who had joined the IRB at the age of eighteen, over forty-five years earlier. He had already served fifteen years in an English prison for his rebellious ways, and he had been anxious to get started once again on the very day of his release.

"Come in, Joe." Pearse stood leaning against the cabinet to one side of his desk. Clarke sat near the opposite wall. Joe took a seat between them, facing Pearse's desk. They spoke for a while about O'Donovan Rossa's legacy and the great loss his death was to the movement. Pearse seemed distracted. He absentmindedly tapped his fingers on the side of the cabinet for several seconds, then got to his point.

"You know, Rossa's wife will be bringing his body back to Ireland for burial."

"It's what he would have wanted," Clarke said, his eyes on the worn, wooden floorboards. He had spent years with Rossa during his time in the United States and thought of him as a friend as well as a legend.

"I've been thinking. The funeral. We have to use it—make it big." Pearse looked straight ahead as he spoke, as if he were looking beyond the walls of their dusty little HQ building into the future. "We'll need more support for the rising, and we need to wake up the people of this city."

Joe agreed. He was glad to hear that Pearse shared his concern about their lack of support in Dublin. Pearse was not always so practical, often transitioning from necessary discussions about budget and strategy into speeches about making the ultimate sacrifice and mystical obligations to the High Kings of Tara.

"It's a great idea, but we need to start today," said Clarke, always a pragmatist and always ready for action. "But I think we need to bring in as much of the country as possible, not just Dublin."

"If we get started on the posters and flyers right away, we can have them on the road before the end of the week," added Joe. He had a printing press out at Larkfield and was already thinking about the layout.

"I think I can arrange to charter some additional trains to bring in people for the funeral once we set a date," said Clarke.

"And you should get started on your speech for the graveside, Pearse."

"How far do you think I can go with it? The speech. We don't want to show our hand, but this will be our only chance to reach most of these people."

"I say, take it as far as you can. This is no time for discretion." Clarke was nodding his head thoughtfully. "Yes. I say throw caution to the wind and get people fired up for rebellion."

"I agree," Joe said. "Make it big. Sure, there'll be spies from the Castle around, but they'll just take it as graveside rhetoric. Don't hold back. Let the people know we need them in the fight." He had risen from his seat and walked to the chair behind Pearse's desk, where he sat and began taking notes of what needed to be done.

Soon Pearse had sequestered himself in his family cabin out west to work on the speech while Joe and Tom Clarke recruited dozens more people to distribute posters throughout the country, charter trains, and organize the procession. Word quickly spread, and by the day of the funeral on August 1, 1915, many thousands had gathered from all over Ireland to pay tribute to the "Unrepentant Fenian," as Rossa had come to be known.

Joe watched the funeral procession from the roof of the Irish Volunteer building. He was alone in the gloomy morning, with cold rain dropping heavily from motionless gray skies. First came the priests from churches all over Ireland. They were followed by groups of kilted scouts of the Fianna, the nationalist youth organization. Next in the procession were the members of the Gaelic League, labor union representatives, nationalist politicians, and business leaders from all over the country, interspersed with decorated carriages and bands of bagpipers. Following them all came the hearse, pulled by plumed, black horses and escorted by armed and uniformed members of the Irish Volunteers and James Connolly's Irish Citizen Army.

Joe was proud and encouraged to see so many civic leaders standing alongside the Volunteers in support of O'Donovan Rossa and his legacy. Even more impressive were the many thousands of citizen mourners that followed, moving slowly through the streets in a long, roughly crescent-shaped route beginning at City Hall on the south side. The crowd of thousands seemed to go on for miles as they turned the corner at St. Stephen's Green and made their way north on Dawson Street like another river flowing to meet the Liffey. They soon crossed the O'Connell Bridge and continued, passing the General Post Office and walking far past Nelson's Pillar before winding west to Glasnevin Cemetery.

Joe wondered where all of these supporters had been in the last few years, when it seemed like almost everyone was opposed to his stance of freedom at any cost. Were these thousands truly standing behind O'Donovan Rossa and his controversial actions, or were they here for the novelty and spectacle? If each person in this crowd had even the smallest spark of sympathy for their cause, Joe felt they might have a chance in the spring.

He knew he should stay away from the cemetery, but he could not resist. He wanted so badly to be at the gravesite to hear Pearse's speech and pay tribute to O'Donovan Rossa. He ran down the narrow stairs and out to where his black 1912 Wolseley 16/20hp was parked. He slid behind the wheel onto the black leather bench seat and drove west quickly, to get to Glasnevin Cemetery ahead of the procession. Once he got there, Joe walked through the entrance and found a spot out of the way but near enough to see the graveside where Pearse would speak.

As he waited, the clouds began to part, revealing patches of blue sky. By the time he heard the sound of approaching bagpipes, a light breeze rustled the leaves on surrounding trees, and the sun was fully revealed.

ᘛᘚ

In some ways, this huge Catholic presence at a cemetery was a victory in itself—a glorious protest. Just a few generations before, it was illegal to perform any sort of Catholic service in public, even when burying and mourning the dead. As Joe looked around today at all the priests and the thousands of proud citizens, that was hard for him to imagine. He began making his way toward the front of the crowd near the graveside just as Pearse started speaking.

As Joe got closer, he could see Pearse above the heads of the crowd. Mary O'Donovan Rossa stood next to Pearse along with Thomas Clarke and some of the others. Joe saw his own father, Count George Noble Plunkett, standing nearby as well, on the other side of the casket.

Pearse took a small sheet of paper out of his pocket and slowly unfolded it. He looked down at the sheet of paper then out over the crowd for a silent moment. He began by humbly asking to be allowed to speak on behalf of a new generation, re-baptized in the Fenian faith.

"I propose to you then that, here by the grave of this unrepentant Fenian, we renew our baptismal vows; that here by the grave of this unconquered and unconquerable man, we ask of God, each one for himself, such unshakable purpose, such high and gallant courage, such unbreakable strength of souls, as belonged to O'Donovan Rossa."

Pearse spoke for several minutes. The crowd was silent as his words rose above them on the breeze. His voice carried strong and clear over the hushed thousands gathered while maintaining an earnest intimacy that seemed to direct his words to each individual present. He clearly meant everything he said, and his passion spread quickly, growing in intensity as he neared the end of his speech.

"Life springs from death, and from the graves of patriotic men and women spring living nations. The defenders of this realm have worked well in secret and in the open." He spoke now of the British Empire. "They think they have purchased half of us and intimidated the other half." At this there were a few defiant shouts from the crowd. Pearse's voice was rising fiercely by this time, and Joe could feel the excitement surrounding him.

"They think they have foreseen everything," Pearse continued, "think that they have provided against everything; but the fools, the fools, the fools! They have left us our Fenian dead and, while Ireland holds these graves, Ireland unfree shall never be at peace!"

The roar of the crowd was overwhelming, starting near the burial plot and spreading through the packed cemetery to the people outside the walls who had not been able to squeeze inside. The whole city seemed to be cheering with joy and defiance. They would not let O'Donovan Rossa's dedication and struggles be in vain but would carry on, re-baptized in the Fenian faith, as Pearse had urged.

As the cheering continued, shots of salute rang out over the crowd and inspired even louder roars of excitement at each volley. Joe inched his way through the closely packed crowd and returned to his car unnoticed. He drove back to Larkfield to prepare for his trip to America.

7

Grace returned home late in the afternoon after Rossa's funeral. She had not been able to get close to the gravesite because of the massive crowd, so she wasn't able to see Pearse or those near him around the casket. She listened to his speech while watching the shoulders and heads of taller people in front of her. She had hoped she might be able to find Joe, assuming he would be up front near Pearse, but there were just too many people.

She knew Joe would be leaving Ireland again soon, and she wanted to say goodbye. She had the impression that he would be gone for quite a while, though he had been vague about the details and changed the subject when she asked for more. She decided that the trip probably involved his work within the nationalist movement; she hoped that he wasn't planning anything dangerous. She was surprised to find herself worrying about this and missing him more than ever, smiling at the thought of his quick mind, his archaically dashing style, and his passionate speeches about … well, almost everything.

She had to admit that she missed him, but she also knew that his work in the nationalist movement would always come before anything else in his life. He was completely immersed. It wasn't until she had started working with him on *The Irish Review* that they had finally become friends, two years after they first met. The *Review* had always been one of the city's more controversial political newspapers, but it had become even more direct, reckless, and radical once Joe had taken over as editor.

The paper was eventually suppressed by Castle authorities after the police confiscated all the copies they could, raided the offices, destroyed the printing equipment, and gave lots of stern warnings. Joe had, of course, ignored the warnings and tried to keep the paper going a little longer, but after the raid there was no chance of a true resurrection.

It had been great while it lasted. Grace worked with Joe on the paper's layout—work she absolutely loved. For quite a while she had been drawing editorial sketches and cartoons, mostly about the political, social, and art scenes in Dublin. One night she brought one in to show to Joe. It was a satire on the employer stance in the labor lockout, and she liked it, but she had never shown him any of her work. She took the sketch out of her folder then hesitantly walked over to where Joe was working. She slipped it onto the table in front of him.

"What do you think? Is it any good?" she asked.

"How come you haven't shown me any of your work before? You've got a great style—it's delicate and cerebral, but your satire is really strong and right on point." He paused, then added, "Can I use it?"

"For what, the *Review*? Are you serious?"

"Of course. I love it. Look, I've got this open space right here, and I have nothing for it yet. And besides, we've got a big piece about the lockout already, right next to it. It'd be perfect."

Grace was standing behind Joe, looking over his shoulder at the empty space where he wanted her sketch to go. It was perfect. Everyone in the movement read *The Irish Review*, and they talked about it all the time. Maybe next week they'd be talking about her work. Before she realized what she was doing, she had reached down and hugged Joe from behind, exclaiming, "Yes, that'd be great!"

His white shirt was crisply starched, and he smelled like leather, cigars, and the fine tweed of his overcoat, which was now hanging near the door. She lingered for just an instant before she let go of him and quickly took two steps back.

"That would be great," she repeated with what she hoped was more restrained gratitude. She then quickly returned to her own work. She was blushing, and she felt like he was looking at her. She glanced up to see him smiling down at the page in front of him.

"No, thanks for bringing it in," he said without looking up. "Really, it'll be perfect."

She worried as she worked. He probably thought it was funny that she was so excited to be published. She didn't think he would judge her for it—consider her to be naive or unprofessional. Working with Joe, she had learned that, although he was the very accomplished son of a count and could be quite intense and driven, he was also funny and cheerful. He loved to talk for hours about all kinds of things. Grace also found that Joe was the most sympathetic and intensely interested listener she had ever met. When she came in to the office of *The Irish Review*, she was sometimes consumed with frustration about her mother or worried about her future. Joe seemed to be genuinely interested and would draw her out, encouraging her to talk about her problems.

He was always curious about human nature, and he asked the kind of questions that helped her to sort out her problem by the end of their conversation. He had studied psychology, religion, and philosophy at great length and used this knowledge in a practiced but unintimidating way to help her, without artifice or snobbery.

Joe was always on her side. He listened with empathy and spoke with understanding and generosity of spirit. She sometimes felt that he understood her more than anyone else she knew. She had never told him that, of course—that would seem far too intimate for their friendship—but she did look forward to going to work at the paper.

One evening she had asked him about one of his poems called "The Spark," which had been published years before. The last stanza read:

Because I know the spark of God has no eclipse
Now death and I embark
And sail into the dark
With laughter on our lips.

"It's such a powerful image, and I like it." Grace tried to explain her feelings about the verse. "I just find it to be so dark and… even a little scary compared to, I don't know, compared to how you are when I talk to you."

"I guess so. I can understand why it would seem that way, but it's not as much about death as it is about faith. The way I see it is, we're all completely surrounded by God's love. Submerged… or immersed. God—or spirit, or whatever word you want to use—is in everything." He moved his chair around so that he was facing her, leaning forward toward her. "Because of this unlimited, protective love that is all around us all the time, I feel like it's possible to face anything—even death—without fear."

Joe's devoted certainty about this direct connection to God was what Grace had always longed for. That same night she admitted to Joe her great desire to convert to Catholicism, even if it meant being disowned by her mother. She told him about everything—her beloved nanny Bridget, and her secret trips to St. Audoen's. They spoke until very late that night, and it was a topic to which they would return many times. They even started meeting often over tea to speak about their faith—without the excuse of working on the paper.

8

By the time Joe returned from his trip to New York in mid-October, things were moving quickly toward the rebellion. When he was not attending meetings and drills or obsessing over maps and planning strategy, he was either with Grace or trying to set up a time to meet with her. She was now diligently studying for her conversion to Catholicism in the spring, so they always had an excuse to meet.

When they did meet to discuss Catholicism, they generally spent at least half their time together chatting about other things, like friends they had in common, Irish independence, and recent ceili dances.

At his first ceili dance since coming back from the United States, Joe sat at a table at the side of the room with Thomas MacDonagh and some other men from the nationalist movement. The band was playing an energetic reel with a melancholy tone, and there were six sets of four couples each in the center of the room, spinning and skipping to the music as they wound in and out, red faced and laughing. Joe and his friends were well into their second pints and were loudly debating politics when he saw Grace enter the hall with her sisters.

"Finally," he said just under his breath, then more loudly, "Tom. See you later." He rose from the table and started across the hall, his eyes on the newly arrived group at the main door.

The Gifford girls were known to brighten any room they entered, with their auburn hair and flowing, fashionable dresses made from delicate gauze, rich velvets, and Parisian silks in all the colors of a spring garden. But Joe only noticed Grace, in a crimson dress and lavender wrap, as she stood with her sisters, catching up with friends. She turned to see him as he made his way through the crowd to her side.

"Joe, you're back! It seems like forever since I saw you. You're not going on any more long trips, are you?" She touched his arm as she spoke, her gaze focused on him like a shiny magnet.

"No, I'm here to stay for the next several months at least, I promise." He stammered a little in response to her smile. He wanted to tell her she looked beautiful but couldn't quite get the words out. "Can I take your coat, or… uh, wrap? Would you like something to drink?" As he spoke, the band launched into a jig.

"How 'bout a dance instead?" She handed the piece of gauzy lavender to Nellie, and she and Joe rushed to find a place in the last formation of couples.

They remained together throughout the rest of the night, talking between sets and dancing for hours that seemed to go by in less than half the time, becoming closer and closer friends.

Grace had missed Joe while he had been out of the country that spring and summer. Now that he was back, they continued where they had left off with their frequent meetings over tea and an occasional evening full of dancing and conversation.

She had started to notice that his face lit up each time he

found her in a crowd. He seemed to be constantly trying to get her to blush with his good-natured teasing, but when she tried to tease him back, he would generally become as bashful and tongue-tied as a teenager. He began sending her letters and notes, often just a brief and friendly greeting or an invitation to tea.

More recently he was sending her poems or pages of his thoughts about mysticism, Catholicism, and the true nature of spirituality. He wrote that the true nature of everything in the world could be found in God or spirit, and that finding a connection to this source was the path to finding perfection and beauty. This perfection was everywhere, and people just needed to recognize it and connect to it.

The expectations of his relationship with spirituality and religion were so much deeper and intimate than those she had been taught in church. Reading and rereading his letters alone at night by the lamplight, Grace could feel the intensity in his handwriting; it was fluid and refined but also heavy and a bit scrawled, giving her a sense of his excitement for the topic.

Joe had been driving Grace home after their meetings for months now. Sometimes they would go for long walks in her neighborhood. One day in late summer as they walked in Rathmines, she stopped to admire an especially beautiful bush of pale roses. The flowers' petals were large and round and were of the palest buttercream—almost white—with edges tinged in gold. The blooms smelled fresher and cleaner than she could have imagined, like sweet citrus and clean air from the countryside.

"I wish Sweny's could make a soap that smelled like that. They make the nicest soap in Dublin—like fresh lemon—but I like this even better."

Joe absently smelled one of the pale roses and then

immediately stopped and seemed to focus sharply. He held the flower in his hand and seemed to stare through it as he moved his thumb slowly across the silky petals. He was so deeply immersed and so sharply focused that he seemed to have momentarily forgotten all about their evening stroll. He lingered a little longer even as Grace began walking again.

"This is what I've been talking and writing to you about," he said, still staring down at the pale petals.

"What is it?" She turned and walked back to his side as he continued.

"The rose. It explains what I've been trying to tell you about mysticism and God... more clearly than I ever could with words. Just this one little rose is... I see it as evidence. It's proof of something vital." He looked at her, his eyes shining. "Don't you see? Its perfection is just one of a million tiny but crucial arguments made every day in support of the existence of miracles and of goodness and... of spirit. Spirit in our everyday lives."

"A flower?"

They began walking again. Joe was speaking rapidly now, words coming easily. "Sure, but not just that. The rolling green hills of the countryside, the theater of a summer storm, and the wild, windy cliffs on the west coast of County Claire. Perfection! No one even sees the miracles, because all of these things have been there all along. But that's the point. It's there all the time. We're surrounded by it."

"What about love?" she offered.

"Yes! Exactly. That's the best example of all. All kinds of love. The constant, sweet loyalty of my father's dogs. They'd do anything for him. And the fact that people seem destined to fall in love with each other—their feelings so strong that they outlast even death." He spoke in a rush. "All this is proof, do you see? Irrefutable proof of the miraculous. It's what I try to show, over and over again in my poems, but I … I can't get it. I just can't find the words big enough to describe it—to contain it."

He seemed distressed by the need to express the way he felt about the wonders of the world—brows furrowed, as if in a debate with a world that chose to remain blind.

"Very few people will even walk down this little side street and have the chance that you and I had to run into this expression of divinity right here in the midst of all of the grit and smoke and stone of the city," he continued. "And of those few people who would walk this same path, how many of them would even see that rose?"

Grace wanted this passionate and faithful way of diving into life with the knowledge that God—or spirit or divinity or whatever people wanted to call it—was all around her. Over time, she'd learned that Joe got just as excited when he spoke of Ireland's independence; it was as if he felt God wanted freedom for Ireland as much as he and Pearse did. In fact, Joe seemed to face almost everything with this type of passion, almost every minute of the day. Instead of being exhausted by this, his excitement and energy seemed to feed on itself and grow.

Every once in a while, however, he would send a note to cancel their meetings, claiming to have a bad cold. This happened more often than seemed natural, and he would sometimes disappear for weeks at a time. Grace began to wonder if there was something else going on.

9

The days hung heavy with gray skies and a persistent, damp cold, which was the worst thing for Joe's health. Throughout the fall and early winter, however, he felt too excited to sleep or rest as much as he should. The strategic plans for the rebellion, on which he had worked for months, were now taking center stage at the IRB Military Council meetings as the time for fighting drew near. Pearse and Tom Clarke seemed happy with his work, and Joe was proud of that.

It was not even possible to boast to anyone else about the important work he was doing because everything was so secretive. The structure of the whole nationalist organization was getting complicated now and seemed to require lying to almost everyone all the time, simply to ensure some measure of security.

Since Joe thought about the plans for the rising more than anything else, he felt the strain of this required silence, but he knew it was necessary. In Ireland's past, too many rebellions had failed before they could begin due to betrayal or intercepted messages. As it was, most of the leaders in the nationalist movement were surrounded by detectives from Dublin Castle, and it was impossible to expect everyone in the Irish Volunteers to keep quiet.

In addition to this, if they had known about the impending insurrection, many of the members of the Volunteers would not have supported it anyway. There are always so many good reasons to postpone risking many lives to stand up to the most powerful empire on the planet; the odds of succeeding were bad, even under the best of circumstances.

The public face of the more radically minded nationalists was the Irish Volunteers. This was the smaller group of members that had broken away from the moderate John Redmond at the start of the Great War in Europe, after he started encouraging Irish men to fight with the British Army. This smaller and supposedly more radical group was officially headed by Eoin MacNeill, who proved to be a disappointing leader for the more extreme members, as he seemed to be in no hurry whatsoever to mount any actual rebellion. He believed that no violence was justified unless it was defensive in nature: after a direct attack from England.

As soon as it became clear that MacNeill would not support a rebellion, a small group of Irish Republican Brotherhood members had taken over certain aspects of the Irish Volunteer organization. This all happened without the knowledge of MacNeill, who still thought he was in charge.

Earlier in 1915 it had been decided that an even smaller, more tightly bound group was needed from among the already very central and elite members of the IRB leadership. This new group of just a few members was responsible for all of the more detailed secret planning that was now becoming necessary. This was the Military Council. When Joe was asked to join several months before, he was one of only three members. No one else in the whole movement even knew the Council existed, let alone what they had planned—not even the other members of the IRB.

Patrick Pearse and Eamonn Ceannt were the other two founding members of the Council. They were among the most central figures in the nationalist movement. Joe had definitely felt outclassed in the beginning, but he was making up for his youth and inexperience with hard work, fresh perspectives, and passionate devotion to Pearse's ideas about personal sacrifice for Ireland. Joe was also fascinated by military history—he had been his whole life. He now spent several hours most nights surrounded by old volumes on military strategy and maps of Dublin and Ireland, drafting plans and plotting out routes.

Eamonn Ceannt was an accountant and musician from Ballymoe, a town in County Galway in the west. He had always been a staunch nationalist. Pearse was a professor and the founder of the Irish-language school, St. Edna's. His passionate and graceful speeches could inspire fervor and loyalty like no others in the movement at the time.

For some moderates and pragmatists, Pearse was a bit too extreme and dramatic at times—speaking at length about blood sacrifice and the divine honor of dying for a great cause. Some thought that Pearse was the type to lead his men into a hopeless battle for an unattainable cause just to achieve a place in history as a noble martyr, but Joe believed in Pearse, and even more deeply, he believed in their cause.

Joe could certainly see the glory and honor of achieving martyr status, like so many of his favorite saints. But what made these saints so extraordinary to Joe was that they stood up for what they believed in no matter what the cost, not that they had suffered and died horrible deaths, which was unappealing no matter what Pearse said, for obvious reasons. But there was no doubt about what Joe believed in; he would stand up to the British Empire at any cost to help win Ireland's freedom.

If they lost? Well, in that case they would have to accept the possible benefits of self-sacrifice and the relatively minor martyr status within the movement that this might accomplish.

If this were their only choice, then they would be counting on inspiring others to finish the job, which was far from ideal. Joe wanted to live to see a free Ireland. He was counting on it.

Soon Joe, Pearse, and Ceannt had recruited Sean MacDermott and Tom Clarke into the Military Council. Clarke was anxious for action. He had worked for Irish independence too long and hard to sit around and wait any longer for Eoin MacNeill and the Irish Volunteers to mount a rebellion. He told any nationalist who would listen that they couldn't let this war in Europe go by without fighting to expel England from Ireland. "Right now," he would say, pounding his fist on the bar, "while the Empire's troops are spread thin. It's our only chance!"

Sean MacDermott was one of Clarke's closest friends and a lifelong nationalist born in a small town in the north called Corranmore, an area filled with remnants and reminders of Ireland's difficult past. While playing in the countryside as a child, Sean would often explore the small, dilapidated homes abandoned during the times of hunger and starvation of the 1840s—starvation that would not have occurred if the British government had allowed the Irish to keep the food they cultivated instead of exporting it for profit. He accepted the invitation to the Military Council and joined in on their plans with a passion.

The Military Council members were anxious to mount an armed rebellion, and they knew it wasn't going to happen with MacNeill in charge.

10

One day, over tea at Sibley's, Joe told Grace about his ill-fated affection for a woman named Columba who had never loved him. He had given up on that long ago and had not even seen her in years.

"The whole thing just makes me feel like such a fool and … and that's why I've never talked about it before, because, I … well, I haven't been able to get totally over Columba until this summer." His chin rested on one fist as he glared down at the fingers of his other hand, tapping quickly on the table. "I just finally came to see that the whole thing was just about … I don't know, attraction and childish infatuation, I guess." He shook his head and furrowed his brow as he paused, his lips compressed into a tight line. "I've just wasted so much time running after a woman who never cared for me."

Grace wanted to say something to make it easier, but she didn't know what to say. She wasn't sure why he was telling her about this, and it made her uncomfortable. She had heard the gossip about Joe being in love with a childhood friend of his family's named Columba O'Carroll. He had apparently written numerous poems about her and had tried for years to win her love.

Grace had been wondering if maybe he had been off visiting Columba during his long absences. Who needed two weeks to get over a cold? But now she realized she would have to look elsewhere for an explanation.

To her distress, Grace had been worrying about Joe and this woman, Columba, quite a bit lately; she knew she was being ridiculous. She told herself sternly that she was not in love with this tall, skinny eccentric, with his capes and rings, who seemed to think of himself as some kind of Arthurian knight! He was such a fervent nationalist rebel and so famously Catholic that her mother wouldn't have even let him in the door if he didn't show up with Thomas MacDonagh. Joe definitely wasn't a good idea for her. Even so, she couldn't think of anyone else she enjoyed being with quite as much.

Before she could decide on the right words, Joe continued. "But now, because of my work with the Volunteers and preparations for—well, the things we're doing in the movement—I've come to see what's really important. Maybe I've grown up a little or something. I don't know."

"You don't need to explain any of this to me." Grace didn't like hearing about his feelings for Columba, and she didn't like watching him struggle with this explanation. "I don't understand why you think you need—"

"No, I do need to explain it, because I know you've heard about the whole thing." He was more direct now, having found some momentum, and his words began to come out in their usual rush. "It was just such a waste of time, and now I don't know what I was thinking. I mean, yeah, sure, I thought Columba was beautiful and charming…"

Grace held her breath and tried not to show how much she hated hearing about this. She wanted him to stop, but he rushed on.

"But I finally realized that she is also just… too empty and superficial," he added.

Okay, this is better, Grace thought. She suddenly wanted to hear more.

"Her main purpose in life seems to be elevating her social position by making the perfect choice of a husband. Any encouragement she gave me was because of my father's title and my family's money." Joe smiled sadly and shook his head. "The things that matter to me mean nothing to her. Probably just an embarrassment to her, if she thought of them at all. To her type, the poetry is just a waste of time, and my politics are a scandal. I don't know how I could have been so stupid! The whole thing is pathetic. But it's over." He took a deep breath and looked at Grace apologetically.

"It's not pathetic at all. I think everyone's acted like a fool because of love." She tried to sound wise, like a supportive friend.

"There was one other reason I couldn't love her anymore, Grace," he said quietly, looking down again and fidgeting with the corner of the white, starched tablecloth. "When I compare—no, I shouldn't say compare. When I thought about a woman like Columba after getting to know you, her type just doesn't hold up too well." He looked Grace in the eyes for a moment then quickly returned his attention to the tablecloth. "See . . . you're as beautiful and fashionable as she is, but that doesn't matter to you. You don't make a big thing of it. There's just so much more to you."

Grace tried to think of something to say in return. His gaze was still on the table, but he now turned his attention to his teaspoon. The little spoon seemed to disappear in his large hands as he turned it over and over restlessly and continued speaking.

"I guess that, once a man meets someone like you, well, he really couldn't love anyone else anymore. You're so intelligent and independent and strong—like you'll make your own way in life at all costs. It almost seems like you don't need anyone at all."

He paused for moment then shrugged, apologetic again. "I guess I've started to hope that you might come to need me just a little at some point. I don't know how to say it, but I just care about you so much. I think about you all the time and… I think about you, and worry about you. I can't seem to stop."

"Joe, I…" Grace wanted to reassure him, somehow get him to look up at her, but he rushed on now with a defeated tone.

"I hate to think that telling you this might ruin our friendship. That means more to me than any of it, but I had to tell you. I don't know why. I'm sorry. I shouldn't have said it, and I have no business saying anything like that—especially now—but I just wanted you to know how amazing you are and how much you've helped me to see what's important."

Grace reached across the table and took the tiny spoon out of his restless hands, putting her own hand in its place. He looked up at her, and after a surprised moment, he cradled her hand between his own. They sat in silence for a while before he left a little money on the table and they stood to leave. They walked through the cool, windy evening, and Joe removed his long, black cape, putting it around her shoulders.

After speaking nonstop for hours over tea, they now walked hand in hand without a word. Grace couldn't stop smiling. She felt like she might be glowing brightly enough to light up the dark evening as they walked slowly through the tumbling, gliding, golden leaves.

11

The political scene in Dublin was becoming more tense and complicated. The city was always buzzing with many small political and paramilitary groups that failed to draw much attention. But ever since the split in the Volunteers during the big war in Europe, the two largest and most well-known nationalist organizations had become more polarized.

The large and relatively mainstream National Volunteers, headed by John Redmond, continued to seek a political approach to Ireland's problems, still hoping to win Home Rule after their support of England in the war in Europe. They didn't want any trouble with the authorities. Because of this, they were increasingly in conflict with Eoin MacNeill's more radical Irish Volunteers, who continued to function as a paramilitary organization, preparing to defend themselves against England if pushed too far. Most now believed that MacNeill would be ready for a fight if England sought to establish conscription in Ireland for additional support in the war.

The Irish Volunteers itself was swarming with internal conflict because of the multiple and secret layers of IRB membership beneath the surface. De facto leaders like Pearse and Clarke were the most radical of all and were not willing to wait for England to give them an excuse to fight. But there was another paramilitary organization led by James Connolly called the Irish Citizen Army.

James Connolly was born in an Irish immigrant slum in Edinburgh, Scotland, known as "Little Ireland." He quit attending classes at the local Catholic primary school at the age of ten in order to find work to help support his family. At just fourteen years old, Connolly lied about his age and joined the British Army out of financial desperation. He served in Ireland, where he often had to support the police while they enforced the evictions of hundreds of poor farming families during the land wars. Connolly learned firsthand how unfair the system could be for the poor, and it was during his time in service that he learned to hate the British Army.

Connolly formed the Irish Citizen Army in 1913. He supported the Fenian tradition of physical force in the name of independence and eventually dedicated the ICA to the rebel cause of establishing an independent Irish Republic.

Because the IRB and the new Military Council had kept their plans so well hidden, James Connolly was under the impression that no one was preparing to mount an armed rebellion. He feared that the nationalist movement would end up languishing while John Redmond continued his waiting game with England.

For months now he had been speaking angrily—and very publicly—about missed opportunities and threatening to go ahead with his own rebellion if no one else was going to do anything at all. At a meeting in December of 1915, Joe and the others in the IRB Military Council discussed their fears that Connolly might lead his Citizen Army into a rebellion any day—right in the middle of the final buildup to the IRB's own uprising in April.

"Connolly's Citizen Army only has about two hundred members, and they don't have enough guns to go around." Clarke paced around Pearse's desk as he spoke. "If they revolt on their own, it'll be a massacre."

"And imagine how much tighter things would get in the city afterward." Pearse sat behind his desk, maintaining his mask of composure. "The Castle is just waiting for any excuse to come out and arrest everyone in the movement. If Connolly goes ahead, it could ruin our chances this spring."

"Can't we let him in on our plans? Bring him in with us?" asked Joe.

"Connolly can be so stubborn," Clarke argued. "And he's so impatient about all of the delay that I don't know if he'd be willing to wait."

"I think he'd wait if we could show him we're serious about it," Sean MacDermott was close to Connolly and knew him better than anyone at the meeting. "And we could use his help this spring. He's an excellent leader and an experienced soldier. I think we should try to get through to him."

The Military Council decided to tell Connolly about all their plans and try to convince him to join them in April. They made many appointments with him throughout December and early January, but each time he canceled at the last minute, apparently under the impression that they were just going to try to talk him out of his own rebellion.

Finally, the Military Council decided that they would have to talk to Connolly whether he wanted to listen or not. Eamonn Ceannt and Sean MacDermott waited for him when he left Liberty Hall. They brought him to a secret meeting at an abandoned home in a little southwest suburb of Dublin. Pearse and Joe were there waiting for them, sitting at a table in the middle of an otherwise empty room.

"So, you're kidnapping me now, that's what it's come to," Connolly said, his words tinged with sarcasm. "There's no use trying to talk me out of it, boys."

"Just hear us out," Pearse answered calmly. "That's all we're asking."

"I'll give you five minutes to state your case," Connolly said to Pearse, but he didn't look all that interested.

Joe stood to speak. It was up to him. These were the plans on which he'd spent so much time over the last several months. "We're going ahead with it this Easter," Joe announced as if it were the beginning of a speech. "We have four Irish Volunteer battalions ready to take over large portions of Dublin by occupying strategically selected buildings in and near the city center."

Connolly looked surprised already, but Joe continued quickly, before he could interrupt or offer any argument, "On Easter Sunday Ned Daly's 1st Battalion will take the Four Courts. That's directly in the path of British soldiers marching in from the Royal Barracks. At the same time, Thomas MacDonagh's 2nd Battalion will position themselves in Jacob's Biscuit Factory, near two more barracks to the south of town." Joe reached for a file on the table, removed a map, and unfolded it as he spoke. "This will enable us to fight any soldiers marching toward the city center from any of the three." He smoothed out the map, then pointed out the locations of the barracks. "Here . . . here . . . and here.

"De Valera's 3rd Battalion will occupy Boland's Bakery," Joe continued, "right here, which you can see is close to another of the British barracks and also stands right on the path to Dublin from Kingstown Port, where England will be sure to land reinforcements." Connolly had walked around the table, closer to the map, scrutinizing it as he listened. Joe realized that he had his attention.

"Eamonn?" Joe slid the map over so that it was in front of Ceannt, who was seated next to him.

"I've got the 4th Battalion," Eamonn continued. "We'll take the South Dublin Union. From there we'll be able to monitor and control movements of British soldiers marching into the city center from two additional barracks."

"We'll also take over some of the rail stations and the telegraph and telephone systems," Joe continued, "as well as the General Post Office, which will serve as headquarters for the whole operation."

"We think we'll have more than 2,500 volunteers for the fight in Dublin," Clarke added, "and we're expecting a massive supply of guns and ammunition from Germany right before the fighting begins."

Connolly was obviously intrigued. He agreed to stay as long as it took for them to give him all the details. Meals were brought in—along with a couple of old military cots, which were placed in the next room for short breaks—and the meeting stretched on for two and a half days.

In addition to relating the details of the rebellion in Dublin, they told Connolly that IRB militias in counties all over Ireland would join in as well, overcoming the relatively small rural British units and then making their way to the city to serve as reinforcements.

They had also made ethical and historical considerations, which they knew would appeal to Connolly. From the first moment of the rebellion, they would be establishing themselves as the provisional government of the new Irish Republic, and their soldiers were to behave like those of a true national army.

"There will be no drinking, no looting, and no dirty fighting, and every attempt will be made to protect civilians and their property," Pearse assured him. "We are all aware that the world will be watching, and in victory or defeat, we are determined to make future Irish generations proud."

After two days Connolly agreed to join in their plans and was brought on as a member of the Military Council. They spent another night answering his questions and considering his ideas and additions. Joe was excited to get Connolly's suggestions on the strategies he had developed, and the two of them gathered over large sheets of paper, where Joe drew out possible scenarios and Connolly praised, questioned, and made changes.

On the third day, Joe drove Connolly back to Liberty Hall. Connolly wanted to check in at Irish Citizen Army headquarters before heading home because he had been gone for so long without explanation. Because of his open threats of an immediate revolution, he had been suspecting someone from the Irish or National Volunteers might attempt some form of sabotage. He had given instructions for the Citizen Army to go ahead and start the rebellion if they suspected this had taken place.

With Connolly gone, Countess Constance Markievicz would be one of the few left in charge of the Irish Citizen Army. She was even more impatient than Connolly and could be extremely impulsive. For a long time now, she had been pushing him to go ahead with a rebellion—looking for any reason at all to start a fight with the Castle.

Although very wealthy herself, the countess had long been a defender of the poor; she funded schools and soup kitchens and also helped to arm and outfit the Volunteer fighters. Over the years she had come to see that it was

England's negligent ruling in Ireland that caused much of the country's suffering. She was convinced that freedom in Ireland would require violent insurrection, so after the war started, she joined James Connolly's Irish Citizen Army. His was the only rebel military force that would allow women to fight on the front lines, and this served him well in this case; the Countess was an excellent shot.

As soon as Connolly had been missing for two days, the Countess had begun urging the other ICA officers to march into battle with her. By now, the morning of the third day, she was threatening to go out and do it on her own, letting them know that they could follow her if they wanted to.

As soon as Joe and Connolly entered the doors of Liberty Hall, they could hear loud voices from the headquarters office downstairs. When they reached the bottom of the stairs, they saw Countess Markievicz on her feet arguing with several men who were seated at a large table.

"Are you cowards or Irishmen?" she demanded. "We have to fight. We can't let them keep us down!" She paced the floor, waving her pistol as she went on. "We must repay our debt to those who have died for Ireland in the past and fulfill our responsibility to future generations!"

"And we will," Connolly announced from the doorway, smiling proudly at the Countess as she turned in surprise. "We will have our rising, all right. And it will be magnificent!"

12

Joe had begun to daydream about asking Grace to marry him. He thought about settling down with her at one of his family's properties, just the two of them. He imagined them talking long into the night, cuddled in front of the fire. He looked forward to entertaining their friends in their own home, or dining together alone, and waking up every morning in each other's arms. He sometimes pictured the two of them living at the house in Donnybrook, near the city, attending concerts and political meetings. Maybe one of them could even run for office. Other times he thought about finding a place to live with Grace in the country south of Dublin, in Kilternan, where he had spent time as a boy.

Joe's dad was an art historian, and in 1900 he had published a very successful book on Sandro Botticelli and Renaissance art. With the money from the sale of the book, Count Plunkett had bought the family a house in Kilternan so the kids could spend time in the fresh country air. Joe's new best friend had been a neighbor boy named Kenneth O'Morchoe. Kenneth's family was Protestant, and he and his brothers had joined the British Army at about the same time that Joe and his brothers had become involved with the Volunteers. Even now, Joe ran into Kenneth out at the pubs from time to time, and it was always good to see his old friend, despite their political differences.

Joe's time in Kilternan had been filled with long days exploring the countryside on horseback with his siblings and friends, far from the reach of his irresponsible and impulsive mother. The area had come to represent freedom for Joe, and he wondered if Grace would be willing to live in the country, so far from the attractions of Dublin.

Either way, they would be together, so he would be happy! The uprising would be complete, Ireland would be starting over as an independent nation, and he and Grace would do their part to rebuild it together.

All of this daydreaming got him nowhere, but it was also free of risk. He had no idea if Grace would have him. He was convinced that he was in no position to ask her to marry him at this point in his life, but he believed that he could make himself worthy over time. There were reasons for him to go ahead and ask her right away. His plans for the revolution in the spring were a big motivation for two reasons. First, he would be facing the imminent possibility of death or imprisonment, and that gave him a reckless courage. Secondly, he was so busy with preparations that, if Grace did not feel as strongly as he did and he was humiliated, he would not have much time to be sad or ashamed.

But there were also practical reasons for the rush. If word were to get out about Grace's confirmation to the Catholic Church, which was coming up in April, there was a good chance her mother would force her to move out of the family home. Isabella was furious in her bigotry against Catholics and made no effort to conceal it. She had said terrible things about Joe's best friend, Thomas, when he began seeing Grace's sister Muriel, even when Thomas was in the same room. This had gone on for months, no matter how much Muriel fretted, cried, and begged her mother to stop.

Joe knew that, as much as she tried to be strong and defiant, Grace often worried about her mother's reaction to her upcoming conversion. She planned to ask Muriel if she could move in with her and Thomas if her mother kicked her out of the house. Joe wanted to create a safe and peaceful home for Grace where she could finally be honest and open and feel free to be herself. He needed to ignore his fears and declare his love.

"Grace, I don't know how to bring this up, so I'm just going to say it."

They sat together on a bench at St. Stephen's Green, wrapped up tightly together in his long, black woolen cape. The sun was bright, but there was a chill in the air.

"I want you to marry me," he announced, adding quickly, "but—but before you answer, I want to tell you that I love you more than anything in the world, and if you love me at all—even just a little bit—I just ask you to give me a chance." He took her hands in his own to warm them as he spoke. "Please let me spend the rest of my life proving how much I love you, making you happy."

Grace blinked and opened her mouth a little, ready to speak, but he cut her off, rushing to make one more point before she gave him an answer. "I know I'm not worthy of you right now. I know it." His mind raced. "I haven't proven myself. But soon—"

"Joe, please stop." Grace was smiling at him. "Of course I'll marry you. When do you think we should do it?" she asked simply. Her dark eyes became more liquid and luminous than usual as they welled with tears, but otherwise she seemed totally composed, as if marrying him were the most natural thing in the world.

He did not feel so calm at all. Waves of joy and relief rushed through him—*She said yes*! But the many reasons why he had no right to ask her to marry him seemed to be shouting at him inside his head, all at the same time. He had no right to pull her into his chaotic world right now, but looking into her eyes and holding her smooth, pale hand, which was warm despite the damp chill in the air, he also felt that he had no choice. He loved her too much to do the right thing and leave her alone.

"But you know, Grace, I am actually a beggar." He winced with the pain of laying out the reasons she should refuse him after trying for months to win her love. "We have all of the property and the family money, but I have no income of my own, and I am earning next to nothing."

Grace smiled and shook her head a little, remaining unconcerned. But he had to continue. He had to be as honest as he could stand.

"And there are other, more desperate reasons to prevent you from marrying me." All the risks involved in the upcoming rebellion clamored for attention and expression. But he could not say any of it out loud to her now. He was too scared of losing her.

He felt that he was never meant to be as happy as he was with Grace. It was as if he had somehow managed to rewrite the plan for his destiny—beating the stars at their own game. The fact that she wanted to be with him forever so overwhelmed him with gratitude that he felt incapable of doing anything that might make that feeling go away. He could hardly breathe with the thought of losing that feeling.

"I'll tell you everything I can, as soon as I can, but for now I can only say that I am terrified that you might end up being very sorry you accepted my love."

Here Grace interrupted him. "I know that you're working on secret plans with the Irish Volunteers." He blinked and stammered and started to speak, but she went on, teasing him. "You look so shocked that I know! It's so obvious, with all of your covert meetings and rushing around all the time! But you don't need to worry about that. I love Ireland as much as you do," she scolded gently. "You know I do! I'm sure I can support what you're doing, whatever it is. Just tell me what's going on when you can."

Joe felt like crying with relief. He had not thought it possible to love Grace more than he already did, but she had proved him wrong. His mind raced with things he wanted to tell her; secrets, poems, every detailed plan for the rising. But Joe was sworn to secrecy. She did not even know about the IRB, let alone the Military Council. He was not sure how long his resolve would hold out—especially now that she had agreed to marry him. It seemed she had the right to know.

For one fleeting second, he was back in Marseille again; he imagined forgetting everything else and running away with Grace. He felt the sun-warmed sand under their feet, far away, where they would be free from all of this—happy with nothing but their love for each other. As he had done many times before, he thought about living a long life with Grace at his side.

They could buy a little cottage near the sea and live there forever; maybe even have a son and a daughter. They would walk to the beach, where Grace could sketch and Joe would write while the kids played in the warm, gentle surf.

Joe could help Grace learn French, and her sisters could come down to visit so she wouldn't be lonely so far from home.

Every time Joe began to enjoy these thoughts, he remembered his love for his country and his oaths to the nationalist movement. But he had another reason to stay and fight. He feared that he might not be worthy of Grace's love if he were to run away. Fighting for Ireland was his chance to distinguish himself and prove that he was capable of doing something big and dynamic and forceful.

He needed to be more than a sickly poet. He thought of how proud Grace would be to stand next to him this same time next year, after he fought for their country and helped to gain its independence. Surely it would more than make up for his inconsistent health and his lack of a career if he were someday in the history books along with the great Irish heroes like Emmet and the Fenians.

"You have my heart," he told Grace, wrapping the cape more tightly around her as a cold wind whisked through the park. "I know that isn't much, but you have it. I hope to become more worthy of loving you very soon, and I swear that I'll make you proud. I just want you to be mine for the rest of my life." He only hoped that he might live awhile.

13

Grace and Joe officially announced their engagement in February with a brief item in *Irish Life* magazine. Traditionally, the future bride's mother placed these announcements in the papers, but Grace knew that Isabella would be fiercely opposed to the marriage. Now that it was in the paper, her mother would find out about her betrothal, but Grace felt that she was ready for the reaction. Muriel and Thomas MacDonagh wanted her to come to stay with them if Isabella threw her out on the street.

As it turned out, her mother did not force her to leave just yet, but Grace soon found out that being thrown out of the house might actually have been preferable. Isabella yelled and ranted and made threats. She said she was sorry she had ever brought Grace into this world, and wondered what she had done to make her daughters go so wrong.

"Every time I turn around, it's another scandal with you girls!" Isabella continued to shout even though she could no longer see her daughter. She was holding a cold cloth over her eyes and forehead with one hand while she waved the other one up and down and back and forth with fierce gestures. All the while, she leaned back against a great nest of pillows that her husband had rushed to prepare for her a few minutes earlier when she had complained that she felt faint after reading the engagement announcement.

"Now that the whole terrible thing's gone public, what am I supposed to say to our guests when they call, Grace?

Can you tell me that? I'll cancel the open house for this week, anyway. I can't stand to go through with it.

"Where's your father? Frederick? Frederick! Frederick! Where are you?" Her husband had quietly left the room a moment earlier and was creeping up the stairs, almost on tiptoe. She removed the cloth, peering about the room like a raptor, then sighed deeply, settling back into the pillows and again covering her eyes.

"Tell the staff to shut everything down for the week. No, no, the rest of the season! No visitors at all. No open houses, no parties, no one over for tea. I simply can't take it! You can take care of everything—the explanations and apologies to practically *everyone we know*—because it's all your fault. No. No, I'll do it! I don't even want you speaking with anyone." She removed the cloth once again, leaning toward Grace and holding up an accusing finger.

"I don't want to see your face ever again. You can either get out right now or stay in your room until you come to your senses and cancel this whole... atrocity!"

Grace was surprised by the fact that she felt so hurt by her mother's tirade. She had known it was coming, but under this constant attack, she had started to feel like a shamed seven-year-old again. As the onslaught continued, Grace wondered why she was still sitting there listening.

"This man's no good, Grace. No good! He's sickly, he's Catholic, and he's in with all those Sinn Feiners. If he doesn't get killed by the Castle for some protest, he's sure to die any day from tuberculosis, and then where will you be?"

Tuberculosis? Joe had said nothing about that, but it would explain why he had to stay home sick for so long at times. Grace said nothing—asked her mother no questions—and tried hard not to reveal her shock at the news. Isabella's eyes were closed, but she had a predator's ability to sense weakness. She did not seem to have picked up on her daughter's surprise about Joe's health, however, and continued shouting as Grace remained seated before her, feeling a little stunned and no longer able to listen.

"Then where will you be, Grace?" Isabella asked again. "I can tell you where you *won't* be—in my home. Not if you marry that … that useless, sickly Sinn Feiner. And of course he's no longer welcome in this house, by the way—even if he comes with Thomas and Muriel. Now that I think about it, I don't want them around here anymore either. Thomas is the one who first brought over that no-good, sickly rebel. And now they're everywhere! Rebels and heretics. It's like a contagion! And you girls have brought it into my house. My house!"

Grace rose silently and started to leave.

"Yes, just go!" Isabella yelled, her eyes still closed and covered with the cloth. "You're such a disappointment—a disappointment and a disgrace!" At this, her voice went up half an octave, and her rant seemed to have reached its climax. She continued, a little quieter now, as if she had used up all of her energy and was once more just the helpless, long-suffering victim of her terrible, unappreciative family.

"Now get out of my sight. Just having you here is making my head pound."

Grace walked quietly out of the room. Her face burned and her hands shook. She was furious with herself for not having said something clever and defiant, then marching out of the room as soon as her mother had started shouting insults. She just felt so small and tired now, deflated.

Grace had been gliding around town for weeks with her secret and exciting plans for the future floating around her like pink and gold balloons, shiny and huge. Now it felt as if they were all gone, lying flat and useless in a dark corner of some grimy street. She felt foolish and alone.

She walked up the stairs on shaky legs, wondering if she was being reckless with this marriage. *What will we do? Where will we live? Can I really be happy without my parents in my life at all? What if Joe does die and I'm left all alone?*

She seemed to love him more every day and become more attached to him every time they met. Grace knew her love and need for Joe would only continue to grow if they were married, so was it safer to leave him now? If he did die of some illness or get shot in a rebellion, wouldn't it only be worse if it happened after more time had gone by and she'd come to love him more?

She was scared by what Isabella had said about Joe's health, but she was afraid to ask him about it. Why hadn't he told her? She also worried about marrying a man who would most likely be on the front lines of the next rebellion, but this was also one of the things she loved about him—one of the many things.

She started to think about Joe—how it felt to be with him, not the myriad details and problems they needed to overcome just to exist in the world together. She thought about how safe she felt with him and how he looked when he smiled at her, like his dark eyes were about to overflow with the joy he felt. If he was with her now, he would hold her and reassure her until she was calmer. Everything was going to be fine. That's what he would tell her. She knew that he would smile and tease her until he got her to smile too, and then he would say, "That's better, my darling Babbaly."

Grace took a deep breath and walked up the stairs to her room. She went to her drawer and took out a bundle of letters she had received from Joe. She needed to feel reassured about what the two of them had planned. She thumbed through the pages, picking one at random and reading it. He wrote about how wrong it was that they could not be together at the end of the day. He wrote that he wanted to hold her "close in his arms through the lovely hours of the night."

Through the lovely hours of the night, she repeated to herself. The meaning of his words sent a little jolt of anticipation through her body that was almost painful and took her mind off of her troubles with Isabella for the moment. Each time she and Joe had kissed, she had wanted so badly to be alone with him to find out where things might go. She wanted to be with him night and day, whether it was for the rest of her life or just a very short time. She continued reading.

"I can never seem to find the words to tell you, but I need you to know: You are wonderful, Grace. You have taken all of the pain from my life and made the whole world beautiful," he wrote. "You have made me so happy—happier than I ever thought I could be. To me, your love for me is another one of those miracles. More evidence of God. That means the world to me, and I want you to promise me that you'll never forget that, no matter what happens." This time the passage struck her a little differently than it had before. What did he mean by "no matter what happens"? Was he writing about his health, or the dangers of an impending rebellion?

14

South of the city in Kimmage, at Larkfield, Joe paced his room. He was getting sick again and would most likely be stuck in bed for the next two weeks or so. This is what generally happened when he let himself get badly run down. During the last few months, he had been running from meeting to meeting almost nonstop without eating right or sleeping enough. He was too busy planning for the rebellion to notice that he had been exhausted for weeks. Now it was the middle of March—just a little over a month until the rising. He could tell he had a fever, and the glands in his neck were swollen again. These were the signs of the beginning of an acute illness that he could no longer choose to ignore.

He could have Military Council meetings at home and work from bed the rest of the time, but he did not want Grace to see him in such a state. He would have to come up with excuses for canceling their plans. He had not told her about his illness yet—something he justified by convincing himself that he had been too busy for such an important conversation. It never seemed to be the right time to tell her that the doctors didn't even know if he would make it through another year. Joe hadn't been to his doctor lately, but he knew the signs. He knew what the diagnosis would be based on so many past visits.

Despite the excuses he told himself, he knew better; he was only delaying telling Grace about his illness because he was afraid that she would break off the engagement. That was not fair to her. But then, he had always made it through the next year no matter what the doctors had told him, and he had every expectation of living a long life despite these occasional spells of serious illness. What good would it do to worry her about it when it was nothing, really?

His serious difficulties with tuberculosis stemmed from the time his mother had stuck him in a Catholic boarding school for months in Paris as a little boy. The original plan was for her to take him to Rome, where it was hoped that the warm, dry weather would help him recover from a long and serious bout with pneumonia. But when they got to Paris, she decided she wanted to stay there instead. She dropped her sick son off at the Marist boarding school in Passy without any warm clothing, and he stayed there for many cold months while she toured museums and attended concerts and parties.

Joe became seriously ill during his time in Paris. Even though he was eventually better after a long period of bed rest, his illness recurred time and again throughout the rest of his life, often requiring surgical treatments when the glands in his neck became too infected to heal on their own. The doctors had told him many times that he did not have long to live, but he had always made it through the next illness to achieve a normal state of health. Once he was well, he could keep up with any of his friends without any trouble at all, playing football or competing in hurling matches all day and staying out at the pubs until early the next morning.

He had no doubt that he would continue to beat the odds and live to a happy old age with Grace at his side, assuming he made it through Easter. He thought it might actually help him to marry Grace. When he was with her, he experienced intense happiness and gratitude that seemed to have a healing effect on him. But if he was honest with himself, he knew that Grace deserved to know everything she was getting into before she was stuck with him forever. This also included his role in the upcoming insurrection. He knew he needed to tell her about it, but he was not allowed to because of his oaths to the IRB. This was a source of great confusion for him.

He was also worried about the timing of their marriage. He thought it was best to wait to marry Grace until after he had survived the fighting in April to eliminate the possibility of making her an immediate widow. But the fact that he could be killed soon also made him feel just as convinced that he needed to marry her right away. Her mother was already on the verge of disowning her, and when Grace converted to Catholicism in April, he knew it would be the final straw. She would most certainly be disowned and thrown out of the family home. He wanted to be sure that Grace had a place to stay and would inherit his share of his family's wealth and property if anything happened to him.

After a lot of thought, Joe had decided that it was most important for Grace to be provided for, and he had been pushing to marry her as soon as possible. He had brought it up the previous week.

"I was thinking that we might have the marriage right after your conversion ceremony," he had suggested, trying for a casual tone.

"But that's on April 7, just a few weeks away… and it's during Lent." She looked bewildered. "Are we even allowed to get married during Lent? It seems a little dismal. Wouldn't that mean we couldn't have a party?"

"I don't know. I don't know. I just don't want to wait—not with so much going on right now." Joe needed to be more careful about what he said. "Besides all that, I'm worried that your mother could throw you out of the house after the conversion. If we were already married, you could come stay with me."

"She is making me crazy." Grace sighed deeply, shaking her head and looking suddenly exhausted. "But another week or two won't matter, and Muriel's all set for me to go stay there." Grace paused for a moment or two, deep in thought. Then her look of exhaustion suddenly vanished, and she sat forward. "Oh, and I forgot to tell you!" She was smiling now, taking his hand. "I spoke to your sister the other day, and she said we should have a double ceremony with her and Tommy on Easter Sunday! Wouldn't that be fun? We were talking about it, and we were thinking we could all have one big party after!"

"Maybe so." Joe didn't know what to say. His sister Geraldine and her fiancé were planning to have a small ceremony on Easter Sunday. Ordinarily it would have been perfect. "That would be nice, but I... well, we'll figure it out soon."

They hadn't spoken of it since.

This was bad; Easter Sunday was the first day of the uprising. The Military Council had set this date months ago, and there were people in the United States, Germany, and all over Ireland who were counting on things going ahead on this exact day. But how could he explain this to Grace if he could not even tell her the details of their plans? He decided that he would have to break his oaths to the IRB and Military Council and tell her everything.

He longed to have her come to stay with him and his family at Larkfield so they could have time and privacy to sort all of this out. But in order to let her stay at his family's estate, he would have to tell her all about the uprising. The property had been transformed into the Kimmage Garrison and had become the main site for many of the preparations for the rising. IRB men from all over Britain had been informed that they were needed to fight for Ireland and had begun making their way to Dublin.

First the estate's old flour mill had been taken over by the Liverpool Volunteers and turned into barracks. They were eventually joined by men from London, Manchester, and Glasgow. Joe's family fed and housed them while his little brother, George, stayed with them in the old mill. He was in charge of keeping the new troops drilling and working. They were a pretty hard and tough crowd, and the family had started referring to them sarcastically as "George's Lambs."

In addition to the barracks, there were munitions and explosives storage sites throughout the property. Shotgun shells were being filled with heavy brass pellets that were made from molds ten at a time. The Volunteers produced primitive pikes made of knives and poles and hand grenades from cast-iron pipes. As the uprising drew nearer, the leaders began to push the drilling and production even harder.

Joe knew that the men living in the old flour mill were beginning to suspect that something serious was coming up soon. That was okay. The rank and file Volunteers still had no specific plans that might be unknowingly or accidentally divulged to a Castle spy. But if they could feel the fight coming soon—if they suspected the time was near—they would be more prepared when the day came.

15

On April 7, 1916, Grace was baptized in University Church at St. Stephen's Green. She was received as a Catholic and thrown out of her home by her mother on the same day. Joe gave her a poem he had written for the occasion. In return, she gave him an antique family heirloom ring that he promised to wear until the day he died.

Joe drove Grace out to her sister's house and helped her carry her bags upstairs to the little room where she planned to stay until after the wedding—whenever it would be. He followed her inside and closed the door. Grace sat on her small bed and watched him pace around the room with a furrowed brow. He seemed to be avoiding eye contact. More than once he stopped, took his hands out of his pockets, and inhaled quickly, as if he were about to speak. But then he exhaled again, shook his head slightly, and continued pacing.

"Joe, what is it? Something's been bothering you for a while now."

"I know. You're right…" He trailed off, continuing to pace.

"I can't help you if you don't tell me what's going on," Grace insisted. She reached out her hand to catch him as he paced by. She held his hand and pulled him over to sit down next to her on the little bed.

"I know. I know. I'm sorry." He sat down and took off his glasses, rubbing his eyes for a moment before replacing them. "I just don't know how to tell you. It's… it's about the wedding."

Grace's chest felt heavy, and she couldn't breathe for a moment. *Had he changed his mind? Had all his beautiful words meant nothing at all?* That didn't seem possible. It didn't make any sense. Joe looked up from his own worries for a moment and saw her face.

"Oh. No, Grace! It's not like that! I'm so sorry. It's just that you want to get married on Easter Sunday, and, well, I don't think I can do that. But I don't know if I can tell you why. I mean, I shouldn't, but I think I have to."

"I thought Easter would be perfect, but it doesn't have to be that day." She watched him as he paused. She could almost hear the thoughts spiraling fiercely inside of his head. "Joe, you know you can tell me anything."

"I know that's true. Usually. It's just that I've been sworn to secrecy. Okay, well, don't tell anyone, but the thing is"—he took a deep breath—"we'll have a rebellion going on that day. I'm going to be fighting."

Grace felt cold and she couldn't move. Intellectually, she had always known that Joe would someday fight for Ireland's freedom, but it had been a distant, romantic idea, not something that needed to be faced and dealt with—certainly not so quickly. She didn't quite know how to react and wondered if she was as pale as she felt.

"Oh. Well, that's fine," she said, smiling faintly. "Of course it's fine. The day doesn't matter. We can do it anytime."

"Thank you, that's great. Listen, I've got to get into the city. I'm already late. But I'll see you tomorrow. And remember, don't tell anyone what I've said." He was already on his way to the door.

"Yes, I understand," she said, absentminded now, her chest tightening at thoughts of screams, fire, and bloodshed. She was Irish; she'd heard all about the realities of revolution.

Then Joe was close to her again, searching her eyes.

"Are you sure you're fine?" he asked her. "You don't look well."

"Really, Joe, I promise I'm fine. Go ahead, and I'll see you tomorrow. I know you need to go."

16

After Joe helped Grace get situated at her sister's, he drove toward the city, thinking about her and her reaction. He was relieved that she did not seem sad or angry with him about spoiling her plans for an Easter Sunday wedding. But she had also been much too quiet, and that worried him as he drove out to the Mansion House to attend a public Volunteers meeting. It was to be the last big public gathering of the Irish Volunteers before the rising.

There had been two detectives from the Castle sneaking around the crowd, but they had been recognized and thrown out near the beginning of the evening. They continued to hang around outside, trying to look casual, like they belonged, as they listened for whatever clues they might overhear. The great main hall was packed with members of the Irish Volunteers, the IRB, Connolly's Irish Citizen Army, and the handful of Military Council members, as well as nonmember supporters. The multiple layers of deceit between all of these different groups were becoming a burden for Joe. He was glad that they only had a few more weeks until everything would be out in the open, whatever the outcome.

Even though the uprising was officially a secret, the hints and allusions in Pearse's public speeches had become increasingly obvious to anyone who was paying attention and knew the Dublin political scene. He told the Military Council members that he wanted to begin to inspire and prepare the

Volunteers psychologically even if they could not literally be warned of what was coming.

This made Joe nervous, though he did not admit to it at the meetings. He was just so worried that something would happen at the last minute to thwart the plans they had worked on for so long now. Eoin MacNeill was already suspicious and had asked Pearse and the others more than once if they were secretly planning something big. Each time they had denied it.

MacNeill was stiff but dignified, as usual, when he took the podium for his speech. He seemed unconcerned with conspiracy and had apparently been adequately reassured for the time. His speech was safe and routine.

Patrick Pearse took center stage next, looking confident, his dark eyes intense as they scanned the large hall. He stood comfortably in total silence for a moment or two until the packed crowd stood silent, waiting for him to speak. He knew how to get their attention.

Once he was sure that everyone in the room was waiting for his first words, Pearse began, slowly and somberly at first, speaking briefly about the situation in Europe and the responsibility of Irish leaders to protect their own. He moved on to speak at length on themes of national pride and the honor of making the ultimate sacrifice in the name of freedom, then built to a crescendo of declarations about the great shame that must be endured by any generation that failed to shed blood in defense of Ireland.

Very subtle, Joe thought tensely.

MacNeill's right-hand man, Bulmer Hobson, rose to speak next, making his way to the stage. Unlike MacNeill,

Hobson did not accept the reassurances of Pearse and the others and was convinced that certain members of the IRB and Irish Volunteers were secretly planning a rebellion. He was sure that they were deceiving MacNeill and—worse yet—leaving Hobson out of all the fun. Pearse, MacDonagh, and Joe had all taken their turns trying to assure him that this was not the case, but he could not be convinced.

Bulmer Hobson used his turn at the podium to go public with his suspicions and opinions. He spoke openly against fighting, advising the Volunteers that they would never be able to successfully fight the English—now or ever. Joe couldn't believe what he was hearing. Hobson was an IRB man who spoke often about using any means necessary to secure Ireland's freedom, including violent insurrection. Now he seemed to be backing down.

After Hobson finished a hush fell over the hall. The Irish would never be able to successfully fight the English? Muttered arguments could be heard starting up throughout the crowd as small groups began to complain and disagree with the people next to them. The quiet rumbling soon erupted into shouts and arguments. Many were yelling angrily toward the podium, shaking their clenched fists, while others in the crowd yelled back, defending Bulmer's statements.

A red-faced man just to Joe's right was yelling something unintelligible in all the noise, his mouth twisted in a snarl. Joe looked over to see the man pull a handgun out of his coat and raise it above the crowd. The man pointed it at Hobson, who was still standing at the podium facing the rising fury before him and shouting his arguments into the crowd. Things began to move slowly as Joe pushed through the throng toward the man with the gun just as a general scuffle broke out all around him. Most people backed or ran away from the man with the gun while his friends gathered around him, trying to calm him down. They got ahold of their angry friend just as Joe reached them.

Joe grabbed the man's gun and handed it to one of the men as the group pulled their irate friend toward the outskirts of the crowd and out of the Mansion House. Things were getting rowdier by the minute. Joe was jostled and pushed as he stood trying to catch his breath. He noticed with surprise that his hands were not shaking yet.

Although most people in the large crowd had no idea what had just happened—of how close things had been to going very badly—the mood in the hall remained heavy and fierce. Father Flanagan, a priest who was heavily involved in the nationalist movement, jumped up on the stage. He launched immediately into a rousing, patriotic, fighting speech that safely released the mounting tensions of the crowd. They were soon unified and cheering again.

Joe saw Pearse and MacNeill near the edge of the stage engaged in an animated conversation. MacNeill's second in command, The O'Rahilly, was standing nearby, listening to them speak. They were too far away for Joe to hear them, but MacNeill's face was flushed and he was gesturing passionately. Pearse had his arms crossed, his jaw clenched tightly shut. He was shaking his head dismissively.

Joe felt sick to his stomach, his chest tight and heavy. If MacNeill found out about their plans, he could ruin everything. He was still the official leader of the Irish Volunteers, and if he contradicted the call-out order for the day of the rebellion, the resulting confusion and political infighting would be disastrous. They would have almost no chance of mounting a significant rebellion if MacNeill came out against them publicly.

Joe watched as The O'Rahilly stepped forward and started speaking with Pearse as well, looking concerned but not as angry as MacNeill. The O'Rahilly was a bit eccentric and an aficionado of linguistics and Irish history. He had added "The" before his name because this was how the clan chiefs were named in the old Gaelic tradition. He had a temper, but he was boisterous, courageous, worldly, and loyal, and if he hadn't been so close to MacNeill, he could have made a good addition to the Military Council.

Joe watched until Pearse walked away from MacNeill and The O'Rahilly. Hoping that no real damage had been done, he worked his way through the crowd, out of the Mansion House, and back to his car. There would be a lot of drinking after the meeting, and things would only get more heated and rowdy as the night wore on.

A group of Volunteers had got ahold of one of the Castle spies out on the street. By the time Joe saw what was going on, they were being pulled off of him by their more sober friends. It looked like they had already beat him badly, and he was still on the ground. As Joe reached his car a few blocks away, he heard two gunshots coming from the direction of the square, and as he drove toward home, he was already dreading what might be in the newspaper the next morning.

17

Joe pulled up next to the house at Larkfield. It was late, and the house was dark except for the lamp on the front porch and a light in one of the upstairs windows. The night was clear, and the indigo sky seemed crowded with silver stars. The chilled air carried the scents of early blossoms and wood smoke, and in the distance, from over the hill, Joe could hear singing and loud conversation from George's Lambs out in the old mill. He smiled, thinking of his even-tempered, soft-spoken little brother being in charge of all those rough, raucous men who had come to fight for Ireland with nothing but what they had on their backs. George had been camping alongside his battalion for months now.

Joe knew he shouldn't have stayed out so late, and he was exhausted. Just a few more weeks to go, and then he would have plenty of time to rest. As he walked slowly up the stairs, he heard his name whispered from amid the small trees to his left. He stopped and peered into the dark as Grace stepped out toward him. She was pale and looked wild hiding there in the shadows.

"I need to talk to you." She was still whispering.

"Grace, what are you doing here? You shouldn't be out here alone. You didn't walk, did you?"

She pulled him by his arm into the darkness at the side of the house. "Please. I need to talk to you. You can't—I can't let you fight, Joe. I mean, I know you have to fight, but I'm just so scared. What if you get—what if something happens?"

"It'll be fine—over before you know it. C'mon, let me drive you home. It's late, and you shouldn't be out walking alone. Besides that, it's freezing." He took her hand and started to lead her to his car.

She pulled him back into the dark and held him so close that her deep-brown eyes were just a few inches away from his. She looked up at him and held his face in her hands. "I wouldn't be okay without you, do you understand? If anything were to happen... I don't think I'd make it. Why couldn't you have told me sooner, Joe?" She began to cry, making no effort to hide it or wipe away her tears. She just stared into his eyes, as if a solution could be found there.

"Oh God, I'm so sorry. I wasn't supposed to tell anyone at all, but I couldn't keep it from you any longer. I was just so scared that you... I was scared you wouldn't want me if I told you the truth. But please don't give up on me, Grace. Please don't hate me."

She wrapped her arms around his neck, her head on his chest against the dark wool of his coat. "Of course I don't hate you. I couldn't hate you now even if I wanted to."

Joe held her close, and her hair smelled like flowers—warm and sweeter than the cool, early spring air around them. "Please give me a chance to make it up to you. It'll all be over in few weeks, and I promise you, we'll win, and... and after that there will be nothing in the world for me to do but try to make you happy—to hold you close, to kiss you and just love you all the time. Please give me a chance, Babbaly."

"That'll be fine, Joe, but I won't marry you until after you finish this thing. You finish it and come back to me, and I'll marry you then."

Joe's relief nearly made him feel lightheaded. Grace already had him pinned against the side of the house, so he closed his eyes and leaned back against the cool wood, holding her against him. He was glad it was dark, because he didn't want her to see that he had started to cry a little too.

"Thank you, Grace. Thank you. Yes, please marry me. I'd marry you now—right this minute if you'd let me." She lifted her face from his chest and started to protest but he kept talking. "But as long as you'll marry me sometime—if you'll still be all mine—I'll make it through this thing, and we can be together forever. That's all that matters to me. You have to understand that loving you is the only thing that will matter after this fight is over."

Grace couldn't hear him anymore. She couldn't hear anything anymore. She was only aware of Joe's dark eyes, his black, messy hair, and his mouth; he was still talking. It seemed like he was always talking. She pulled his face down toward hers and kissed him. He looked down at her in surprise for a second or two. He started to open his mouth, like he might speak again, but seemed to think better of it. Instead he kissed her back with a gentle hesitation that melted away by the second.

Then his arms encircled her completely, and he was a different man, pulling her so tightly against him that they felt locked together like pieces of a puzzle.

He lifted her off the ground just a little and turned so that she was against the side of the house then pressed himself against her, kissing her the whole time with a desperation—as if her body against his was the only thing in the world that made any sense at all. She was glad she had the wall to lean on because she felt weak and a little dizzy. The stress that had consumed her during the walk to his house had melted away as she held him. She kissed his mouth and face and throat, and it seemed like there was no one else in the world but the two of them. There was nothing else, and there was no other time.

18

Joe got interesting news when he went in to Volunteer headquarters the next afternoon. The IRB had a trusted supporter named Eugene Smith who worked as an official at Dublin Castle. Over the years he had reached a high security access level, and despite his job with the British government, he remained loyal to the cause of Ireland's independence. Early in April he had notified his IRB connection that he had come across a document that included a list of the addresses of almost every leader in the Dublin nationalist movement, as well as that of Volunteer headquarters. Along with the list were plans to round up and arrest everyone found at any of these addresses who was known to be involved in "antigovernment activities." In other words, anyone associated with the Irish Volunteers or other nationalist organizations.

The document had come across Smith's desk on its way to the Chief Secretary in London, and he had memorized the main points and written them down after work. He had delivered his notes to his IRB connection, who then translated them into code so that they could be delivered safely to the leadership. Being arrested while carrying this kind of information could cause trouble for everyone, including Eugene Smith.

One problem with the document was that it did not indicate when the arrests would take place. Smith believed that the arrests were being planned in advance in case England decided to impose conscription in Ireland in support of the Empire's fight in Europe. The Castle knew that this would cause a tremendous uproar, and it would want to keep things as peaceful as possible. Rounding up all of the Irish Volunteer leadership would keep the protests and rebellion to a minimum.

While it was possible that these plans were being made in advance of an eventual establishment of conscription, it seemed just as likely to Joe that the general wanted to go through with the mass arrests very soon.

Joe wanted a copy of the document as soon as possible so that he could disperse it throughout the membership of the Irish Volunteers. The document could engender more support for the rebellion. Even more importantly, the people on the extensive list needed to be warned of their coming arrests. The Volunteers had been making plans and collecting weapons for years, and if they were all thrown in prison before the insurrection, it would be a very long time before they could get to this point again.

It was decided that Eugene Smith's IRB contact would pass the coded document to Joe's aide-de-camp, Michael Collins, at St. Stephen's Green that same day. After that, Collins would meet Joe on the north side of Grafton Street for the hand off.

Joe was so sick by this time that his body hung with exhaustion, despite his excitement about the document and the insurrection plans in general. He quickly drank two more cups of strong tea as soon as they had cooled down enough and then tried to focus on some paperwork while waiting for his meeting with Collins. If the document indicated any kind of planned aggression or mass arrests by the Castle, as he had been told, they would release it as soon as possible—and not just within the IRB and the Irish Volunteers. They would try to get it published in the nationalist and general press so that everyone in the country could see it. With less than two weeks until the uprising, they needed to encourage support however they could.

Late that afternoon he met with Collins and received the encrypted message. By the time he got back to Larkfield, it was almost time for dinner. Grace was just arriving in response to his invitation to dine with his family. Now that he had told her about the upcoming insurrection, he did not need to keep her away in order to hide the bustling activity at his family's estate. Drills were going on for hours every day, and the munitions production was almost constant by now. As they went in to the dining room, he whispered to her that he would like her to help him with some work after dinner.

Later in the evening, they went upstairs to his room, where they worked for hours, sitting side by side on Joe's bed. He read each word aloud as he decoded, and Grace took notes. The document supplied a long list of organizations whose members were to be detained. There was also a list of addresses of various nationalist headquarters that were to be watched almost constantly so that members could be arrested while coming and going.

Among the addresses listed was 2 Dawson Street, Volunteer headquarters, and Liberty Hall, headquarters for the Irish Citizen Army. There was a second list of addresses of locations that would be surrounded and isolated completely during the entire operation, preventing any communication from going in or out. The address of Joe's family estate, Larkfield, was among those on the second list. If the Castle were to carry out these plans before Easter Sunday, the rebellion would be impossible. The whole movement could be set back years.

As Joe had been expecting, the document gave no timeline at all. In addition to this, it was quite long and had been written down entirely from memory. Because of this, it seemed like there had to be mistakes, additions, and omissions. Then there was the fact that the Volunteers could not name their source; Eugene Smith needed to be protected. This would invite questions about accuracy and accusations from the British government that the document was a forgery.

It was after midnight when Joe got Grace back to Muriel and Thomas's house. As he drove back to Larkfield, he thought about how they could best use the information in Smith's notes. It was far from perfect and not quite as potent a piece of propaganda as he would have liked.

At the next day's Military Council meeting, however, he argued that the document needed to be released as soon and as widely as possible. It was also important to somehow accentuate the possibility that the Castle would go through with the arrests at any time. It was decided that, where the document was missing information about timing, they would go ahead and imply that the actions planned by England were imminent. In addition to garnering more support from within the movement, it would help to pacify MacNeill if he were to find out about their plans.

Many times, MacNeill had very publicly stated that he would support an uprising in the face of any outward aggression by England. Now MacNeill would have his direct and looming threat of outward aggression from the English, and he would have to support the Military Council and their rebellion. Joe wrote up the document from his deciphered notes and included a map with all of the targeted addresses marked. He then sent for some Volunteers, who came to print up hundreds of copies on the press Joe and his brothers kept on the estate. The document was soon read aloud at nationalist meetings and gatherings throughout the city and published in the papers.

ൽ

Although Castle authorities claimed that the document was forged, this was no surprise to anyone, and the reaction within the nationalist movement was swift and fierce. The Volunteers were ready to fight. Orders went out for all Volunteer and Citizen Army members to prepare for maneuvers on Easter Sunday, and rumors were running rampant that this was not just a drill but a full-on rebellion.

The rumors eventually got around to MacNeill and his supporters. He, Bulmer Hobson, and The O'Rahilly started numerous confrontations with members of the Military Council. Eventually, it was decided that they needed to tell MacNeill and his closest supporters about the thousands of guns and cases of ammunition that were already on their way from Germany. This, combined with the information in the document from Dublin Castle, finally convinced MacNeill to reluctantly support the Military Council in their rebellion.

19

Although it was the last thing he wanted to think about now, for some time Joe's illness had been getting steadily worse. The glands in his neck were swollen and painful, and he had been running a fever for weeks. The usual accompanying fatigue had rarely been present until very recently, because he was so caught up in the excitement and chaos of planning for the uprising. As usual, he had been trying to ignore his illness completely and going on with the plans for the uprising as if he felt fine—but this was getting harder every day.

Because his health had been bad from time to time throughout most of his life, Joe had learned to ignore his symptoms and discomfort. This would generally continue until a friend or relative forced him to go to the doctor or slow down and rest. As he saw it, he couldn't just wait around, drowsing by the fire, until he was healthy enough for adventure and travel. If he were to do that, then he would have spent a good portion of his life sitting around doing nothing.

But a week before Easter Sunday, things had become too bad to ignore any longer. His sister Geraldine had confronted him about his health as he was putting away his coat after coming in late from a meeting at Volunteer headquarters.

"Where have you been, Joe? Why aren't you upstairs resting?" She spoke with an accusatory tone, but there were tears in her eyes.

"I'm fine, Gerry, don't worry. Really, I'm going upstairs right now. I won't go out at all tomorrow, I promise. I just couldn't get out of this one—"

"No! I won't let you do this to yourself again." She was almost shouting at him now. "You look terrible, and I can see it's getting worse!"

"I know. I know you're right," Joe almost whispered, as if admitting it out loud would make it true.

"I'm just afraid that you might not make it through this time," she said softly now as well, tears filling her eyes. "If you wait any longer, it might be too late."

Seeing how worried his sister was, Joe couldn't bring himself to offer any more excuses or arguments. He agreed to go to the doctor the following morning.

The doctor poked and prodded and asked a lot of questions, then directed Joe to a seat before a large, oak desk, cluttered with folders and a couple of thick medical volumes. He moved the volumes to one side and retrieved Joe's file from a small stack. He made a few notes, then leaned forward over his desk, looking steadily into Joe's eyes.

"I'm afraid you've let things get pretty bad this time," the doctor said somberly. He took a deep breath and continued. "To be honest, I don't know if you'll make it through this time, no matter what we do. But if we don't immediately operate on the glands in your neck to treat the infection, I don't think you'll live more than a few more weeks."

"But I don't really feel that badly at all, and there's no way I can go in for surgery right now. See, I'm ... I'm getting married on Easter Sunday," Joe insisted, naming the only excuse he could admit to. "It can't be that bad. Can't I just wait a couple more weeks?"

"I'm sorry, but it is that bad. Even with the surgery, it might not be enough. But if everything goes well and you do everything right afterward as far as your recovery goes, you could very well pull through."

"What do you mean, do everything right?" Joe hated to ask, since he was pretty sure that launching a revolution against the British Empire was not going to be on the doctor's list of things to do after an operation.

"That means total rest—starting out at the nursing home until you're stable. It means lots of sleep, staying warm, eating healthy, regular meals—which I don't think you've been getting, by the way—and no alcohol at all. No going out. None of it. After that you could have six months, or maybe even years. I just can't tell you at this point until we get in there and find out how far the infection has progressed."

Joe left the doctor's office after promising to return first thing the next morning for surgery. Stunned, he wandered the neighborhood for a while before he could remember where he had parked the Wolseley. He needed to get home, but he couldn't think straight, his mind awash with despair and rage. He felt like he could just as easily collapse in tears or start a fight with a stranger. When he finally made it home, he refused to answer the greeting or questions from his father or Geraldine, who met him in front of the house. He strode past them without a glance, trying to get to his room—to privacy—before he lost control.

Generally, Joe tried to be good-natured and accepting about his frequent bouts of ill health; being in a rage all the time never made anyone feel any better. But this was too much, coming up right in the middle of everything. He had been working toward this rebellion for years, and he knew it was his destiny—the one thing he had to offer the country he loved.

Being so sick once again also underscored his fears that he wasn't good enough for Grace. If he couldn't go through with this fight, he would have no way to prove himself to her. But having this surgery now threatened to keep him out of things entirely.

When he got to his room, he clenched his jaw and fought back tears and pounded his fists on his desk. He felt as if he could cry but feared that if he let himself start, he might sink into despair and give into his illness. He cursed his pointless and useless body and even sent angry prayers to God, which he had never done before.

After several moments of this, he stopped and took back his angry prayers. He said one more—a quick prayer asking for help and guidance—then took some deep breaths. He began packing a small bag to take to the hospital in the morning. If they must do the surgery, they could go ahead and get it over with, but no one could keep him at the hospital after it was done. He would have until Sunday to recuperate, and that would have to be enough time.

The surgery went well, and there seemed to be some hope for Joe if he would only follow his doctor's orders. The procedure was a serious one; the glands at the side of his throat had to be cut open and cleaned out in hopes of relieving the infection.

The problem was compounded by the fact that he had waited so long to see the doctor, and after the surgery was over, he had little time to rest.

Lying in his narrow bed in Mountjoy Square Nursing Home, he received a message that gave him more reason for despair. Earlier in the week, five IRB men, including a wireless expert named Con Keating, had traveled to the southeast corner of the country. The Military Council sent them down to Cahersiveen to steal some radio transmission equipment and then drive it to Tralee and reassemble it there.

The hope was that they would be able to establish communication with the German ship that was scheduled to arrive any day with the additional weapons for the uprising. If Keating could get through to the ship's captain, it would greatly simplify and facilitate the hand-off of the guns and ammunition.

The five of them stopped briefly in Killarney, where they met supporters who supplied them with two cars and drivers. They continued their trip to Cahersiveen late Friday night, navigating the winding, narrow country roads in a punishing rainstorm. On the way, the second car took a wrong turn in the darkness and plunged off the road and into the harbor below.

No one in the car up front saw the others go off the road, and they continued driving for some time before they noticed there were no longer any headlights behind them. After stopping to wait for a while, they retraced their path and found the wreckage in the cold water of the harbor. The driver was still alive, but all three of the IRB men in the car, including Con Keating, were already dead.

The mission was abandoned, and word was sent to Dublin. This was only the tragic beginning to a series of events that would threaten to defeat the rebellion before it could begin.

20

On Saturday it was decided that everyone on the Military Council would stay the night away from home, both to be nearer to Liberty Hall, where they planned to gather for the rebellion, and in an attempt to thwart any last-minute group arrests that Castle authorities might have planned. Joe had spent the days after his surgery in the nursing home in recovery, but now he moved into the Metropole Hotel in Sackville Street. Even in his current weakened state, he could make the walk from the hotel to Liberty Hall in a few minutes.

Joe was at Volunteer headquarters that afternoon, attending to some last-minute details, when a few of MacNeill's supporters rushed in, The O'Rahilly among them.

"The ship. With the German weapons. It's gone." The O'Rahilly was out of breath after running up the stairs.

"What are you talking about?" Joe asked suspiciously. He wouldn't put it past MacNeill and his supports to come up with a trick to delay the rebellion.

"The German ship full of weapons. It was sunk near Cork Harbor. They're saying she showed up two days early, several miles off from the rendezvous point, so no one was there to meet her."

"You're serious." Joe felt weaker than before, and his stomach tightened. "All the weapons? They're gone?"

"That's what they're saying." The O'Rahilly's mouth was set in a thin, straight line and his cheeks were flushed. He seemed genuinely distressed by the news. "Two British naval trawlers saw the ship waiting off the coast and tried to force them into the base at Queenstown."

"So the captain scuttled the ship to keep the weapons out of the hands of the British Navy," Joe finished the report himself. No German captain could allow a boatload of weapons and ammunition to fall into the hands of the British right now.

"What's the plan now?" The O'Rahilly demanded. "Surely you can't go ahead with things tomorrow!"

"Of course we will. There's no question of that," Joe responded with as much confidence as he could after this latest blow.

The O'Rahilly and the others continued pressing Joe with questions about the insurrection, then they turned to the issue of the document from the Castle, claiming now that it was a forgery, as British authorities had insisted from the start. They were caving under the pressure of losing the weapons, looking for any excuse to force the Military Council to cancel entirely.

Nothing Joe said could calm them down. When they rushed out the door a few minutes later, Joe was certain they were headed straight for MacNeill's, which would only cause more trouble. He needed to find Pearse and the others. The rising was only one day away, and now they would have to find a way to contain MacNeill and his followers in addition to everything else.

Joe didn't know if he would have a chance to see Grace, and he was worried about what might happen in the city during the fighting. Before he left headquarters, he sent his aide-de-camp Michael Collins with a small package for her. He placed all the money he had with him in a little bag, along with a small, loaded gun, and then quickly wrote her a short note.

Holy Saturday, 1916
My sweetest Grace,

I have been running nonstop since this morning and have not had a minute to sit down to write to you until now. We go out to fight tomorrow. I know things will be fine, but I will worry about you anyway. I want you to hold onto this gun during the whole thing. Keep the small bar under the word "safe" pushed down unless you need to shoot it. I'm sending a little money as well, in case you run into any problems with supplies.

I'll see you soon, my darling. All my love forever,
Joe

After spending a few hours tracking down members of the Military Council to update them on the news of the ship, Joe went back to the hotel to rest. That night Thomas MacDonagh showed up late at his room with more bad news. MacNeill had decided that the Castle document was a forgery and now believed that there was no plan for mass arrests of the nationalist leaders. Because of this—and the sunken German ship—MacNeill had changed his mind about supporting the rising. He had written up an order canceling their instructions to the Volunteers to show up at Liberty Hall on Sunday. Thomas thrust a small piece of paper to Joe with MacNeill's countermanding order:

> *Volunteers completely deceived. All orders for special actions are hereby cancelled, and on no account will action be taken.*

MacNeill had his order distributed throughout the city and sent The O'Rahilly to travel all throughout the country with special orders to alert supporters that the planned Volunteer maneuvers were canceled.

There might still have been time for the IRB to send out more messages canceling the countermanding order, but the resulting confusion and chaos would be devastating. It was the night before the insurrection, and with such a short amount of time, there didn't seem to be any way to recover from this latest setback.

MacDonagh left quickly to attempt to round up the other members of the Military Council for an emergency midnight meeting. Joe carefully wrapped more gauze around his neck then slowly and stiffly got dressed. The pain was a constant, dull ache that intensified terribly whenever he moved, shooting from his throat through his head and upper torso. He half-filled a small water glass with whisky, drank it in one painful swallow, then left for the emergency Military Council meeting at a supporter's home in Hardwick Street.

Lighting up the house of a known supporter of the Irish Volunteers at this hour could draw police attention, so they sat in the dark, holding flashlights and small lanterns. The discussion and argument went on for hours but got nowhere. Mounting an insurrection with no fighters was pointless, and it seemed that MacNeill might have gotten his way after all.

21

Joe felt completely defeated. He was in constant pain by now, and it looked like he was losing his only chance to fight for Ireland and prove himself to Grace. He had seen her when she stopped by his hotel for a short visit earlier in the evening but hadn't been able to tell her about their latest setbacks. Although she told him she didn't want him to fight, she had looked at him with such pride for what he was about to do. She had no idea that it might all end in humiliation and failure. In addition to missing her, he feared that he might lose her after all.

His excitement and his will to keep moving forward at all costs had held his exhaustion at bay all day long. Now, after so much bad news, it rushed over him like a river bursting through a dam. He collapsed in bed, totally unconscious until dawn, when a message arrived calling all Military Council members to Liberty Hall for yet another meeting.

Joe felt a glimmer of hope that gave him the strength to rise once again. Perhaps someone had come up with a solution. On his way out, he received a message from Grace, but he decided to answer it after the meeting. He was not ready to admit to failure, and he might have good news soon. *At any rate*, he told himself, *it can't get any worse.*

He arrived at the hall Sunday morning to find nothing but more bad news. MacNeill had somehow managed to get another version of his countermanding order into the *Irish Independent*, which went out all over the city and much of the country. It read:

> *Owing to the very critical situation, all orders given to the Irish Volunteers for tomorrow, Easter Sunday, are hereby rescinded and no parades, marches or other movements of Irish Volunteers will take place. Each individual Volunteer will obey this order strictly in every particular.*

Connolly's daughter made everyone breakfast, which they ate in ravenous silence. Joe could not remember the last time he had eaten solid food and had not even realized he was hungry until he smelled the bacon and eggs. The Military Council struggled through their anxiety and exhaustion, arguing for four hours about what they could possibly do now to resurrect their plans. Every man at the table had dreamed for years—perhaps his whole life—of standing up for Ireland against the British Empire. It had been each man's chance to take a place in history and represent his own generation in this struggle that had gone on for so many generations.

Joe thought about Grace, wondering if she would still look at him in the same way now that he had even less to offer her than before. Without his part in the rebellion, he wondered again how he would ever prove himself worthy of her love for him. He had no career, no plans, and was in terrible health. She told him she would always love him, but he still felt that it might be too much to ask.

He hoped to live through this last illness, but even if he did, what would be left for him? If he did live and was not arrested and imprisoned or exiled by Castle authorities, could he go back to his studies and poetry with any satisfaction now that his dreams had been destroyed?

Canceling the insurrection was not an option for any man at the table. Clarke wanted to go ahead and start it that very day, as originally planned, but the others thought that was impossible now. They also knew that they could be rounded up and arrested by the Castle authorities at any moment, so they could not postpone for weeks or months to regroup and try again. Clarke having been outvoted, the Council decided to go ahead with the rebellion one day later than they had originally planned. They would take the city on Monday at noon.

The Council next turned to finalizing the proclamation they had drafted announcing their new, independent provisional Irish government. They all signed it at the bottom, securing their place in history, but also most likely condemning themselves to execution if the rebellion failed. They sent the proclamation to Larkfield, where hundreds of copies were printed up to be posted and handed out all over the city as soon as the rebellion began.

Eventually the Council broke up the meeting and began sending out messages and orders. For the rest of the day, Liberty Hall was packed with supporters scurrying from place to place making preparations and adjustments. Some worked in quiet dejection, holding back tears, while others ranted loudly about MacNeill's betrayal.

The worst part of the day was watching as one person after another showed up with their gear, ready to fight. Volunteers were posted out front to turn them away with the explanation that maneuvers were postponed until the following day. So many showed up—even after MacNeill's countermanding order. *Was Clarke right? Should they have gone ahead with the original plan?* Joe forced himself to stop second-guessing their decision. They would move forward tomorrow, whatever happened. Feeling somewhat hopeful again, he decided that he would spend the night in the nursing home where he had been recovering from surgery. It looked as if the rebellion would go forward after all, and he would need his strength.

George and his Lambs were there helping with preparations. Before leaving, Joe pulled his little brother aside and asked him to serve as a witness while he wrote out his will on a small piece of paper. He left everything that he possessed—and everything that he might come to possess—to Grace. Joe then signed the will and had George sign as a witness. He thanked his brother and let him get on with his own long list of tasks to be completed before the following day.

Joe read the little document again, then folded it carefully and put it in his pocket. He had known that their plans for the insurrection were real, and he had always been aware of the fact he might be killed before it was over—in some ways, he was expecting it. Nonetheless, writing out his first will made that reality feel closer than ever.

Part Two

22

Joe arrived at Liberty Hall on a bright and sunny Easter Monday after two weeks straight of sullen, rainy skies. Every few seconds a Volunteer raced down the front stairs with a new dispatch or order, taking off across the city on a bicycle. People chatted and laughed as they worked, and Joe was greeted with salutes and smiles as he walked inside.

Just as he was about to enter the hall for a Military Council meeting, he saw The O'Rahilly drive up and park near the building. Joe had hoped there wouldn't be any more trouble with MacNeill and his supporters; once again, he was filled with dead. He reminded himself that there was nothing more MacNeill could do to them now. The rebellion was going forward no matter what the consequences. Sean MacDermott, the Military Council's most natural diplomat, walked over to where O'Rahilly was now getting out of his car. Joe could see now that the car was loaded with rifles. MacDermott and The O'Rahilly spoke for a moment or two and then they shook hands.

The O'Rahilly had spent the last two days and nights driving all over Ireland at MacNeill's insistence, delivering the countermanding order to put a stop to their revolution. When he got back into town, he heard that they were gathering at Liberty Hall and saw that he and MacNeill had failed. Now that things were going ahead, he wanted to be a part of it. Everyone on the Military Council knew that The O'Rahilly would be a great addition, and he was welcomed to join in without hesitation, despite all the work he had done for MacNeill to stop them. It was decided that he would leave his stash of weapons in the car and drive them over to the General Post Office when they were ready to go.

The O'Rahilly was polite, but formal and reserved, with the Council. Joe couldn't tell if The O'Rahilly was angry about the insurrection or just hurt that they hadn't included him in the planning. But he seemed heartened by the warm welcome he received, and once he got to work helping the Countess Markievicz with preparations for the march to the General Post Office and other positions in the city, he cheered up. He stated out loud for all to hear that he was confident that they would lose—and lose badly. He said he didn't expect the fight to go on for long, but if it was going to happen, he was going to be there.

"It's madness," he told the Countess, "but it's glorious madness."

It was time to go. Each of the men took two grenades from a large barrel near the entrance of the hall, and then fell into line. The grenades had been manufactured using condensed milk cans. The men added the grenades to the many other supplies they had tucked into their haversacks and stashed in their belts and in every pocket. Few had adequate military packing gear, and their civilian jackets bulged awkwardly with required personal supplies—including towels, soap, candles, blankets, and spare socks—in addition to their weapons.

At about ten minutes before noon, the whole group began their march to the GPO. A large crowd made up mainly of family and friends that had gathered in front of Liberty Hall cheered them on. At the head of the procession were Connolly, Pearse, and Joe, followed by a four-wheeled cart that was stacked so high it swayed precariously, groaning under the weight of weapons, ammunition, explosives, and other supplies. George's Lambs followed behind the cart, armed with shotguns, pikes, and whatever other random weapons could be found, including a large ax that one Lamb carried.

"Into line! Left turn!"

Joe watched the Volunteers pivot to the left and snap into position to face the imposing main entrance of the General Post Office. At three stories high and a block wide, it had six massive, white Ionic style columns, each over fourteen feet in circumference. There were smaller entries on either side of the building as well as a walled courtyard in back. Only about 150 men had shown up for assignment at the GPO, and they were mostly made up of George's Lambs.

"A-Section, right wheel!"

As George shouted a second command, Section A of his Lambs took off in a run around the right side of the building, toward the Henry Street entrance. The tone of George's voice drew looks from previously uninterested bystanders. Dublin citizens had been watching the Volunteers marching through the city in drills, maneuvers, and parades for years, and they generally paid no attention anymore. But today George's voice carried tension and the weight of the responsibility he had taken on by giving these first orders. He had run the same drills dozens of times at the Kimmage Garrison, but he was now beginning a process that could lead to the death of some of these men.

Still, he was firm and strong, as if he had been giving commands to commence battle for years, well aware of the nightmare he was about to unleash. His battalion's instant obedience and near perfect formation showed they were serious, despite the fact that only one or two of the battalion's soldiers could come up with a complete uniform. The rest were dressed mainly in street clothes.

"D-Section, left wheel!"

Joe could not help but be proud of his little brother as George continued his command and Section D ran south toward the O'Connell Bridge. They were to guard the bridge and take over Hopkins and Hopkins Jewelers and Kelly's Gun Shop at the south end of Lower Sackville Street. Joe worried as the men in D-Section ran off toward the O'Connell Bridge. Overall, far too few people had shown up for the morning's events, and Joe knew they had not sent enough men to hold these three positions.

The leaders wanted the O'Connell Bridge totally secure so that no British troops would be allowed across, but with just a few Volunteers sent to guard it, that seemed impossible. The bridge was almost 165 feet wide—even wider than it was long—as it stretched across the River Liffey. He worried about their ability to hold their position against an attack from the south while he and the others prepared for an extended occupation of the post office. As soon as D-Section took off, George continued in his strong, clear voice.

"B- and C-Sections…" and then his voice seemed to break and lose most of its strength as he said, at an almost conversational level, "charge."

The remaining Volunteers heard him well enough nonetheless and ran at full speed through the main entrance of the General Post Office. Almost immediately there were sounds of angry shouting and broken glass from inside. In their many lectures on urban warfare, the Volunteers had learned to eliminate all of the glass windows right away to minimize injuries from flying shards during battle. After that they would use everything they could find inside to build barricades at the windows and doors.

To Joe it felt like time had been speeding by for weeks, but at George's first shouted command, it had slowed to a crawl. He and the other leaders followed their men inside. After the initial charge, the sound of smashing glass formed a wall of sound that went on and on without pause as Joe and the other leaders tried to get the post office customers to vacate the building. For the most part, they were met, not with respect or fear, but with confusion and annoyance.

Some customers insisted on remaining in line at the counter even when surrounded by armed men smashing everything in sight. As he watched Dublin citizens argue for their right to buy stamps in the middle of his revolution, Joe felt that the fulfillment of his destiny was getting off to a ridiculous start. Eventually, he heard someone fire a shot at the other end of the building—just a warning, he hoped. The main room on the ground floor was as big as a ballroom, and it was crowded. There was no way to see what was going on at the other side. At the sound of the shot, people stopped arguing and allowed the Volunteers to herd them toward the main entrance and outside into Sackville Street.

Several of the customers were British soldiers who needed to be taken prisoner. Everyone had been commanded to treat all prisoners with respect, and this was the first test. Joe watched as two Volunteers escorted their captives upstairs with apparent professional courtesy. Some of the other Volunteers were gathering money from the tills and depositing it all in the post office safes as had been ordered. It was important to all of the leaders that there was no looting, theft, or needless destruction by any participant in the rebellion. All felt it would be wise to secure the money right from the start. That way there would be no suspicion or temptation.

Having removed the last of the civilians from the GPO, The O'Rahilly secured the massive front doors. The sound of smashing glass tapered off as the troops turned their attention to building barricades at the windows. Upstairs, Volunteers were preparing the headquarters kitchen and dining area. Screens were arranged to set up a small hospital and armory, and a storage area was stocked with extra clothes and other personal supplies.

A small group was sent up to the roof to raise two flags, one at each side of the building. The first was the Tricolor, divided evenly into wide stripes of green, white, and orange. The white symbolized peace between the green for Catholics and the orange for Protestants. The other flag was one of a kind, created specifically for the rebellion. It portrayed a golden harp set against a green background with the words "Irish Republic" painted in gold.

Downstairs, Father Flanagan arrived and was setting up his space in a secluded corner of the building for prayers, confessions, and blessings. Joe knew the Father would be busy.

Of the Military Council, only Joe, Patrick Pearse, Tom Clarke, Sean MacDermott, and James Connolly were stationed at the post office, and they began to set up their workstations on the main floor amid the chaos. The O'Rahilly continued to keep his distance from the other leaders and climbed the stairs to the upper floors.

Joe found a table and spread out his maps, notes, and field message book. He began to record which locations should have been taken throughout the city by now if things were going as planned. But he only had about half the fighters he had been expecting to take the GPO, and there was no telling how many had shown up at the other locations. It was very possible that many of their plans were being changed or sacrificed at this very moment all over the city.

After settling in, Joe gathered his corps of new communications experts and gave them their orders. He had been training a small group of Volunteers in the use of wireless and telegraph equipment. This had been a hobby of his for years, and it seemed like the perfect opportunity to take advantage of what he had learned. It was important that the world know what was going on here in Dublin, especially in the rest of Ireland and in the United States, where the nationalist movement had so many supporters. Telegraphed messages were fast, and they were the only way to get around the British censors, besides sending someone personally with a verbal message, which took too long in most cases.

His little communications corps was to take over Atlantic College, the nearby wireless telegraphy school. They would receive dispatches regularly from headquarters and were instructed to send out telegraphs reporting the progress of the insurrection continuously for as long as they could hold their position.

Just as his communications corps left the building, Collins walked up, dragging a small mattress and flung it down next to where Joe was working.

"Lie down, sir. You need to rest."

"Thanks, Mick, but I don't need that!" Joe was determined not to show how exhausted he was. Although he was touched by his aide-de-camp's constant worrying about his health, he didn't want to be seen lying around—even if he was recovering from surgery.

"You've got to. We hope to hold out here for quite a while, and you'll need to keep up your strength."

Joe thanked him and agreed to sit down on the mattress while he worked, taking some of the maps and notebooks with him.

As foreign as the whole situation was, Joe felt oddly at home here in the first stages of the long-awaited rebellion. As he organized plans, discussed developments with the other leaders, and gave orders to the busy Volunteers, he was surprised by how natural it all felt. He was more energetic with each passing minute, and the core of melancholic brooding that often inhabited his heart had disappeared completely. He felt more focused than ever before, and instead of the anxiety he had been expecting, he felt only optimism and excitement—almost elation.

He was also taken by a cheerful fatalism that eased the doubts and ruminations that had troubled him about all of the difficult decisions he and the other Military Council members had been forced to make over the last few days. Regardless of the outcome, this is what needed to be done, and they were doing it. It was as simple as that. Everyone would do their best, and that was all that anyone could ask, so there was no longer any reason at all for fretting, second-guessing, or regretting the many mistakes and failures that had occurred—or those they were bound to face in the coming days.

Once the leaders had things somewhat organized and the Volunteers were constructing barricades in the windows, Joe saw Clarke hand a copy of the Proclamation of the Irish Republic over to Pearse. This was the document that Pearse had written with the help of the Military Council stating the ideals and aims of their new republic—the document that they had each signed the day before, as the members of the new nation's provisional government. Hundreds of copies had been printed out overnight, and soon their declaration of a new, independent Irish state would be passed out to people all over Dublin. It began with the line:

> *IRISHMEN AND IRISHWOMEN: In the name of God and of the dead generations from which she receives her old tradition of nationhood, Ireland, through us, summons her children to her flag and strikes for her freedom.*

The document went on to describe the training of their troops by the formerly secret revolutionary organization, the Irish Republican Brotherhood, and then declared the right of the Irish people to the unfettered control of their own destinies in this new sovereign and independent state. It guaranteed religious and civil liberty, equal rights, suffrage, and equal opportunity to every Irish man and woman and promised that the soldiers in this rebellion would fight with honor, valor, and discipline.

If they were to lose the fight this week, the seven signatures at the bottom of the proclamation would most likely assure the execution of each member of the Military Council.

Joe knew that Pearse was about to read the proclamation to whomever happened to be out in front of the GPO. This would be the official and public declaration of their intent to take back their country from England. He watched as Clarke unlocked and slowly opened one of the heavy wood doors to the front entrance then stepped outside, followed by Pearse and an armed guard.

23

About an hour after Pearse read the proclamation, Joe heard a Volunteer running down the stairs from the roof, out of breath from excitement, calling out, "Lancers! Lancers!"

Just seconds later the same call was taken up by the men at the windows on the main floor. Joe grabbed his Smith & Wesson revolver. He felt like running over to the windows to look—the first direct British opposition he would ever witness—but he knew that would show his inexperience, which could affect the confidence of the men. He walked over to the window as if with casual curiosity.

The Lancers were a reserve battalion from the Royal Irish Regiment—infantrymen recruited in Ireland by the British. Although they were still close to a hundred yards away, Joe could see a small battalion riding toward them on horseback down Sackville Street from the north. They were in full military dress and coming on quickly with their weapons out and ready.

This is it, Joe thought, *our first real challenge.*

Everyone on the ground floor looked prepared, hunched down behind the window barricades with their weapons aimed and ready. Since the men on the roof had seen the Lancers first, Joe had every reason to believe that they were ready for the challenge as well.

They all watched and waited in silence as the mounted battalion of Lancers moved toward them. It looked like there were about twenty-five men. They were coming on fast, and soon Joe could hear the pounding of their horse's hooves. The Lancers needed to be taken by surprise, so until the riders reached a position that would enable the Volunteers to get in some good shots, no one moved a muscle or said a thing. Joe could not even see anyone breathing. The whole post office battalion froze as if posing for a photograph.

The only movements were occasional, split-second glances. The Volunteers looked to George as they waited for the command to shoot. George, on the other hand, stole occasional nervous looks over at Joe. George knew that he was about to give an order that would result directly in death. It would be his first order of the kind. Joe could see this knowledge in George's eyes, and he smiled almost imperceptibly in support, thinking, *You can do it, little brother.*

As the Lancers passed Nelson's Pillar and drew almost parallel with their position at the windows, George glanced at Joe one final time. Joe nodded, and his brother immediately turned to the window and gave the order to fire. Almost before the end of the word *fire*, a sound like thunder broke out. The Lancers scattered in confusion. A good portion of them looked to be hit and had either been knocked off their horses or were bent over in the saddle. The rest seemed to be riding in all directions at once, eventually recovering their composure and heading north again, back up the street.

Most of the Lancers who had fallen off their horses were able to remount and were soon following the others in retreat at a fierce gallop. Two men were lying still in the middle of the wide street in front of the GPO and did not move again. A third, who had landed on his stomach, seemed to be trying to get his arms underneath his body to crawl. One of the horses was hit and lay there as well. Her chest heaved, and she moved one of her front hooves a little in useless effort. Her rider's leg was trapped under her, but he soon wriggled free and was allowed to retreat on foot as the Volunteers held their fire. Sackville was several times wider than a usual avenue, and the poor man seemed exposed for a long time, darting about in a panic, expecting them to fire on him at any second.

As the man scurried for cover, Joe turned away from the window. It was surprisingly easy to engage the enemy, but once a man was on the ground writhing or crawling, he just did not seem like an enemy anymore. And the horse—Joe had not really thought of having to watch the horses die.

The Volunteers erupted in relieved and excited cheering. Joe quickly recovered himself so that he could praise and encourage the men with a sincere spirit. And he was sincere; this had been a small challenge, but it was a start, and Joe knew it was good for morale and confidence. The Lancers had been so surprised and confused that they had not had the chance to do much of anything but retreat, so none of the Volunteers had been shot. Most of the men had never fought before, so coming out of this initial confrontation without any wounded was a huge relief. But it only delayed the time when they would be forced to come to terms with the realities they were to face.

Actually, they did have some very minor injuries—mostly cuts from all the broken glass, which seemed to be everywhere. Things were getting a little out of control with celebration by the well-trained but largely inexperienced men. Joe winced as he heard a couple of accidental shots go off amid the jubilation. He went to the window and saw that two of the men and the horse were still lying in the same position near Nelson's Pillar, just north of the main entrance to the post office. He sent two Volunteers out to get the third man, who was still attempting to crawl for safety but had made no progress at all. He would be the first patient in their GPO hospital.

They had killed at least two of the Lancers and had obviously wounded many more. This was a victory, but everyone needed to calm down and get ready for whatever response this would bring from the British, who would not allow themselves to be surprised in this manner again.

Things got very quiet for a while. Joe had predicted that they would do a lot of waiting for the first couple of days while British soldiers and supplies were brought in from England, but many of the men seemed disappointed by having a lull after such a quick start to the action.

After a while without much to do, George and two of his Liverpool Lambs came to Joe with an idea. One of the Dublin city trams had been abandoned and was sitting to one side of Sackville Street, blocking most of Earl Street, which was just across from the post office. They wanted to try to get another nearby tram moving and then crash it into the first one so it would be immovable and could serve as a barricade, blocking an approach from Earl Street. It was a great idea, and Joe went outside with his brother and the two other Volunteers.

As quiet as it had been inside the post office for the last couple of hours, it was nothing compared to the hush out in the street. The main boulevard for the entire city, Sackville Street was generally active and chaotic. There was always something going on, day or night. This was the street where all the people of Dublin came together, often without much harmony. On one side the "proper" citizens were safe to stroll. Businessmen, couples, ladies with their shopping bags, and nannies followed by their tiny battalions of children wearing school uniforms or the season's latest from Clerys Department Store.

When these fine citizens had to cross to the other side of the street, it was a minor adventure. This is where the other half of Dublin walked. That sidewalk was for the "shawlies," poor women from the slums of Dublin who were named for the tattered shawls they wore around their shoulders. On that side of Sackville, there were beggars and stumbling drunks. Little children wandered alone, and older kids ran wild in groups as they played, taunted, and fought loudly.

Now the whole street was empty and silent. The dead and injured Lancers had been taken away, but the horse they had left behind still lay in the spot where it fell. It seemed lonely and humiliating to be left there in the middle of the street, and Joe wished that there was something he could do to move it out of the way. He supposed that, if he had any real military experience, things like this wouldn't bother him so much, so he shook off his melancholy thoughts and said nothing, turning his attention to the trams and the barricade they wanted to create.

The two Volunteers with George focused their attention on the second tram that had been abandoned near Nelson's Pillar, located halfway across Sackville Street's wide expanse. They tried to get it moving so they could crash it into the other one that sat blocking Earl Street. Thinking that there had to be a better way to do this, Joe watched as the Volunteers struggled with the controls of the tram. It was such a relief to be outside that he did not mind the wait at all. The sun was still shining brightly, and there was a light breeze blowing in from the sea.

He turned back to look at the General Post Office. He remembered his awe of the giant building when his father had brought him as a child. His favorite part of the GPO had always been the three statues created by sculptor John Smyth placed high above the entrance pediment. On the left stood Mercury, and on the right was a statue of a woman representing Fidelity. In the center was a fiercely noble personification of Hibernia, a name for Ireland from the time of the ancient Greek explorers.

Even though the GPO was built during the time of England's oppression in Ireland, this representation of Hibernia wore a Greek war helmet like Athena and defiantly held a long spear. She also carried a harp, a symbol of Ireland since before written history began. High atop the pediment, Hibernia gazed with confidence over the empty street, flanked by the clear blue sky. She seemed to see what Joe and the others were doing there that day—seemed to approve of their stand for freedom. She was proudly Irish, and she had come ready to fight. Now she would have her chance.

Joe was called from his thoughts by one of the Volunteers' shouted warnings. The Volunteer was about to throw one of his grenades into the tram. They all took cover and waited, but the grenade failed; silence continued to prevail over the empty street. Joe asked the other Volunteer to get one of the small bombs from the GPO basement. He lodged the bomb in the workings at the bottom of the tram that was stopped on Earl Street and told everyone to get back.

They walked back across Sackville Street toward the post office, seventy-five feet or so, until Joe could just barely see the bomb. He got out his semi-automatic Mauser pistol—his most accurate gun for distance—and aimed carefully. He shot once, and there was a huge explosion. One of the Volunteers cheered as they all stepped back a few more feet, feeling the rushed force of heat from the blast, and watched as a plume of black and gray smoke billowed up into the sky.

Once some of the smoke cleared away, they walked over to the tram to see if it had worked. The chassis had been totally blown out, and the tram car now rested on the tracks, blocking much of Earl Street and totally immovable. They went to work arranging some of the disconnected pieces of the chassis and other objects to block the rest of the street.

Later that same afternoon, the looting started up on Sackville. Some Dublin citizens were taking advantage of the relative chaos of the situation and had started breaking into stores up and down the wide main street, grabbing whatever they could find. It was like a tawdry circus.

Little kids dragged brand-new, expensive golf bags down the middle of the street, acting as caddies for their dads or older brothers, who were hitting golf balls in all directions. The men were dressed in motley collections of whatever they had found in the shops, wearing top hats with football jerseys and tailcoats. Joe saw a little girl of about nine years old running through the streets wearing a long fur coat that dragged behind her, her arms dripping with jewelry and expensive watches, her dirty face beaming. She wore a huge, feathered hat like a lady might wear to the races.

Clerys Department Store, directly across the street from the GPO, was hard hit and received most of the damage that first day as looters smashed windows and crowded into the immaculate aisles. Joe and Connolly repeatedly sent groups of Volunteers across the street to try to quell the looting. The men shouted orders and even fired warning shots into the air, but the scavengers were fearless and determined, refusing to stop no matter what threats were leveled at them.

"Shooting over their heads is useless. Unless a few of them are shot, you won't stop them," complained Connolly, who was frequently impatient and easily annoyed. "I'll have to send someone over there who'll deal with these looters!" He did not specify who, exactly, would be willing to shoot into the crowds of citizens. Thankfully, he never followed through on his threat.

24

Grace watched everything from the window of her second-floor room at the Imperial Hotel. The hotel was directly across the street from the General Post Office, and she watched as Joe marched into Sackville Street with Pearse and Connolly followed by the carts and Volunteers. Joe was beautifully dressed, almost as if he were playing a military leader in one of the plays at the Abbey Theatre, with his boots, sword, and officer's tunic. As usual, he was wearing some of his jewelry. Most of it was exotic, from his travels in northern Africa, but he also wore the family ring that she had given to him on the day they were engaged.

Joe knew that some of the men joked about his jewelry, which was not at all common for a man to wear in Ireland, but he didn't care about that kind of thing. He told Grace that he had always felt like an outsider and was comfortable with it as long as he had a certain number of friends in the world who understood him and appreciated him for who he really was.

He had explained to her once that he so valued the ideas, experiences, and perspectives that he had gained during his travels that it was comforting and inspiring to carry some concrete reminder with him in the form of a bracelet or ring. He had also spent a great deal of time studying the Celtic warriors and knew that they had worn jewelry.

He had looked so fragile when she last visited him in the nursing home, and she felt weak with worry and empathetic pain as she watched him marching up Sackville Street. He walked as if nothing were wrong, but this did little to console her; when Joe was excited and inspired, he felt little pain and practiced even less caution. She knew that his powerful and enthusiastic mind had hidden his weakness and exhaustion even from himself so that he could play out this moment, which he felt would somehow make his life worthwhile—no matter how it ended.

She watched as the Volunteers charged in to take the GPO and down toward the river to take the shops on the quays. She watched Joe enter the GPO, forcing herself not to think that it might be the last time she ever saw him alive. She saw the customers ejected, and when the large door of the main entrance to the GPO opened a short while later, she felt her heart grip, thinking she might see Joe again.

She was surprised to realize how important one more glance of him was to her as she strained to see who would emerge. But she quickly corrected her thoughts once again, telling herself she was being silly. A momentary sighting from across the widest street in Europe was nothing to be excited about when she and Joe would have their whole lives to spend together.

Only Patrick Pearse, Tom Clarke, and an armed Volunteer emerged from the door. She leaned out of the window as far as she dared, trying to hear Pearse as he read aloud from the Proclamation of the Irish Republic to the passersby and the few people who had gathered. Most people took no notice of Pearse as far as Grace could tell, but she knew about the proclamation and what it meant. Joe had told her all about it. It was quite daring and would cause a lot of trouble with the authorities at Dublin Castle. Now that the Volunteers were mounting a rebellion, she supposed that shocking the

Castle was the least of their worries, but it still filled her with excitement and fear to know that Pearse was reading it out loud in public.

Pearse read it right outside the door of the GPO. She couldn't hear him. There were no stairs at the entrance, so he was largely hidden from view as people walked by or stopped to listen to him. But he then walked a ways into the street and read the proclamation again, louder this time, and she had been able to hear a great deal. It felt like a dream—or a nightmare—to hear such closely guarded secrets read aloud to anyone who happened to walk by.

First of all, the proclamation revealed the existence and intentions of the secret Irish Republican Brotherhood. She had been in the nationalist movement for years but only knew vaguely of the IRB's existence until recently, when Joe had spoken with her about the plans for rebellion. Pearse went on to claim Ireland as a sovereign and independent state and to demand the allegiance of every Irish man and woman, promising in return civil rights and equality to all its citizens.

At the end of the proclamation, Pearse spoke of the necessity of the people of Ireland to sacrifice themselves for the common good. This made Grace feel a little sick, given the circumstances.

She wished that Joe would have come out for the reading so that she could see him again. She remembered how difficult it had been for him to tell her the IRB's secrets. He had paced and delayed until she said that maybe he shouldn't tell her at all—whatever it was—if it was going to cause him so much pain.

Once he had finally told her just a couple of the Military Council's secrets, it had become easier for him to tell her more and more. The first had been necessary so that she would understand why they could not be married on Easter Sunday and why he was always running off to meetings, day and night. But after Joe made the decision to break his oath and talk to her about the rebellion, he began telling her more and more every time it came up.

He seemed to be relieved to unburden himself. He spoke of all the guilt he had felt over the last few months, keeping these secrets from her as they became closer. Telling her seemed like the right thing to do, despite his vows. He knew for a fact that Tom Clarke was reporting everything to his wife, and he guessed that some of the other men were doing the same—although no one would admit it.

In the afternoon Grace watched the Lancers fall. It was like nothing she could have imagined. It was so easy to talk about rebellion being the right thing to do for Ireland—and she still believed this—but it was quite different to watch men and horses fall, writhing in pain in the street, right before her eyes.

She had never seen anyone die before. She simply could not fit it into any historical perspective about the foreign occupation of Ireland or England's years of abusing her people. A violent death was so final and disturbing, no matter whose, and she knew that people on both sides would fall before the rebellion was over. Since none of the Lancers had got off a shot, it was clear that no one in the post office had been hit, and for this she felt relief.

But she couldn't feel joy or jubilation to watch what had happened. One man tried to crawl to safety, but his arm was hanging uselessly at an unnatural angle, and he was leaving a trail of smeared blood drops as he struggled, dragging himself toward the cover of buildings that he would never be able to reach.

Another man lay motionless and was bleeding badly. Grace watched as blood flowed from his chest, spreading bright red against the pale stones of the street. None of it seemed real. She found herself hoping that she would wake up soon.

She stood at the window for a long time, watching as the Volunteers brought the living men into the GPO and the British came for their dead. For a while she waited for the horse to get up and walk away. Then she began to wait for the British to take it. No one came.

Later in the afternoon, Joe came out with his brother and two other Volunteers. They fiddled with two stranded trams for a while. She didn't know what they were doing. Eventually Joe somehow managed to shoot one of the trams from all the way across the street, causing it to explode. It appeared that the wheels were gone, and the tram rested on its axles.

After Joe went back inside, Grace decided to go home. She had insisted on staying nearby for the very beginning of the rebellion but had promised Joe she would go home if it got too dangerous. After the confrontation with the Lancers, she had seen enough action and didn't feel safe, so she got her bike and made her way to Muriel and Tom's on the south side of the city.

She spent a restless afternoon trying to help around the house, but she couldn't concentrate. She knew she was no good to anyone. That night the usual rainy April weather returned. Grace lay in bed most of the night listening. In the darkness, along with the sound of heavy rain, she heard frequent bursts of gunfire coming from various directions all over the city. Every shot made her want to cry, but she refused to let herself start. She was afraid that if she did, she would not be able to stop for as long as this rebellion lasted. Instead, she swallowed her fear and the lump of dread in her throat and lay staring at the ceiling. As cold, gray light began to creep over the city several hours later, she was finally able to fall into a short bout of sleep filled with dreams of flailing, injured horses, and rivers of blood as wide as the River Liffey.

25

Monday night Joe lay awake on the mattress in the GPO. Cold rain had fallen, heavy and ceaseless, for hours. In the distance he could hear occasional exchanges of gunfire coming from the south side of the city. He had even heard several bursts from a machine gun. These were obviously—and unfortunately—coming from English forces, because the Volunteers and IRB had no machine guns. The intermittent firing went on throughout the night. He tried to guess where the fighting was taking place based on the directions of the sounds and the dispatches he had received throughout the day.

He had learned that Dublin Castle had not been taken after all. This was unfortunate for symbolic reasons more than anything else. The Castle was the heart of Britain's power in Ireland, and if the armies of the new Irish Republic could have taken possession of the whole complex, it would have made a huge statement. But it was a large structure surrounding a huge courtyard. With the small amount of troops that had shown up today after the confusion caused by MacNeill's countermanding order, it would have been hard to hold onto.

Sacrifices and last-minute changes had been necessary on Sunday night and Monday morning, and he had no doubt that this would continue. Instead of the Castle, Volunteers had taken City Hall next door to it. Thomas MacDonagh was in possession of Jacob's Factory to the south of the Castle. Joe wished that Tom could be fighting with him at the GPO, but although most of the Military Council was there at headquarters, both Thomas and Eamonn Ceannt were not. He assured himself that he and Thomas would survive and, when all of this was over, he would see his best friend again.

West of Jacob's Factory, Ceannt had taken the South Dublin Union, which was one of the largest poorhouses in the world. This was perhaps too large a task for the turnout they had that day, and Joe worried about this position in particular. The Union was home to Dublin's most ill and poverty-stricken citizens, and it included administration buildings, housing for officials and nuns, and dormitories for thousands of inmates, as well as churches, workshops, and hospitals.

It was strategically important because it overlooked Kingsbridge railway station and was directly in the route that British soldiers would have to take from Richmond Barracks into the city center. But after separating his forces to take several necessary outposts nearby, Ceannt would probably have only about thirty men to occupy what was basically the equivalent of a small town with grounds covering fifty acres.

On the same side of the river as the General Post Office, Ned Daly had taken the Four Courts. Eamon de Valera had taken over Boland's Bakery, which was on the south side of the river, on the east side of the city. Almost directly to the south of the GPO, over the Liffey and through the city center, Michael Mallin and Connolly's Citizen Army had occupied the large city park, St. Stephen's Green. Joe could not help but feel badly for that particular group of soldiers, having taken the one position that could provide almost no cover from this weather. He thought that the park must be a cold and muddy mess by now and felt thankful for the cover of the GPO building, even with its high ceiling and drafty, stone interior.

Other than the looting, he felt that things had gone well on their first day of revolution. Joe had even had the chance to see his father, who showed up unexpectedly at the GPO that afternoon asking to fight alongside his sons. The Count always had a stable and reassuring presence, and Joe was happy to see him. Joe loved his father, and he was proud that the Count was there asking to fight on the front lines with the others; but he couldn't let him stay. Joe just couldn't take it if something were to happen to his father, and he had eventually convinced the Count to go back home. There was too much work that needed to be done at the Kimmage Garrison anyway, because ammunition production would need to continue during the fighting.

People had continued to bring in more ammunition throughout the day. Some were Volunteers making deliveries from various munitions stores around the city, but there were also citizens who came by with whatever bullets they could find in their homes. In addition to this, their numbers of fighters and support staff at the GPO had increased substantially, growing to almost double the size as when they started at noon that day.

Many Volunteers who had initially obeyed MacNeill's countermanding order had changed their minds and come to the GPO asking to be included in the fighting. Members of the Hibernian Rifles joined in as well, once they found out what was going on. The Hibernian Rifles were a group of exiled Irish Americans who had formed in opposition to British rule of Ireland years before, while still living in the United States.

James Connolly's assistant, Winifred Carney, the only woman to start out the day with them at the GPO, had been joined by members of Cumann na mBan, a woman's auxiliary group of the Irish Volunteers. Many of the women showed up armed and asked to fight, but Pearse had refused to allow it, relegating them all to necessary support positions like nursing, cooking, or running or riding bikes back and forth between the rebel-held positions with dispatches.

There were also plans to send members out to gather additional arms and ammunition from the remaining stashes throughout the city. Joe knew many women of the Cumann na mBan were fighting on the front lines along with Mallin and Countess Markievicz at St. Stephen's Green, but this was not the case at the other positions in Dublin.

Some of the women had complained, stating that they wanted to fight and be a real part of the revolution, but Pearse held his ground. Joe disagreed with Pearse, but he was also glad he wasn't the one who had to make that decision. He was a military strategist in this fight and little else, so questions of personnel were not technically any of his business.

One of the main features of their proclamation was equality for all people in Ireland, and this expressly included women. Didn't they have the right to the satisfaction of fighting for their country as well? Joe had to assume that, as Irish citizens, these women felt the same rage that he did about the hundreds of years of oppression and occupation their country had endured.

This was 1916, not the dark ages. Things were changing for women, and while the new Irish Republic claimed to be on the forefront of those changes, it seemed that Pearse might not have the stomach for it after all. In a way Joe could understand Pearse's unwillingness to have the women fighting on the front lines. The very thought of Grace or his own sisters being in any danger at all made him forget all the recent advances.

Joe knew this was wrong, and he felt ashamed for his unenlightened thinking. He didn't want to see women getting shot and killed, but as it was, the Volunteers had teenage boys fighting all over Dublin. Wasn't that worse? He knew Connolly agreed with this. Women were included in the ranks of his Irish Citizen Army and were trained to fight. Joe thought about Markievicz and some of the other women fighting alongside the men at St. Stephen's Green at that very moment. From what he had heard, the Countess was one of the best shots they had.

All the same, he was glad that Grace was far away from the GPO by now. After the Volunteers had actually taken over a good portion of the street and fought the Lancers, Joe began to worry that the British response might not be as controlled and focused as they were all expecting. The leaders at Dublin Castle and Westminster Abbey might just be furious about the rebellion and respond with rage, causing widespread destruction instead of fighting with a more logical and strategic approach at close range. This would mean bombs, incendiaries, and cannons, which would cause much more destruction and many more civilian deaths.

James Connolly had ordered a large barbed wire fence to be put up all along the front of the GPO, encompassing a good portion of the wide street. It would keep out the scavengers and help to slow down a direct frontal ground attack—but Joe was beginning to wonder if that would ever come.

Connolly, the devout, lifelong socialist, was totally convinced that an imperial capitalist nation like England would never seek to destroy the actual buildings of Dublin because they viewed the city as their own valued property. Connolly expected close-up—even hand-to-hand—fighting, with lots of shooting and death but little shelling or use of explosives or fire to destroy the actual structures. In many ways the rebels were pinning their hopes on this belief when they made their strategic decisions since Connolly had joined the Military Council. Joe almost always agreed with Connolly, but he wasn't sure about this idea of his that the English wouldn't try to destroy the buildings of Dublin.

Either way, Joe hoped that Grace was now out of the area entirely, especially with all the looting that had started up that afternoon. As the first day of the rising came to an end, Joe rearranged his inadequate blanket, wrapping it as tightly around him as he could. Since they had broken the glass out all of the windows at the GPO, it almost felt like he was sleeping outside. It was a cold night, and the rain continued to fall heavily. In the distance he could still hear occasional bursts of gunfire coming from different positions throughout the city.

26

On Tuesday, dawn emerged clear and bright, as if winter might be giving up early. There was a chill in the air, but the sky was bright blue and sunny, with drifts of cottony white clouds. Overnight more troops had arrived by train from Belfast. By morning 1,600 men had arrived from Curragh to support the British. Soon these forces were joined by another thousand soldiers from the 25th Irish Reserve Infantry Brigade, bringing the number of new troops arriving on Tuesday morning to over 3,000. This flood of new arrivals meant the rebels were already outnumbered by more than four to one, and it was just the first day of reinforcement. Britain already had many more regiments preparing to set sail from Wales, and they were just getting started.

The military authorities had finally caught on to what was happening in Dublin, and they were beginning to take things seriously. There had been numerous spies on the streets for over a year, and the Castle had been censoring mail for longer, even succeeding in intercepting a number of letters directly relating to plans for the rebellion. Even so, they had failed to grasp the immediacy of the situation.

They knew about the IRB, for instance, but most intelligence reports claimed that the secret society was inactive. The few detectives who had urged the authorities at Dublin Castle and in London to take the threat of insurrection seriously had been ignored. But now the response was in high gear, and despite the resources needed for the war in Europe, England was sending heavy forces to fight the insurrection in Dublin.

All was still at the GPO except for the slight breeze coming in through the glassless windows and quiet conversations between small groups of Volunteers. It was the second day of the rebellion, and things were beginning to feel somewhat organized. The kitchen was already busy serving breakfast in shifts, and the smell of fresh biscuits and grilled bacon made its way down the stairs. Separate storerooms had been set up for ammunition, grenades, and other supplies, and the hospital was full of beds from the Metropole Hotel, where Joe had stayed just two nights before. Women from Cumann na mBan were continuously on the move, touring the city for updates from the other garrisons. Regular shifts were established for security guards surrounding the GPO. So far, the looters hadn't shown up again; apparently they weren't early risers.

Outside, the street was completely deserted. No one had removed the dead horse left behind by the Lancers, although its harness and saddle had long since been removed by scavengers. It lay there alone, surrounded only by a blanket of white paper. The previous day the Volunteers had stacked hundreds of notebooks full of documents and accounting books in front of the windows to create barricades, and a good deal of paper had blown out through the windows, covering the ground outside like a fresh snowfall.

Normally Sackville Street would have been bustling by now with carts, horses, trams, and the few cars that belonged to Dublin's more affluent families. The shop owners would be opening their doors as people made their way to school and work. But this morning nothing moved but the breeze.

It stirred the flags atop the GPO and lifted a corner here and there of the scattered pieces of white paper. Even the birds wouldn't come near the area. The silence was complete.

As the sun moved higher in the blue sky, the wide avenue began to stir once again. A group of postal workers had gathered down the street near Hopkins Jewelers. They stood around for quite a while in serious discussion and seemed to be trying to decide whether to make their way through the new barbed wire fence and into the GPO to begin sorting mail for their routes—in the middle of a revolution.

Eventually, one of the mailmen moved away from the group and up the street, squeezing under the fencing and carefully approaching the post office. A rifle-wielding Volunteer walked out to meet him before he got near the building.

"Sorry, but you all need to leave. It's not safe."

"But what about the day's mail? We need to get it out."

"There'll be no mail today, sir," explained the Volunteer. "The post office is closed. It's … it's the new republic," he finished awkwardly.

The rejected mailman crawled through the barbed wire and walked back to his colleagues who were waiting just down the street. They continued to discuss the matter for a few more minutes, then they all walked away.

The next visit was from Grace's sister, and Thomas MacDonagh's wife, Muriel. Joe had no idea how she had made it in, but he rushed to her with questions.

"Muriel! How did you get here? Is something wrong? Grace and Thomas, has something happened?"

"No, everyone's doing well," she assured him quickly. "They're fine. I've just been to see Thomas at Jacob's Factory, and Grace is at our house."

"Don't let Grace try to come over here or get close to any of the fighting," he insisted. "Don't let her, no matter what. She's stubborn, and she'll do just about anything."

"Yes, I think it might run in the family... with the girls, anyway. You know Nellie's fighting at Stephen's Green, don't you? There was nothing we could do to keep her from going."

"She's with Mallin and Markievicz. She should be perfectly safe out there." He was trying to be reassuring, but they both knew this was not necessarily true. "But what are you still doing, running around the city? Please promise me that this will be your last trip out here, will you? Things might seem pretty quiet right now, but it's only because we took them by surprise. It'll be wild soon enough."

"I know, I know. It's just driving us crazy to be stuck down there in Ranelagh with no idea of what's going on up here. But this is my last trip, and I promise to keep Grace away as well."

"It'll all be over before you know it, and Thomas will be home with you soon. And... could you give Grace a message for me?"

"Of course. What is it?" Muriel looked worried, as if she expected him to launch into some kind of dramatic last statement.

"Please just let her know that I still want us to be married as soon as possible. When this is over—even if I'm in prison—please ask her to find a way to get to me so that we can be married."

"I'll tell her."

"Please be sure of it, Muriel, will you?" He almost pleaded. Then he added more quietly, "If I wasn't so sure that Grace and I would see each other again and be married... I don't know that I'd have the courage to go through all of this."

Not long after Muriel left, the looters returned. First there were just a couple of more industrious, relatively early birds easing themselves through the broken glass of the doors and windows of the shops up and down Sackville Street and picking through the items left behind in the chaos of the previous day's scavenging party.

But before long the crowds returned, talking, laughing, and fighting loudly as they waded through the mess, grasping everything they could find that could be used or sold. Many had come prepared this time with bags and carts, having learned from Monday's improvised and gleeful—but less focused—foraging. Soon people were running down the street pushing carts filled with toys, housewares, hats, and clothes.

Joe could see the frustration in the eyes of the Volunteers as they manned their posts in the GPO windows, watching the savage greed and disrespect playing out before them in the street. He knew it was the worst thing for morale. These were the citizens that they were fighting for, and it was hard to watch such depravity. But there was nothing they could do to stop it, short of shooting into the crowd.

Joe began setting up phone lines throughout the GPO so that the leaders could communicate with the Volunteers all over the huge building, even running wires up to the roof so that Connolly could stay in touch with his Irish Citizen Army snipers. Volunteers and Cumann na mBan members were sent out once again to gather additional ammunition and rifles from arsenals throughout the city, and vehicles were sent down to Joe's family estate in Kimmage, where production of grenades and shotgun shells continued.

Joe continued to receive dispatches from throughout Dublin and the rest of the country, and by midmorning it was becoming clear that Ireland as a whole had not risen up in rebellion as planned. The confusion caused by MacNeill's countermanding order had proven too much to overcome. Most had not received word of the last-minute changes, and even though many had mobilized on Sunday—contrary to MacNeill's orders—they had been sent home again by their local leaders, who told them the insurrection was canceled.

Even in the counties where they did get word of the late changes and tried to mount rebellions, the men were very poorly armed. The interception of the German ship full of weapons made nationwide plans almost impossible. These were the rifles that had been intended to arm regiments outside of Dublin.

In County Galway, for instance, where almost seven hundred men had gathered to fight, they had done so with only twenty-five rifles and three hundred shotguns. The rest carried pikes and axes. With such a shortage of arms, they had not been able to overthrow the local authorities. Like the rest of the country, they would not be descending on the city. The leaders in Dublin had been counting on troops from all over Ireland to join them in Dublin after mounting local rebellions throughout the country. Without these reinforcements, there was little chance they could hold out for long against British forces.

They would just have to do what they could with the numbers they had. From the dispatches he had received throughout the night and morning, Joe estimated that they had about one thousand troops altogether.

At the GPO and surrounding buildings, they were now up to almost three hundred troops, including support staff.

These troops were spread out still further, however, as Connolly began ordering small groups of Volunteers to occupy Clerys Department Store and the Imperial Hotel, directly across the street from the GPO, in addition to the positions they already held all the way down to the river. After these locations were secure, they would hold a large part of Sackville Street.

Since the time of their first charge on Monday, when a small group of Volunteers had taken the bridge and the two shops at the river's edge, they had been breaking through the walls of connected buildings, occupying each one as they went. It was slow and difficult work, but they continued to burrow their way through the walls of the shops on Sackville Street toward the GPO. Now that more Volunteers were taking over the buildings across the street, Joe was beginning to feel more secure and prepared for the onslaught they would undoubtedly face anytime now.

There had been a lot of British activity to the north, on Great Britain Street, all afternoon. Although it was hard to tell for sure, they seemed to be occupying some of the buildings that were very near the post office. Joe paced back and forth to the windows; waiting to see what they were up to was the hardest thing of all. He had to hope things would be okay as long as their own forces could hold onto the area from the GPO down to the river. But this plan had its drawbacks too. That was a lot of territory to cover with less than three hundred men, and if they had known about the low turnout in advance, they probably would have made plans for a more compact strategy.

Shortly after the buildings across Sackville Street were occupied, a Volunteer ran into the GPO to report that British forces were bringing in a cannon so large that they were pulling it behind six horses. They were attempting to position the large weapon a few blocks to the north, at the Parnell Monument, at the intersection of Great Britain and Sackville Streets, and it looked big enough to fire eighteen-pound cannonballs.

As soon as the leaders got word of this latest development, they called up to Connolly's snipers, who went to work immediately. Mauser rifle fire thundered from the roof of the GPO, as well as the newly taken positions on top of Clerys and the Imperial Hotel across the street, killing or wounding anyone who got close enough to the eighteen-pounder to get it positioned and ready to fire. Eventually the British gave up on the cannon, and all was quiet for a while.

Soon, however, British reinforcements arrived and started setting up again, despite the major losses they were facing as the snipers continued their bombardment of anyone who came near the cannon. They eventually got the eighteen-pounder ready and attempted to fire at the GPO. After the sound of the cannon fire, everyone braced for the impact, but nothing happened. They had missed the GPO, instead hitting the YMCA nearby, which, as it turned out, had already been occupied by British troops.

The building was badly damaged—so badly, in fact, that the men inside immediately evacuated, thinking that they were under attack by the rebels. As they ran out into Sackville Street, the snipers started up again. Then the other Volunteers joined in as well, and the government troops suffered heavy casualties as they ran out the front doors of the YMCA.

Prisoners were taken and the wounded brought upstairs to the GPO hospital. Then things got quiet again. The Volunteers had sustained very few injuries, none of which were serious, so the mood was cheerful at the GPO as the sun moved lower in the sky. The daytime security guards came in, and their reinforcements stepped out into the cool, still night.

Dinner was served in shifts, and groups of Volunteers talked and laughed while singing continued almost nonstop in other parts of the huge main room on the ground floor of the GPO.

Frightened away by the cannon fire, the looters had returned once the firing stopped. They spread into Lawrence's Toy Store, continuing to ravage it like a swarm of roaches. After they had finished with it, they set the store on fire. One group of looters found a huge display of fireworks and brought them all outside. A group of children worked dutifully as darkness fell, stacking all the fireworks into a pile almost as tall as some of the youngest. After they had all the fireworks piled as high as they could get them, they set fire to the whole batch.

The Volunteers had a lot of explosives on the roof of the GPO, and this latest development made everyone nervous. Soon dense and continuous sprays of sparks and fire were exploding over and over again into the evening sky from just yards away from the GPO. There were sky-rockets, starbursts, Catherine wheels, Roman candles, and every other firework made, shooting off in every direction with thousands of tiny flames cascading down onto the roof of the GPO, right on top of their stashes of explosives. The Volunteers scurried around on the roof with water buckets putting out sparks and still-flaming firework cartridges.

This constant barrage of blasts, fire, and explosions of the fireworks went on and on. Volunteers stationed on the ground floor ran up to the roof with extra fire extinguishers and new buckets of water to be sure nothing was set on fire. Joe went up to help as well and remained there until the fireworks show was over and things calmed down once again.

Lawrence's Toy Store continued to burn, and in the sudden quiet Joe could hear the crackling sounds of the fire and the destruction it caused as inner structures crashed to the floor. The sounds of the looters laughing and fighting continued in the darkness. They had long ago broken into liquor stores and bars, and the street had become a chaotic free-for-all, even worse than on the previous night.

In the distance the steady sounds of heavy fire south of the River Liffey continued nonstop as other rebel garrisons fought the British with all they had.

27

Throughout Tuesday night and Wednesday morning, British troops were landing at the port at Kingstown, southeast of Dublin. Some of the men in these reinforcement battalions had been in uniform for only eight weeks, had barely finished with their training to fight in the war in Europe, and had seen no combat at all. Many of the young soldiers had been misinformed when they boarded the ships at Holyhead, Wales, and when they disembarked in Ireland, they thought they had landed in France.

The sun rose bright in the clear blue northern sky as British troops marched toward Dublin on their way to quell the rebellion, receiving cheers from people gathered along the road to greet them. Entering the city, they were met by larger and larger crowds of Dubliners, who welcomed them with sandwiches and tea. Citizens filled them in on rumors regarding the locations of the various rebel positions. They even handed out gifts to the soldiers, like field glasses and Dublin maps.

Many people who had been totally uninvolved and uninterested in politics before now had strong opinions. They just wanted the rebellion to end so that they could get back to their regular lives. The previous two days of fighting had already had an impact. Most food shipments from the rural areas had not been able to get through, and people were finding that some of their favorite items were missing from store shelves.

Traffic was diverted, and the newspapers hadn't been delivered at all that morning. The *Irish Times* had published the Tuesday edition on the previous day, but they mentioned very little about the rebellion, so the city was running on rumors.

At the GPO the leaders and Volunteers woke up to the sound of heavy fire. Joe watched as just about everyone who was not already on duty rushed to the windows, ready to defend their position. He had finally fallen asleep not long before dawn; he guessed that was about two hours ago. Even though the days had been beautiful and warm for April, the early mornings were still dark and bitterly cold and damp in the high-ceilinged, cavernous stone rooms of the GPO.

Joe ached from the cold and lack of sleep. The few times he had allowed himself to lie down and rest for more than a few minutes, he had come out of it feeling exhausted and heavy, as if someone had laid boulders on top of him. When he did try to start moving again, just sitting up felt like an all but impossible task. He felt that his body had pretty much given up on him because of its exhaustion; now his mind was running the show entirely.

The way he saw it, even though his tank was completely empty and his engine was beyond repair, he would tow, push, and pull himself through to the end of the rising no matter what came. He was inspired enough to run solely on excitement and the duty he felt to complete a good and honorable fight. As he sat up slowly and carefully, trying to reposition his bandages to cover the still unhealed surgical wounds at his throat, he thought about his doctor's orders. There was really nothing much he could do about them now.

Among many other things, he had been told to have his bandages changed regularly, remain in bed at all times possible, eat hearty and regular meals, stay warm and dry in front of a fire, sleep as much as he could, and avoid any form of physical exertion. So far he had been able to do none of these things. The only instruction he had even attempted to follow was to take care of his bandaging—he had gone up to the hospital once to have them replaced.

He winced a little as he thought about how unhappy the caring women from the nursing home would be with him right now if they knew how badly he was taking care of himself. Even worse, there was no way he could hide what a terrible patient he was because his own doctor—the same man who had performed his surgery—was currently upstairs in their post office hospital attending to the wounded.

The doctor knew full well that Joe was ignoring all of his orders and had given up on asking him to quit the fight and take care of himself. He had insisted numerous times that Joe might actually pull through if he went back to the nursing home immediately, but even he'd had to admit that at this point it might not make much of a difference what Joe did.

The look in the doctor's eyes when he spoke of this was chilling. It was full of concern, pity, and regret, and it made Joe feel more exhausted and pathetic than anything else he was going through. He shook it off and pushed it out of his head. He would remain until the end in victory or defeat, no matter how long it took. If it turned out that he was wrong and he couldn't make it to the end, then he would die trying.

Every once in a while, Joe would see the doctor's face in his imagination and feel that chill creeping back into his consciousness. This was a distraction he did not need. When it came up, he said a quick prayer and got back to work. He tried to focus instead on the gratitude he felt for getting the chance to be a part of the big fight of his generation. This was it. It was all that mattered.

Joe sometimes thought that all of this physical suffering actually made things easier for him—not harder. He had come into this fight with all of the loyalty and devotion in the world, but he had only recently begun to understand that he might already be—in a way—dead on his feet. He now had nothing to fear. He marveled at the idea that something so completely negative—his terrible health—had enabled him to dedicate himself even more completely to the dangerous task at hand. He truly felt no fear. Instead of fearing that he would be shot, he was just glad he had made it through another night to continue fighting.

He didn't even worry about the miserably distasteful possibility of having to surrender, or the fact that he and the other leaders would most likely be quickly executed if they did. Even in that worst-case scenario, he would just be thankful to have lived long enough to be executed, so that his death would mean something in the big picture. If he could make it to the end of the rising and the British had to kill him, then his name could be added to the long list of martyrs in the cause for Ireland's freedom.

The doctor's sad and pitying eyes were not the only thing Joe had to force from his mind. There was another pair of eyes that haunted him and at times made him almost give in to his exhaustion in the darkness. When he thought of Grace and her gentle, trusting love for him, he felt that he could almost completely collapse in tears—not just tears, but outright weeping. Although he never succumbed to it, he felt a heaviness in his heart that he could hardly endure when he thought about her dark eyes, the warmth of her hand in his own, and the softness of her pale skin.

Grace was the only thing he did not feel prepared to leave behind in the name of this rebellion. This is why he had tried so desperately not to fall in love with her. No, he hadn't tried for long, but that was only because he had seen that there was no point. He couldn't resist loving her, and he couldn't keep himself from telling her how he felt. He knew he would not turn back from the fight now, but when he remembered their walks in late summer—and thought that they might have been their last—he felt raw and hollowed out inside, a lingering and empty heaviness settling deep in his chest.

The thought of Grace was one more reason that it was best to keep moving. Even during the first two days at the GPO, when they spent most of their time waiting and preparing for battle, he kept busy with his notebooks, strategies, and conversation as much as possible.

Despite the fact that resting seemed to make things worse, Joe did feel very lucky just to have the little mattress Mick Collins had brought him on the first day. Most of the other men got what little sleep they could while curled up on the floor under a desk or table. None of the men had enough blankets.

The seriously injured stayed in the makeshift hospital upstairs and were the only people who had a comfortable place to sleep, with hotel beds and enough blankets to stay warm and dry. This included the wounded prisoners as well as their own Volunteers, since the leaders had given strict orders regarding the treatment of any soldiers taken prisoner. In the hospital their wounded opponents were treated like their own men, and everyone got the same food and other rations. Joe had even seen a British officer in the mess hall upstairs eating dinner with some of the Volunteer officers.

After the first rush to the windows at the sound of heavy gunfire that morning, things calmed down a bit, but everyone was chattering excitedly like little boys, looking wide awake and ready to fight. As it turned out, it was the Imperial Hotel across the street that was coming under heavy fire. When some of Connolly's men hoisted a flag with the Starry Plough emblem high above their new hotel garrison, they received a fierce and immediate response from the government forces on early morning duty.

The Starry Plough was the flag used by Connolly's Citizen Army. It consisted of a green background with stars in the shape of the constellation Ursa Major, which was known in Ireland as the Plough. The men stationed at the Imperial Hotel would have known that putting up a rebel flag in another building was just the kind of thing that would infuriate the British. It was pretty much an invitation to start the day with some serious fighting; their invitation was accepted with enthusiasm.

The Starry Plough was one of three flags the rebels were using at the time of the rising, but the sight of any flag at all going up at another rebel position caused the expected violent reaction from British snipers. It seemed that the men in and around the GPO were tired of waiting and wanted to get on with the fight. Joe smiled, because after listening day and night to the sounds of almost constant heavy artillery in the distance, he felt the same way.

The sniper fire from British forces made it dangerous to cross Sackville Street with dispatches, so it was decided to tie a long cord across its very wide expanse. Written messages were placed in little cans and tied to the cord then pulled quickly between the GPO and the Imperial Hotel. The first couple times messages were sent across the street, British snipers fired at the can, but it was moving quickly and none of them could hit it. Eventually they gave up on even trying to hit the cans.

Just as Joe had gone back to his maps and notes, he was alerted again to the sound of heavy shellfire from somewhere near the River Liffey to the south. The crashing booms were loud enough for him to know the shots were coming from cannons. It was decided that one of the Volunteers would make his way toward the sound to find out what was going on then come back with information.

They sent a man out, and he was gone quite a while before returning to give his report. When he had made it to the garrison at Kelly's Gun Shop, which was now being called Kelly's Fort, he was told that the British had actually brought a gunboat up the River Liffey. Cannons on the British naval vessel, the *Helga*, were bombarding the riverfront at Liberty Hall, where they had begun their march on Monday.

James Connolly was well-known to British authorities, and since Liberty Hall was headquarters for his Irish Citizen Army, they apparently thought that the building would also be the central base of operations during the rebellion. It was, in fact, totally deserted throughout the week, other than a caretaker who had remained for just the first day or two. From the Volunteers' angle at Kelly's Fort, it was impossible to safely view the shelling, but one of the men had created a makeshift periscope from a little mirror and an old broom handle.

The Volunteers were shocked and a little unnerved by the fact that the British had brought out their navy in such an enclosed, urban situation and were using such big guns so early in the fighting. The great ship was intimidating, and the twelve-pound shells shook the ground near the river as they smashed into buildings just blocks away.

Despite great powers of intimidation, the *Helga*'s cannons were having a hard time actually hitting Liberty Hall effectively from her angle near the Custom House. Nonetheless, the cannon fire continued to knock down whatever walls it could hit. It was all hard to ignore. Before long, shells were coming from somewhere else farther away, on the south bank of the river.

Cannons near Trinity College joined in the bombardment of Liberty Hall. Soon the great, abandoned building was reduced to charred ruins with only some jagged outer walls remaining, blackened and crumbling.

28

By midday on Wednesday, British machine gunners on top of Trinity College swept Sackville Street continuously with a horizontal shower of bullets. While it had been dangerous to try to cross the street between the GPO and Imperial Hotel before, now it was impossible. The college was several blocks to the south, but the powerful metallic shivering sound carried easily to the GPO. Snipers continued to fire on anything that moved. All of this sound was drowned out only by the frequent crashing booms as cannons on the *Helga* and near the college continued to fire at a regular rate for hours, destroying the buildings all along the north side of the river.

The British cannons were still unable to hit the GPO directly because of their angle as they aimed up the street. The men at Kelly's Fort maintained their position despite the heavy shelling at the river, blocking any advances, but Connolly was starting to talk about pulling them back and stationing them somewhere a little farther up Sackville Street, closer to the GPO. This would not just be safer for the men now stationed near the river, it would also compress and strengthen the rebel position generally. While the top floor of the post office was still not in the line of fire of the cannons or the machine guns across the river, Volunteer snipers on the roof traded shots with government forces situated at Amiens Street Station to the east, Great Britain Street to the north, and Findlater Place in the northeast. This continued throughout the morning and into the afternoon.

At about two that day, there was a booming explosion so big and loud that it shook the GPO on its foundation. Some men thought that the bombs stored in the basement must have exploded; surely there was nothing else that could shake the building like that. But there soon came a second and third earth-shuddering impact, and they realized that it must be the British cannons. After a short time, a Volunteer from Kelly's Fort on the river came to report that they were being shelled directly by heavy artillery. The plaster was crumbling from the ceilings of the former gun shop, and the top floor was on fire. It was decided that they would abandon the position—at least until the shelling died down.

A few hours later, Hopkins—just across Sackville Street from Kelly's—was also abandoned. The GPO remained relatively safe for the moment, still out of the range of the big guns. Despite the lack of fighting within the building, there was a constant bustle as its inhabitants continued to make preparations, care for wounded, and lend support and relief to the men on the roof, who were still engaged in an almost constant exchange of gunfire with British snipers stationed in windows and on roofs throughout the area. It was clear where this firing was coming from. They were receiving no hits from the west side of the building.

Joe decided it would be good to know if there was a British presence on that side. He wanted to be alone and get outside for a short time anyway. The constant beehive-like activity of the GPO was exhilarating, but it had been going on constantly for days now. He needed a break.

The area around the GPO wasn't safe, and there were buildings held by the British within easy range of fire, but Joe guessed he could make it out if he left by the side entrance then crept down Prince's Street to Abbey Street. They had to scout for British positions out there because there was no other way to know where they were or how close they were getting.

"I need to go out to explore the situation on the south side of the building—and out back, if possible," Joe told Connolly. "I shouldn't be out there long."

"You should stay here. Send one of the men," Connolly insisted. This would be safer for Joe, and it would be expected that they would send out a Volunteer instead of one of the leaders. But that wasn't necessarily the way they were doing things in this uprising. The handful of leaders at the GPO were constantly putting themselves in dangerous positions to fight alongside their men, and Joe assumed this was the case in garrisons throughout the city.

With Connolly there was something more. Since the IRB's mostly friendly abduction of the Citizen Army leader from in front of Liberty Hall just weeks ago, he and Joe had become close while working together to refine strategy and plans for the rising. By the time they marched side by side to the GPO on Monday, Connolly had proven to Joe that he was all dedication and intelligence. Whether or not he would admit it, Connolly had a big heart.

On the outside, Connolly's charm could be hard to appreciate. He could definitely be described as a diamond in the rough. His uniform was made of bottle-green serge—a lightweight and coarse fabric, which made for a bad fit. It pulled uncomfortably across his very prominent belly then continued its awkward drape down his skinny, bowed legs. He was sometimes gruff and impatient and could be thoughtless in the way he gave his sometimes rather harsh opinions.

"I promise to stay close, and I'll be back soon, whether I find their positions or not," Joe assured Connolly, then made his way to the side entrance. The main entrance—and everything else on Sackville Street—was off limits as the intermittent machine gun showers persisted throughout the late morning and into the afternoon. Sackville Street was both wide and in range of British snipers from several directions, and there was no good cover at all. Even the looters seemed to have given up for the day because of all the shooting. Though it was possible that they had already taken everything there was to take.

Joe stepped carefully into the doorway on Prince's Street. He took off his hat and waved it a little in view of any snipers who might be on this side of the building. Nothing happened; no shots were fired. He snuck out into the street and down the block. The narrow street was totally deserted and as still as a cemetery. Joe could hear his own footsteps as he made his way west with his back to the wall. Reminding himself to breathe, he turned down the alley and made it to Abbey Street. On the corner was a pub. The door was open to the fresh, summer-like air of the afternoon, and he could see inside. They were open for business, as if nothing out of the ordinary were going on. The owner was wiping down the bar, chatting with two older men in caps who were seated with their pints of stout in front of them—a normal afternoon scene.

Joe was getting used to the sudden crashing and booming from explosions and shelling and was expecting to be shot at while coming around each corner, but the calm and ordinary scene at the pub took him completely off guard. He stayed in the doorway a moment too long and was seen by the man behind the bar, who stopped speaking, causing the other two men to turn. The bartender motioned for Joe to come in and offered him a pint.

"No charge for you," he said, with a motion toward Joe's Volunteer officer's uniform. Joe must have looked stunned, because the man smiled and continued, "Name's Brian. This here's Patrick and Brendan, and you're welcome here—probably even safe for now. C'mon, have a seat."

Joe couldn't turn him down. He felt like he had turned a corner and walked into last week. He was surprised at how good it felt to be in a more routine situation again. He thanked Brian and sat at the bar near the other two men as they continued their conversation.

One of the men was from Galway, and they were debating the relative virtues of the Galway and Dublin hurling teams. Brian took his time, pouring the stout just right, and Joe could feel his mouth water as he watched the tiny pale bubbles rising through the blackness, gathering thick and creamy at the top of the tall glass.

Drinking any alcohol was strictly forbidden during the rising. The rule was that any Volunteer caught drinking was to be shot. But Joe didn't care about that right now. He had a strong feeling that this might be his last pint—might be the last time he would ever have the opportunity to just sit in a pub and listen to old men arguing about sports. Soon they would probably move on to local politics. Things were so quiet and easy here, and Joe longed to go back to any of the hundreds of times he had been in a similar situation so he could pay more attention—appreciate it more.

The smell of the wood pub interior had such warmth when compared to the stone walls of the GPO. The wood mingled with scents of tobacco, wood smoke, years of daily simmering pots of lamb stew, and warm slices from golden loaves of fresh-baked soda bread. There was a Tricolor flag on the wall, along with the ubiquitous Guinness signs with the pelican and the old horse cart, as well as the two crossed hurleys hung over the bar.

Joe was lost in the past now. He felt gratitude that was beyond words for being here with Brian and his perfectly poured pints, listening to Pat and Brendan discuss team trades as if they were the most important thing going on in the world. But it also made him very sad. He had been thinking a lot about how much he missed Grace and his family. They had risen to the surface of his thoughts many times over the last couple of days, momentarily weakening his will and distracting him from the task at hand—just for a moment or two. But he had never really given any thought to the normal things in his life and how good they had been. So many moments that had seemed ordinary and unimportant took on greater meaning for him now.

He felt his eyes well with tears and blinked them away, thinking back to the evenings out with Thomas MacDonagh or his brothers, George and Jack, drinking, eating, and talking for hours at the pubs. As it got later, the fireplace would come to life, followed by the fiddle, whistle, and button accordion. A session would start up, with the music going into the early morning hours.

These memories all seemed like they were from years ago, from a great distance, even though some of these scenes were from only a couple blocks and a few days away. He was lost in thought when the bartender brought over his pint. Joe figured he must have been looking pretty tragic, because Brian reached over the bar to pat him on the shoulder with fatherly affection.

"There'll be another pint waiting for you when all of this is over. On me. Welcome any time." Brian smiled and handed him the big glass. Joe was so exhausted and happy in the moment that he felt a little overwhelmed by the bartender's kind words.

"I'll be back as soon as I can," he answered, keeping it short, afraid his eyes might well up of he tried to thank Brian or say much of anything at all. He took the first creamy drink of what might be his last pint of stout.

Halfway through the glass, Joe reluctantly rose to leave, thanking Brian for his hospitality.

"You'd be best off staying out of Abbey Street. We've heard shooting down that way," one of the two old men at the bar told him. Joe couldn't remember if it was Patrick or Brendan. "We heard it from the west, down at the end of the block, and we don't think you boys have anyone down there, do you?"

"No, we don't. I'll hold back. And be careful walking around out there. They seem to be firing at anything that moves—and I think things will get a lot worse soon."

"I don't see any reason to do anything but stay where I am for now," the old man answered, totally relaxed and unalarmed, draining his pint and motioning to Brian for another.

As he went out into the alley and walked toward the corner, Joe wondered what these men had seen in life to make them feel so comfortable in the midst of all this. He took off his hat and waved it out into Abbey Street. After less than a second, he heard a spatter of rifle shots from the west and decided he'd had enough of a break from the GPO. It was time to go back.

29

When he got back to the GPO, Joe received a dispatch from the south side of the River Liffey. There had been heavy fighting at the Mount Street Bridge all afternoon, and it was still going on. The handful of Volunteers who held the buildings in the area estimated that at least two hundred British had been killed already.

Troops from England had landed at Kingstown Port the previous evening, where they camped and prepared for battle. That morning a large group had made their way into Dublin, planning to cross at the Mount Street Bridge.

While the River Liffey cuts through the center of the city, the Grand Canal encircles it, separating the center from the outer neighborhoods. The Mount Street Bridge is one of many small bridges that cross the canal and is in line with the most direct route into the city from Kingstown. This was the way Joe had expected British troops to take, and he had made plans to have the whole area near the bridge covered. Due to the low turnout on Monday, only fifteen Volunteers were stationed in homes and other buildings overlooking the bridge and the approaching area.

As the several hundred British soldiers arrived at the Mount Street Bridge, they did exactly what they had been trained to do, charging in small groups when alerted by the sound of an officer's whistle. For hours the little groups ran for the bridge and were mowed down by the handful of

Volunteers, armed with only one rifle or revolver each. The British continued to charge straight ahead at the sound of the whistle until there were great piles of dead and dying soldiers covering the bridge and surrounding area.

Joe made an announcement about what was going on at Mount Street, and there were cheers that broke into songs and general happy conversation throughout the main floor. Joe was worried, however. Standing at the postal counter with Dublin maps, dispatch notices, and strategy notebooks spread out before him, he soberly considered their situation.

After this massive defeat at Mount Street, there was no way the British government would try the same tactics again. They wouldn't come charging at the post office with rifles and bayonets, and this was the only kind of fighting the Volunteers were really prepared to face. They had trained for months to fight against this kind of challenge in an urban environment, and they were good at it—as the Volunteers at Mount Street had proven. Unfortunately, Joe doubted there would be another chance. Instead, he expected more bombs, cannons, and incendiaries. The rebel fighters had no good options to defend their position against that kind of attack. He found Connolly nearby and pulled him aside.

"This attack at the Mount Street Bridge is the first time they've fought the way we expected them to," Joe said in a hushed voice.

"And look how it turned out," Connolly replied with an easy smile. "We massacred them, Joe! It went better than we could have expected."

"Yes, but they won't try that again after that kind of defeat. That kind of rifle-to-rifle, eye-to-eye fighting—it's what we were prepared for when we planned this thing, but I think that's the last time we'll see anything like it."

"Just give the men a moment to celebrate, and then we'll decide what to do next." Connolly was more serious now.

"I know. You're right. We had a big win today at Mount Street. But we won't have that chance here. The enemy is keeping their distance here—staying out of range," Joe argued. "We don't have any defense against the cannonballs and shells."

"This building is strong. There's no way they'll bring it down," Connolly insisted.

"You might be right about that, but what about the incendiary bombs? What'll we do if they try to burn us out of here?"

"If they try, then we'll face it. We've got buckets, hoses, and a good water supply," Connolly assured him.

Joe had other worries, but he kept them to himself. It was now clear to him that the rest of the country had not risen with Dublin. There would be no wave of support coming in from the towns and cities in the west.

Pearse was still making rousing and optimistic speeches about the many hundreds of Volunteers currently marching toward them—due to arrive at any minute. He spoke of a German submarine that would soon be landing in Kingstown with reinforcements and heavy artillery. At first the speeches were encouraging and exciting for everyone, but they were starting to make less sense now. Joe knew for a fact that there was no German submarine; he was the one who had been in Berlin when plans were made, and this was never even a possibility.

He began to wonder about Pearse, who had been entirely unable to sleep since Sunday night. While most of the Volunteers and leaders had been able to get a couple of hours of sleep here and there, even in the midst of the excitement, Pearse had seemed too overwhelmed to relax at all. He was clearly suffering from exhaustion. Joe was glad that Connolly, Clarke, and MacDermott were there as well. They had maintained their stable and practical leadership roles while remaining optimistic about the situation.

The unexpected arrival of The O'Rahilly had been a big help as well. He was a steady and brave leader who never seemed to tire or doubt. He had a boisterous and cheerful personality and could often be found leading the men in songs about the rebel heroes of past generations. He had spent much of his time on the roof and upper floors, however, and seemed to be avoiding the other leaders, probably still hurt by the fact that they hadn't let him in on the planning for the rebellion. Just the same, it was good to have him there, and everyone had done their best to make him feel welcome, especially with their lower-than-expected numbers.

It was evening by now, but darkness refused to descend because of the fires across the street. Despite the flames surrounding the GPO, it was cold on the stone floor. Joe's mind was full of worries about tomorrow's attacks and the effects of his illness on his ability to fight. He thought about the damage the chilled, damp nights and lack of rest must be doing. He distracted himself by thinking about his travels to faraway places. He daydreamed about the hot, dry air of Cadiz.

After his trip to Germany that summer to secure the shipment of arms, he had sailed to Barcelona then traveled west to Cadiz, Andalucía's major sea port. One of the oldest cities in all of Europe, it is thought that Cadiz was first settled by the Phoenicians over a thousand years before the birth of Christ. Greek legends claim that Hercules founded the city after slaying Medusa's grandson, the monster warrior Geryon.

Many nations had claimed Cadiz since then, but the influence of its several hundred years under Moorish rule seemed to be the most notable. Joe only had a short time in this ancient city, and the mystery and romance of its narrow, winding maze of streets filled him with the desire to stay longer and explore. The whole walled city was at the end of a tiny peninsula, and for the few hours Joe had in town, he walked through the alley-like streets, heading as best he could in the direction of the Atlantic Ocean.

Most of the walls of homes and shops were either pure white, pale pink, or the toasted golds and light browns of late summer barley. They were contihuous and packed together, each home sharing a wall with its neighbor, with no break until the next narrow street sliced between them, separating block from block. Also continuous were the wrought iron railings of the tiny balconies that went on as far as Joe could see on every floor of almost every building.

Ropes were tied between the black balcony rails and strewn with brightly colored drying laundry, which unfurled and waved like hundreds of little flags. The high walls on either side of the street were so close to each other that much of Joe's walk was spent veiled in shade, despite the fierce midday sun.

The shade was a break from the heat, but after a time in this shadowed labyrinth teeming with shoppers, vendors, families, and strutting groups of young people, Joe was relieved to step unexpectedly into the bright open space and fresh air of Plaza San Antonio. He walked straight across the city's vast main square, past the neoclassical mansions and two towers of the church, before diving again into the shadowed streets on the other side.

Joe wandered some more through the dim, bustling maze before he emerged with a view of the Atlantic and breathed the clean sea air. Dozens of tiny blue anchored boats bobbed in unison on the gentle swells of the cobalt water. He sat in the sun and enjoyed the view for a few moments before heading back across town to the port. He had then completed his trip home, sailing to England, then traveling through London, back up to Holyhead, and across the water to Dublin.

Joe looked past the men stationed at the GPO windows—black silhouettes against the fiery glow outside. Many of the buildings across Sackville Street were already dangerously ablaze, but Volunteers could still be seen in the windows of the upper floors, firing toward the river. He could hear the British returning fire from at least six different directions.

It was clear that they were now surrounded. The firing was fierce from all sides. In between bursts of nearby gunfire, he could hear the booms, snaps, and rumblings coming from rebel-held positions in the distance. One sound layered over the next and over the next, creating a constant, multi-dynamic storm of noise that rose into the sky to hang over the city.

Joe could usually guess where the sounds were coming from based on the dispatches he had received throughout his days at the GPO, but it was increasingly difficult for messengers to get through to him at headquarters. It seemed that the government forces were attempting to isolate them, cutting them off from support and information. He had heard nothing from Grace since her sister made it through the previous day. He could only pray that the fighting and looting had not spread to where she was staying in Ranelagh, south of the city.

30

On Wednesday morning the government had proclaimed martial law in the city. All citizens were ordered to remain indoors between seven o'clock at night and five o'clock in the morning. The darkness was filled with sounds of fighting. This was when things were especially difficult for Grace to endure. No one in the house could tell for sure where the explosions and gunfire were coming from, though they sat in the dark and did their best to guess. Muriel's husband, Thomas, was in command at Jacob's Biscuit Factory. Eamonn Ceannt's wife was staying with Muriel as well. Her husband was leading the garrison at South Dublin Union, and she did not want to wait out the rebellion alone.

There was almost no news about how things were going; what they did hear was not reliable. Sleep was almost impossible at night, but Grace tried to remain unconscious as much she could. When she was awake, she could feel every second creeping by with excruciating monotony, broken only by the jolt of another explosion or the ruthless spatter of a machine gun in the distance. These sounds scared her more than the firing of rifles because she knew that Joe and the other rebels had no cannons or machine guns.

Daytime was a little easier. Grace could find lots of ways to pass the time and stay optimistic. Muriel was on her own with the two babies, so there were always plenty of things Grace could do to help out around the house. She also rode her bike around the neighborhood trying to find out what was happening at the General Post Office and other garrisons. She was nervous about going too far outside of the neighborhoods south of the Grand Canal and hadn't gone near the River Liffey since she left Sackville Street at the beginning of the week. As scared as she was, she probably would have ventured nearer the river anyway if Joe had not made Muriel promise to keep her away.

When Muriel returned with her message from Joe on Tuesday, Grace had felt terror and relief, fear and joy, well up inside her all at the same instant. She was so happy that he was still thinking about their wedding, but she hated to hear him talking about imprisonment. Although Joe had mentioned the possibility of defeat from time to time—suggesting that he would likely be deported in such a case—when they spoke of the rebellion, it had generally been with victory as the only likely outcome. They had always talked about their future together in a new independent republic where they would have long and happy lives in a truly Irish Ireland. Now he was speaking of the possibility of defeat.

She needed to get out of the house. Since Muriel had the two kids to look after, Grace had appointed herself chief forager. She needed to come up with enough of everything for the five people who were staying regularly at the house. With no public transportation available, a good portion of the day was spent just gathering necessary supplies for the evening and following morning.

Almost all of the shops were shut down in the city center. On Tuesday there had been food shortages throughout Dublin, but by Wednesday morning things were worse. Now even the people in the neighborhoods south of the Grand Canal were struggling to find food and supplies. Next to nothing was getting into the city from the rest of the country, and the regular distribution system had almost totally shut down. The bread in the city seemed to be totally gone, and with most of the flour and meal sold out as well, it was getting harder to find supplies for home baking.

Grace had seen entire stores commandeered by British officers to supply the government troops, and now some citizens were hoarding in a panic. On Tuesday she had seen people running through the streets with huge carts full of food and candles and other supplies, looking like it was the end of the world.

She had even seen her mom walking awkwardly through Rathmines with a number of bags over her shoulders. Grace watched as a cabbage dropped from one of the bags. Isabella bent over and lost her hat as she tried awkwardly to catch the cabbage, which had rolled away from her and into the street. Grace almost felt sorry for Isabella, but not quite enough to go over and help her.

When Grace thought about the names her mom had called her and the insults she had shouted when she found out about her conversion to Catholicism, she doubted if Isabella would even accept any help from her anyway. *Let her figure out how to get the cabbage home on her own*, Grace thought. Her mother had never had to go to the markets to buy her own food, and it would probably do her good to find out how difficult it could be for people who had to exist without a small army of servants.

Ordinarily, the shop women, farmers, and bakers came to the outer neighborhoods, carrying their fresh vegetables and baked goods in huge baskets for the ladies of the house to inspect, selecting what they liked. If anything else was wanted, there was always the kitchen or house staff to go out for it.

The women hadn't shown up with their baskets of bread and vegetables since the fighting started on Monday, and there were no deliveries of coal or other necessities.

It wasn't just the deliveries to the wealthy that had stopped. There simply wasn't much food left in the city at all, and not much was going to get through for a while. Because of the short supplies, the shops that did have something to sell had quickly raised their prices. Basic necessities like milk, eggs, and butter had doubled or tripled in cost in just the two days since the insurrection began. Vegetables were almost impossible to find at any price. Some of the city farmers who supplied markets in the outlying areas of the city had heard about the shortages and high prices and had started bringing in carts of produce from nearby towns. Even out in the country, people were experiencing looting from hungry foragers and were forced to patrol their gardens at night.

Grace had heard rumors that new distribution routes were being arranged by groups of shopkeepers in some neighborhoods—that a ship had been sent to Liverpool for supplies while more food was said to be coming from Belfast. But rumor was all they had. The only news about the situation in the paper the previous day was a few lines about a "Sinn Fein" rising in Dublin, with reports that the authorities had everything under control. The writer had passed on the Castle's assurances that the rest of the country was peaceful and quiet. Today there had been no paper at all.

There was no delivery or pickup of letters or messages, and there was almost no way of getting any information about what was going on. Even the phone system was partially shut down, and no one in Dublin could make calls. It was still possible to receive calls, but since no one in the city could place any, that didn't seem to matter much at first. As news of the insurrection spread, however, friends and relatives began calling from elsewhere in the country to ask for details of the rebellion.

Grace was glad that her sister had made it all the way up to the GPO the previous day to get some idea of what was going on, but they had heard nothing reliable since then. Hoping to find someone who could tell her more, she rode her bike north into the city center, finding that most of the shops were closed and locked. There was almost no traffic whatsoever in the streets, so things were oddly quiet—other than the distant sounds of gunfire and explosions.

The Dublin Metropolitan Police force had been called off the streets as soon as the fighting began on Monday, so there was no one in the city keeping the peace. Looters were taking advantage of this state of anarchy, and she saw a lot of broken shop windows and people walking by with carts or huge bags full of brand-new goods.

Nonetheless, it was a beautiful day, and there were many people out walking around in the quiet streets. Most were uncommonly friendly and cheerful—as if they had been brought together by the chaos and destruction. There were groups on the corners debating politics. Most of the people she heard were angry about the rebellion, speaking with hope that the British would stop it soon and string up every one of those troublemakers. Grace shuddered to think that, if defeated, Joe and the others would have to face not only the punishment of the government but rage from the vast majority of Dublin's citizens as well.

She heard several young people run by her shouting that they were headed up to the river to watch the fighting. Grace headed in the opposite direction toward St. Stephen's Green, where her sister would be. She did not have to get close at all to see that things had been bad. There was no one in the park anymore—they seemed to have moved into the surrounding buildings—but there were men's bodies and a dead horse lying at the entrance, and no one was doing anything about it. Barricades had been constructed from cars and benches and garbage, and there was a lot of firing. She decided it would be a good idea to keep her promise to Joe and stay away.

As she headed south to cross the Grand Canal, she could hear unremitting and intense firing from the direction of Mount Street. The fighting seemed to be going on everywhere, and spooked by the feeling that she could be hit by a stray bullet at any second, she sped away to look for food and supplies closer to home.

That night she lay awake until after three o'clock listening to the continuous fighting. Even with the curtains drawn tight, she could see the red glow of the sky reflecting the light of the fires raging throughout the city. She tried to keep her mind on her prayers as she squeezed her eyes shut tightly and listened to the cracks and bangs of the rifles, the pounding of the cannons, and the metallic convulsion of machine guns in the distance. She prayed only that things were quiet at the GPO and that Joe was so safe he had nothing to fear but boredom.

She tried to pray for everyone else she cared for, but no matter how hard she tried, her mind kept returning to this single prayer for Joe. She continued to repeat this prayer to herself until, not long before dawn, she finally melted into a short sleep filled with broken glass and bodies in the mud of St. Stephen's Green.

31

Dawn broke on Thursday morning with a riot of fire and chaos. The General Post Office was soon immersed in showers of metallic hail, the calm shattered by the now familiar sound of machine gun fire from the southeast. Volunteers stationed in the GPO windows fired back and were soon joined by the other rebel outposts. Within seconds every British machine gun in range was emptying ammo belts into the GPO, countered by fierce and rapid firing from every Volunteer stationed in the area, including the rebel snipers.

The British were now heavily concentrated in College Street and Trinity College to the south, across the river; the Custom House and Liberty Hall to the southeast; and Amiens Street farther to the west. Although the government had not yet established any positions directly to the west at this point, they had troops moving to that area, and they had completely occupied the buildings to the north from Great Britain Street down to Findlater Place.

All of these positions were heavily manned and armed. As British troops steadily advanced toward Sackville Street, they tightened their grip in a slow suffocation of Volunteer forces. There was no longer any ability to send or receive dispatches, and leaders at the GPO were totally cut off from the other rebel positions throughout the city. Joe had no information, and the isolation unnerved him.

British forces repeatedly attempted to break through to

Sackville Street from the blocks just to the southeast. Often they would make some progress, hidden by thick billows of dark smoke from the fires raging on the east side of the street. But government troops were ultimately repelled again and again by Volunteers who fired so relentlessly in defense of their positions that their outdated Mauser rifles overheated. The guns were so hot they could not be touched or fired safely.

There were not enough weapons to go around, let alone any backups to use while their guns cooled, and holding fire was not an option under such heavy attack. Having no proper gun oil, sardine tins were drained, and the gunmen were forced to use fish oil to wipe down the overheated barrels.

Volunteers were now stationed at the Imperial Hotel, just across Sackville Street from the GPO, and it was also under heavy fire. At one point a huge rooftop water tank was hit by a shell fired from a British cannon. When the tank burst, waves of water flooded halls and stairs and rushed through a room on the ground floor where Volunteers were repairing their rifles. The wall of water washed the Volunteers out of the room and down the hall, upending and jostling them like toy soldiers.

Joe sat at a table on the ground floor scrutinizing his maps, trying to determine what might be going on throughout the city based on the last information he had received. He barely noticed the sound of the constant, heavy fire that had been going on all morning. At about noon there was an explosion that shook the walls of the GPO with such power that it startled everyone. He jumped from his chair, grabbed his Smith & Wesson revolver, and ran to join Connolly and some Volunteers at the windows to see what was going on. The government forces were bombing the offices of the *Freeman's Journal*, right next door to the post office. This intensive shelling continued, bombarding the buildings all along the blocks to the south.

Nearer the river, the Metropole Hotel was in trouble as well. It was under such heavy attack from across the Liffey that the ceiling collapsed, destroying the inner structure of the top floors and sending up billows of black smoke and fire as all the men of the garrison scurried downstairs.

However continuous and fierce the shelling, the British cannons had not managed a single direct hit to the GPO itself. It was riddled with bullet holes, but the structure was still completely intact.

During all of this, a civilian somehow managed to get though all of the surrounding chaos and make his way up to one of the ground-floor windows of the post office. Joe and Connolly were speaking nearby when they saw the man appear outside the window and speak to two Volunteers, who were holding him at gunpoint. One of the two Volunteers came over and told Connolly that the man outside the window wanted to join the fight. They reported that they had told him to go home, but he wouldn't leave until he had a chance to plead his case to Connolly.

Joe followed Connolly over to the window, where the other Volunteer—a man who had trained at the Kimmage Garrison—still had his gun pointed at the visitor. Connolly told the Kimmage man to stand down and asked the visitor what he wanted. The man outside the window spoke at some length about how much he wanted to join the fight, explaining why he had not tried to get in sooner and speaking of his love for Ireland. Judging from his accent, Joe could tell he was local.

The visitor explained that his grandfather had fought with the Fenians, and he needed to be a part of the fight as well. He had tried to avoid politics all his life, but he was outraged now. Just the previous day, he had seen government forces on King Street mowing down groups of unarmed civilians from the cover of an armored vehicle—an old truck armed with tanks commandeered from the Guinness brewery and cut to fit over the bed.

"There were women and children—even a very old man. A totally unprovoked attack. I... I just stood there watching. I couldn't move. Couldn't do anything," he explained breathlessly, crouching near the ledge of the window below the sight of British snipers. Glancing from side to side at the sound of gunfire, he shouted, "I need to fight with you now. I just need to do something!"

Joe watched as Connolly leaned over the high window barricade of ledgers and books, totally ignoring the bullets hitting the building near his head. He reached down to shake the man's hand and looked him steadily in the eyes, telling him quietly, "Go home while you can, man. We thank you, but it's too late now. I'm afraid it's a hopeless cause."

Joe glanced at the two Volunteers standing next to him to see if they had heard Connolly's words. It was clear that they had. One of them—the Kimmage man—looked straight ahead, somber and matter of fact. His face had a look of determination and intelligence and showed no surprise at Connolly's words. This was a man who had known well what he was getting himself into before joining in the fighting that first day.

The men who had trained at the Kimmage Garrison had been waiting for real battle. For months their days and nights had been dedicated to training and manufacturing weapons and ammunition. They were anxious for the insurrection and had been expecting it to start any day. George had reported that, after the countermanding order canceled the mobilization on Sunday, his Kimmage men were so angry and ready for a fight that he feared they might go out into the streets and start a revolt on their own.

But the other Volunteer was local, and he hadn't trained at Kimmage. When he turned up on Monday for maneuvers, he likely had no idea that a real rebellion was planned, expecting only parades and maneuvers. He blinked quickly several times at Connolly's words then looked at the ground, shifting his weight from foot to foot and fiddling with his rifle. Joe could see that until that moment, this man had believed in Pearse's latest speeches about the many hundreds of supporting troops marching to Dublin from the all over the country, and the German relief forces in submarines that were due to arrive at Kingstown Port at any minute.

As the Volunteer pretended to focus on his rifle, he seemed to deflate a little. When he glanced up at the others for an instant, his eyes looked stunned and blank, leaden with early surrender. Joe felt for him, thinking it was possible that the young Volunteer hadn't even considered the possibility of death or defeat until this very moment. Joe thought of the months and years he'd had to prepare himself for the many possible outcomes, good or bad, and wondered how he might feel if similarly taken by surprise.

For many of the Irish Volunteers from Dublin, things had been very different than they had been for the men training at the Kimmage Garrison. The locals had been at home with their families when they received mobilization orders just days before. Other than requiring each Volunteer to carry a longer list of items than usual, there was not much to distinguish these orders from the many that had come before, which had resulted only in a day of military drilling. While rumors of rebellion were rampant, there was no way for the men to know for sure that this time it was the real thing.

In most of the garrisons—the GPO included—Volunteers had been given a chance to turn back and go home once the reality of the situation was revealed, but almost no one chose to leave. Some very young boys had shown up wanting to fight and had been forced to go home against their will. All the men had stayed, but for many of the people fighting right now, it had been a sudden realization that this time it was not a drill. There hadn't been any time to adjust to this reality before they marched from Liberty Hall and the fighting began.

32

By Thursday afternoon it appeared that the British finally had the GPO surrounded. At about three o'clock, Joe received a report that troops were preparing to march on the GPO from the northwest side. This was a first. Every available Volunteer ran from posts on the east side of the building to take up new positions. There was a lull in the firing, and everyone was left waiting with no idea where or when it would start up again.

The O'Rahilly had come down from the upper floors, apparently no longer holding a grudge against the leaders who had left him out of the planning. He led a group of Volunteers in singing, his smile and booming, resonant voice encouraging even the most reticent, fearful, or dejected of the Volunteers to join in. In addition to being a linguist, he was a well-known songwriter. Many of the men present had learned and sung his songs in pubs and halls over the years, so when he broke into his most popular, "Thou Art Not Conquered Yet, Dear Land," there were cheers of recognition:

Though knaves may scheme and slaves may crawl
To win their master's smile,
And though thy best and bravest fall,
Undone by Saxon guile—
Yet some there be, still true to thee,
Who never shall forget
That though in chains and slavery
Thou are not conquered yet!

Pearse took the opportunity of a break between songs to make another inspirational speech, hoping to boost the morale of the men.

"All of our targets throughout the city are now under rebel control," he spoke loudly as the cheers for The O'Rahilly began to die down. "The rest of the country continues to rise as well, and a huge force of Volunteers is now marching from Dundalk to Dublin to aide in our final defense!" There were shouts of celebration.

Based on the dispatch Joe received earlier in the week, he knew this just couldn't be true. He knew it was important to keep up morale, but he wasn't sure that outright lies would help.

"In addition to our victories throughout the city and the new troops arriving anytime, there is more good news." Pearse looked pale, his eyes fierce and glittery black. "Now that we've held out this long, our new republic has lasted for three full days." The crowd looked at him expectantly. "Under international law," he explained, "our new Irish Republic is entitled to send a delegation to the peace conference that will inevitably take place at the end of the war in Europe!" More happy shouts, even from the men who knew nothing of delegations or the politics involved.

"We have fought well and bravely. We deserve this victory, and we will have it, even if we must win in death!" Pearse hadn't been sleeping at all, but he was a natural orator and, as he spoke to the Volunteers, the weight of his exhaustion began to lighten. His energy had clearly returned as his words came to an end on a triumphant note.

"Now we have all redeemed Dublin from shame and made her name splendid among the names of cities!"

A huge cheer erupted throughout the crowd surrounding

Pearse and then spread and echoed through the building. Joe wondered if Pearse believed help was coming or if he was merely saying that because it was what the men and women present needed to hear. Interspersed throughout the speech were phrases that caused Joe to think that, despite his optimistic tone, Pearse was aware of the dire reality of their situation. He spoke of "final defenses" and "winning in death."

Either way, focusing on impending failure wouldn't help. As the heavy shelling started up again a short time later, Joe was busy getting around to all the men with encouragement and gratitude. Everyone had given up so much to be there to fight for Ireland, and Joe was overwhelmed by their support and sacrifice. He needed to be sure that every one of them knew that their service was essential to the nationalist cause. The Military Council could plan rebellions all they wanted, but without the hundreds that had shown up to fight, nothing would have come of it.

The British began their next bombardment using howitzers to lob shrapnel shells right onto the roof of the GPO. These cannons could shoot at high trajectories and hit places they could not reach before. While the men on the roof were distracted by the shelling, the British snipers had picked up again. The whole unit on the roof was quickly ordered downstairs to take cover. This heavy shelling continued throughout the rest of the afternoon, and the garrison hospital was truly busy for the first time since the rebellion began.

Connolly was shot in the leg while running around outside under heavy fire trying to set up and secure barricades. It was a serious injury—and his second, as it turned out. The previous day he had been shot in the arm but had kept it a secret. It was not a serious wound, and he had refused to stay out of the action. He let the doctor patch up that first injury only after he promised not to say anything about it to anyone.

This second wound could not be ignored, as almost two inches of his shinbone had been completely shattered. This was bad for him and the whole garrison. Connolly was an experienced commander. His confidence was a great comfort to the Volunteers, and his influence was dearly missed. After being treated by a captured British Army doctor, Connolly was injected with morphine and was out of the action for the rest of the day.

After the afternoon shelling died down, the men returned to the roof. The British shelling and sniper attacks continued incessantly throughout the evening. Soon the fires across the street had grown to an inferno, spreading through the whole block facing the GPO. Flames spread from the buildings to barricades then on to the adjacent blocks while the constant shelling continued to set new fires.

The shells eventually reached Hoyte's on lower Sackville Street, a building that included a pharmaceutical chemistry lab with a glass and oil warehouse. Some barrels of oil were hit, and night turned to day as a sudden wall of blinding-white flame shot hundreds of feet into the sky with a blast that shook the walls violently for blocks around. Explosions of flames and showers of sparks in every color followed the initial blast, shooting into the air over and over again as the various chemicals and oils combusted.

Even 150 feet away at the GPO, the men at the windows were hit with a wave of heat like a solid force that knocked them back from their positions. There was no time to recover. Millions of sparks and flaming bits of debris had shot up with the flames and were now descending in heavy showers, igniting the barricades. Dazed and red-faced, the men stumbled for buckets of water to drench anything on fire. The water hissed into steam the second it landed on any surface near the windows.

Next came a succession of explosions when hundreds of oil drums burst in the flames, one after another, as the inferno spread, consuming every building nearby. Finishing quickly what other fires had started, it spread to the Imperial Hotel and beyond. Soon the huge plate-glass windows of Clerys Department Store were melting into a stream and running onto the sidewalks.

33

The fires across Sackville Street faded throughout the night, having already consumed most of what there was to burn. The blackened stone shells of buildings glowed red with tired flames lighting the walls of the GPO as if by some hellish dying sun.

The night was relatively quiet, but there was little rest. It seemed fairly clear by now that the British forces were not going to charge up Sackville and fight the rebels face to face. Instead, it seemed they would continue their barrage of shells and incendiaries from a great distance at sunrise and stick with this approach until the whole area was destroyed. There was a good chance the GPO would be in flames soon. All of the munitions stores needed to be moved from the roof and upper floor down into the large basement room that extended to the north underground, below the Henry Street sidewalk.

This preparation started just after midnight and went on for hours. It wouldn't keep the Volunteers safe for long, but it would buy them some more time at their present location. In the midst of getting ready for the fires—just when they had totally given up on the idea of the British ever coming up to fight them in person—they heard the sound of many horses galloping up Sackville Street at full charge. Cavalry.

Volunteers ran for positions at the windows. In the dash across the room to get situated, someone dropped his gun. It went off, and the bullet ricocheted off the stone floor, causing more chaos and increasing the rush. But there was no more firing when they reached the barricades. When Joe got to the window, he would see why.

There was no charge of cavalry at all. At least a dozen terrified and riderless horses—apparently set free from one of the flaming buildings in the area—were thundering up the street, their hooves pounding and clattering against the stones. Although they were silhouetted in the dim red glow from the dying fires across the street, Joe could see the panicked whites of the horses' eyes against their dark faces. They moved as a group, running all but blindly through the night like thundering shadows past Great Britain Street and beyond to the north. The sound of their hooves followed far behind them as they receded into the darkness.

All was quiet again, and Joe returned to his little mattress toward the back of the room where he had been resting. Without warning a wall of fatigue as heavy as stone began to crush him. The surgery, the many days of excitement, and the lack of sleep and food were all catching up with him, but he could not let himself be overcome. He would see this thing through to the end. After that he only had to stay upright long enough to marry Grace, and then he could rest. The doctor believed that it was too late for him to recover from his illness and surgery, but Joe didn't believe it. And if the government didn't hang him or shoot him, he felt that he could rally and get his health back. Eventually.

No matter what happened to him later, he would face it as Grace's husband. *Grace's husband*! What a sweet phrase! It made him feel a luscious comfort, like being held in her arms, as if he belonged to her already and she would be his forever.

There had already been talk of retreating from the GPO, which certainly sounded like the beginning of the end of things. But no matter what happened next—whether they won or lost—he had done all he could, and no one could ever take that away. Now there were only two things he had to do: live through this rebellion and get to Grace.

34

In the cold, pale predawn light, the east side of Sackville Street was forlorn and gray. There was nothing left but bare, outer walls, smoky and blackened. All was silent except for an occasional shot from a sniper or the sound of a section of stone wall finally giving up its position and crumbling to the ground. The flames were barely visible now, sullen and defeated in the damp air. But heat still radiated from the entire block, steam and smoke rising in slow, dismal swirls from the charred ruins of stone and debris. There was nowhere to go to get a breath of clean, cool air.

Just before dawn, Joe, Clarke, MacDermott, Connolly, Pearse, and Pearse's little brother Willie met privately in a small room near the front of the building to discuss what should be done if the fires got bad at the GPO. They all agreed that, if the British were able to successfully bombard their side of the street as well, they would not remain to be incinerated. Everyone would retreat from the GPO and find somewhere else to gather and regroup, possibly at the Williams and Woods Factory up on Great Britain Street, just a few blocks to the north.

After that it might be possible to make it past the government forces at some point, even though they seemed to be completely surrounded. If they could, they would head southwest to join up with Ned Daly and his 1st Battalion at the Four Courts. Communication between the rebel positions had been cut off for some time, but for now, at least, they would assume that was still an option.

Throughout the day the Volunteers defending the other positions on Sackville Street would be brought back to the GPO so that everyone would be together when and if the decision was made to leave. After the meeting the leaders took their positions and waited to see what would come first—fighting against the British troops or fighting fires.

ஐ

At sunrise the government forces started firing at the west side of Sackville Street, as expected. Even though the rebellion had only been going on a few days, it felt like a sort of surreal eternity. Joe had come to associate the rising sun with the sounds and smells of gunfire and explosions, smoke and gunpowder.

Connolly had demanded to be on the scene despite his injuries, and since his bed had coasters, two Volunteers were wheeling him around the ground floor as he shouted orders and encouragement to the troops. He seemed so happy to be back in the action. Joe could tell he wasn't ready for it to end, but he was wearing out quickly. At one point, everyone who could be spared was gathered together, and it was announced that Connolly had written a message he wanted to have read aloud. He wasn't sure if he had the strength to get through it himself, so O'Rahilly stood at his bedside and read it to everyone present in his deep and resonant voice.

"First of all, welcome to the fifth day of the New Republic," The O'Rahilly boomed. "For the first time in seven hundred years, the flag of a free Ireland floats above our heads. I, and all of the leaders, want to thank everyone at the

GPO—all of the men and women who served here—for your tremendous bravery and sacrifice over the course of the week."

Although The O'Rahilly was doing the speaking, Connolly's eyes shone with tears of pride. Joe saw him silently mouth an occasional word or phrase as The O'Rahilly spoke them. "I would also like to take a moment to recognize the bravery of the other commandants who have led the fighting at rebel outposts throughout the city throughout this fateful week. Soon we shall be united in victory!"

This was heartfelt and moving, and Joe was a little sad that they would most likely have to leave the GPO soon. But as the message went on, he began to feel uncomfortable and even a little shocked.

"Outside the capital our whole country now rallies to our cause, and more troops are marching on Dublin. Elsewhere in the city," The O'Rahilly continued, "our garrisons are standing strong, impervious to all British efforts. The rising will be victorious!"

As the speech ended with O'Rahilly shouting, "Courage, boys. We are winning!" a triumphant cheer broke out among the men and women present. Joe clapped and smiled with the rest of them despite his unease. He understood the need to keep up morale, but he felt it was time to stop speaking of the hundreds of reinforcements who would arrive at any time from the countryside. And as far as the other garrisons? The government forces had the GPO so isolated from the rest of the city that Joe hadn't received any dispatches recently. They had almost no information, other than what they could guess from the distant sounds of fighting.

There were about thirty women who had served in support positions throughout the week, and Pearse now gathered them all together. When he told them that it was time for them to leave, there was a serious uproar. They swore that they would not go. They intended to stay with the men and fight until the end. This seemed to be a unanimous refusal, and Pearse seemed unsure of what to do. Surely they had every right to stay and make the same sacrifices as the men did, but all the same, retreat was imminent and dangerous, and he couldn't agree to let them stay.

Three of the nurses, a small number of women from the Cumann na mBan, and Connolly's loyal secretary, Winifred Carney, were allowed to stay. The nurses insisted that they would stay until the end because the number of wounded was growing more quickly every day. The members of the Cumann na mBan would stay with the prisoners and Volunteers who were already seriously injured. The women could then accompany these wounded men if it became possible to get them out and to the hospital at some point. Winifred Carney had been with Connolly throughout the week and no one would be able to convince her to leave his side; Pearse didn't even try.

The rest of the women were finally convinced to go. They accepted hastily written notes from Volunteers with desperate and grateful requests to deliver the messages to wives and families. Despite their disappointment at being forced to leave, the women graciously took the notes. After putting out the Red Cross banner in Henry Street at the north side of the building, the women exited carefully. This time, thankfully, the government forces honored the momentary ceasefire.

35

Although the British started getting some direct hits to the GPO by mid-Friday, the serious fires didn't start up until later in the afternoon. Volunteers and leaders alike were constantly running with buckets and hoses, putting out flames on the roof. Soon the shelling was coming on faster, and a new fire or two would start before the last one was put out. The snipers from Connolly's Citizen Army, who had done such a thorough and unrelenting job of cutting off enemy fire and holding back advancing government troops, were now having trouble seeing through the smoke. They were in danger of catching on fire themselves and soon had no choice but to give up the positions they had ruled all week long.

Eventually even the hoses lost water pressure and the men could no longer get water up to the top of the building. Soon the entire roof was on fire, and everyone was ordered to retreat to lower floors. The last of the men were forced to leap through the trap door in a free fall to the story below to avoid the exploding flames. The upper floor was on fire as well and too hot to take for long. Large pieces of the roof were collapsing onto the floor, the smoky sky visible beyond twisted girders and flames. Even on the two lower floors, the walls were too hot to touch, and most of the barricades in the windows were smoldering or on fire.

All of the men from the surrounding rebel positions were back at the GPO now, but there still were not enough men to deal with the fires and hold back the enemy, and less attention was paid to the window positions. This, plus the absence of the snipers, gave the government forces the opportunity they had lacked all week. They began a slow but steady advance into the areas the rebels had easily held for days from their post in the GPO.

Soon British forces had taken up positions nearby in Abbey Street. For the first time all week, machine gun fire was coming through the windows of the ground floor and the story above. Men were getting hit while walking inside the building, far from the windows, an area that had been safe all week. There was so much smoke and chaos that they received some serious casualties before it even became clear what was going on.

Whenever possible, people at the GPO now stayed along the back wall of the huge main room. But some men were still needed at the window positions, behind the burning barricades, to return fire and hold back the enemy. Getting to and from these positions was the most dangerous part of the situation. The fighters had to crouch or crawl, staying low to the floor, well below the level of the windows. By now, that meant crawling through several inches of water.

The water from intense firefighting had flowed down the stairs for hours, and now the ground floor was flooded. Steam came off the walls from all sides, and flaming debris floated on the water. There was an attempt to build new barricades farther from the windows, but this was soon abandoned. It was time to leave.

Leaders pulled as many of the men as possible away from the windows and out of the building. They began to gather in the courtyard in back—well away from Sackville Street and the advancing British troops. The prisoners, who had been kept in the basement for their safety, were brought out as well, both to be taken along in the retreat and to get them away from all of the ammunition stored down there. Just a few hours ago, the basement was safe and secure. Now the heat and flames were too near the door, and occasional sparks descended the old iron stairway and disappeared into the relatively cool darkness below.

There was no telling how long it would be before the flames would reach the basement and ignite the hundreds of pounds of ammunition and explosives. The advancing troops continued to fire through the ground-floor windows and had hit some of the men as they brought prisoners and supplies up the stairs. At that point it was decided to get the remaining men out of the building and into the courtyard.

Once they had all gathered outside, it was almost dusk. Pearse told Joe he wanted to wait until later to try to make it out under cover of darkness. With the flames now beginning to engulf the building and growing brighter every minute, Joe wondered if it would be much darker at night than it was right now. They all agreed to evacuate the seriously wounded at this point. The women who were to leave with these wounded men accepted more notes from some of the men who were staying behind. Joe watched as Tom Clarke approached one woman to relay a message. His face was businesslike and composed, but his eyes swam with emotion.

"If you see my wife, tell her that the men fought… " He was unable to finish the sentence and turned away quickly. He walked to the other side of the courtyard and remained there for some time, arms crossed, speaking to no one.

When Joe saw this exchange, he felt like he might pass out. Exhaustion was gnawing at every inch of his body and mind, and just the thought of sending a "goodbye" message to Grace was more than he could stand. It wasn't over, and he decided resolutely that he would refuse to think that way. There was no question about whether he would see her again. *Of course I will,* he thought. *I won't be sending out any sad farewell messages. Not yet.*

The second he had made this resolution, it began to wither in the heat of the fires. The chances of making it through this alive were getting worse every minute. Maybe he *should* send a message. A young woman walked right past him at that moment, and he almost said something to stop her.

He wanted to say, "Please go to my Grace and tell her I love her more than anything in the world, more than the stars, more than myself, even more than Ireland. Tell her I'm so horribly sorry that I dragged her into all of this and I want her to try to forget me as soon as she possibly can. I want her to do whatever she needs to do in her life to be happy. Please tell her that the last few months with her have been the best of my life and I never knew I could feel the kind of joy I have known in loving her. I have never done anything to deserve the happiness that Grace brought into my life."

But he said nothing. He took a deep breath and clamped his jaw tightly and let the young woman pass by. He would tell Grace all of these things soon. He would tell her soon. Face to face.

36

"Stop!" a Volunteer shouted at the little white house. "You're firing on your own men!" But the rifle fire continued, halting the retreat from the GPO.

Joe couldn't believe the situation they were in. They had all made it out of the Henry Street exit on the north side of the building, where they immediately encountered heavy rifle and machine gun fire. A few men were hit but not too seriously, and the wounded were able to continue with assistance. Connolly and the others who couldn't make it out on their own were carried out. They were badly jarred in the dash across Henry Street without cover while the enemy continued to fire without pause, even at the men carrying stretchers.

There was just no other choice but to make a run for it. Henry Street was too wide to try to put up barricades, and there wasn't much time. The heat was becoming unbearable at the GPO, and the flames that had begun on the roof were engulfing even the ground floor. Pearse took up the rear after making one last trip around the flaming and flooded building to be sure no one was left behind.

After everyone made it across Henry Street and into its narrow, alley-like offshoot, Henry Place, they were out of the direct line of fire and safe for the moment. But there wasn't much time. The leaders suspected that they were surrounded and feared that government troops would most likely advance up and around the corner into Henry Place soon, to fire on them from behind. Everyone was too spread out, and no one was in charge.

Henry Place makes a hard left turn about a block from the GPO, and Pearse and Joe had decided that they would try to take that way to cut across to the west to Moore Street. They ran into trouble right away at the turn as they started to cross another alley-sized street called Moore Lane. Once they reached this point, they were suddenly facing fire from two directions once again. Everyone backed up quickly and bunched up together in the corner. Most of the men from the GPO were packed in the corner, and they couldn't stay there for long. They stayed as flat as they could against the brick walls with all the supplies and stretchers.

In addition to heavy rifle and machine gun fire from a British position up Moore Lane, the Volunteers in front determined that shots were coming from a little white house on the corner, just across the street. From the sound of it, whoever was holed up in that little house was firing Mauser rifles, which were much louder than anything the government was using, with a distinct explosive sound. There appeared to be a confused or panicked group of Volunteers shooting at them from the little house, and they had everyone else pinned into the corner, making it impossible to get to safety.

People continued to shout at the men in the house, trying to get them to understand that they were firing on their own men, but the shooting persisted. Everyone from the GPO was trapped in the open. British troops could come around the corner from Henry Street at any moment.

With the help of Collins, Joe selected some Volunteers to establish a rear guard back at the street's entrance so that they would not be taken by surprise. They also decided to release any of the prisoners who wanted to go. A few of the captured

British soldiers made their escape and tried to get back to their brigades.

The O'Rahilly wanted to form an advance guard as well.

"Sitting here trapped in the corner is getting us nowhere," he shouted over the clamor of gunfire. They were risking everything to get up to the Williams and Woods Factory on Great Britain Street to the north, even though they had no idea what they would find when they got there. "The factory might already be occupied by the enemy. Someone needs to go find out before we're all trapped up there!" He decided to go back in the direction they had just come to Henry Street and then cut across to the west and head straight up Moore Street.

The Volunteers were already facing heavy fire from the north, up Moore Lane. If there were British at the top of Moore Street as well, they would need to know before everyone tried to get up that way. Even if it turned out that Moore Street was already occupied, a smaller group might be able to make it through, because they wouldn't have to move all of the supplies or wounded.

The O'Rahilly called for twenty men who had rifles with bayonets to follow him. No one stepped up right away, and two or three even dropped their weapons surreptitiously in an attempt to avoid the call, which seemed to many to be a suicide mission.

The firing continued coming from the little white house. If there had been no way to convince them that they were not facing advancing British troops before, it seemed hopeless now. After seeing the freed British prisoners run by in enemy uniforms, they seemed more convinced than ever of the danger they were in, and the firing was coming more rapidly. In addition to this, the British were still firing on anything they saw come from behind the buildings and into Moore Lane. Trapped, the men continued to huddle in the corner.

The O'Rahilly taunted and shouted at the Volunteers about their lack of courage. "What's wrong with you all? Are you even Irish men at all? You won't charge?"

Eventually, he got close to twenty men to step up. They gathered together at the corner and crouched against the wall, bayonets fixed. Some looked determined and resolute, but others had that same lost look of terror that Joe had seen in the eyes of the panicked horses galloping up Sackville Street through the smoke and flaming buildings just the night before. The O'Rahilly shouted, and the little group left the protection of the buildings and ran back toward the GPO, which was completely engulfed in flames. They turned onto Henry Street and disappeared from view.

A couple of minutes later, there was a lot of shooting from a block over on Moore Street. The gunfire lasted just a short time, and then it all stopped suddenly. No one came back from The O'Rahilly's group, but Joe clung to the possibility that some were taking cover where they were. There seemed to be little chance of getting up to the factory on Great Britain Street. Since there were now British troops in every direction, they would all need to find cover closer to where they already were. Meanwhile, the shooting had stopped coming from the little white house. The men inside had either been hit or had finally realized that they were killing their own men.

A few Volunteers tried to break down a door nearby to get out of the heavy British fire. They were in a chaotic rush, panic at their heels, and no one could reason with them or get them to slow down. They were using their rifle butts, smashing them against the heavy wooden door over and over again when one of the guns went off—shooting another Volunteer in the face. He dropped, heavy and silent. A large part of the back of his skull was no longer there.

The Volunteer's body lay at their feet. Those who had been trying to break down the door stopped trying. The man whose gun had gone off looked empty and defeated, the panicked edge and rush of his movements drained in an instant. Joe could feel the tension rising among the men as everyone huddled together with the dead body and the wounded. He needed to come up with a plan to get across the alley, past the little white house, and into one of the buildings on Moore Street.

Finally, someone got into a building through a nearby window and opened the door to a tiny entryway. The wounded were brought inside until a plan could be made, but they could not stay much longer. Heavy machine gun fire was still coming from the British positions up Moore Lane, and after The O'Rahilly's charge, it had increased considerably. *It can't end like this*, thought Joe, *huddled and trapped in the corner like rats.*

Now that the little white house seemed to be quiet and the firing was only coming from one direction, it seemed like the time to go. Moore Lane was relatively narrow, and they might be able to get across under the cover of some kind of barricade. He ordered a large cart to be moved into the lane. It was upended to provide the most cover.

Mick Collins located some barrels and had the men roll them into position just past the cart, then replace them upright so they were high enough for people to crawl or run, crouched down, behind the cover. There were some gaps, but they had to get out of there quickly and there didn't seem to be any other options. They couldn't stay in the corner waiting for the enemy to catch up with them from behind. They needed to get across Moore Lane and onto Moore Street now; this was all the cover they were going to get.

37

"C'mon, everyone line up here in groups of five. I need you to go on my signal," Joe shouted above the sounds of gunfire, which was still coming on heavily from the north. But his directions weren't being processed by many of the men. They just huddled against the wall, staring at him. They didn't seem to believe that he wanted them to run straight across another stream of gunfire. They'd just done the same thing getting out of the GPO and barely made it through alive.

They'd had enough of this, he knew it. The men just needed to have a little time to rest up in a building that wasn't catching on fire above their heads. But they couldn't have that now. Not yet. The enemy could come up behind them from Henry Street at any time, and if they stayed in this corner any longer, they could be trapped. They would have no chance at all and would be wiped out entirely within minutes. Joe couldn't let that happen after they'd fought so hard all week long.

Joe considered the situation as his men stared at him blankly, miserable about what he was asking. They needed to get across the street, and he knew they could make it. They must make it.

"Now! You can do it!" He tried again, shouting louder this time. The men reluctantly organized themselves into groups of five. This was good enough for Joe. He continued, "Good! You won't just sit here waiting to die! Don't be afraid. Don't be cowards, any of you. Now, go! Go! Go!"

Each time he shouted for them to go, another five men ran across Moore Lane. The alley seemed as wide as a boulevard as the men ran and crawled behind the hastily constructed barricade. A few were hit but not seriously wounded, and everyone made it across, including those carrying supplies and stretchers holding their wounded.

There was still too much chaos, and some men weren't thinking straight. They encountered heavy fire once again when they got to Moore Street, and there was a sort of frantic rush to get into one of the buildings. Rifles went off accidently, and more were injured. Soon a small group was able to break into a house on the corner. The Volunteers and leaders put up barricades in the windows, while others went outside to set up another large barricade at the corner of Henry Place and Moore Street so they could not be so easily taken from the direction they had just come.

It was a small space, so some Volunteers broke through the walls to the next apartments to make more room. After that, they were able to rest for a while. It was getting late, and there was very little food. Mick Collins tried cooking the rations he had brought from the GPO, but a British sniper shot hit the smoking chimney. The result was a frying pan full of soot and ash that billowed out into the room. This resulted in a barrage of taunts and complaints from the other men, so Collins gave up on eating anything but the small, hard biscuits they had packed.

Mattresses were found for the wounded, and everyone else found other places to try to sleep for a couple of hours. Joe sat at the foot of Connolly's mattress in a small room with most of the other leaders and one wounded British soldier. The soldier's injuries were serious, and he was upset to the point of delirium. He seemed to be calmed by Connolly's presence, so they had placed him on a mattress nearby. Pearse did his best to soothe the injured prisoner then left the room and crawled through the holes in the walls to visit the others, checking to see how people were doing after such a long day.

When Pearse returned from his rounds he joined Joe, sitting at the foot of Connolly's bed. Joe had the wall to lean on, but Pearse sat stooped and exhausted, his head down.

"What about tomorrow?" Joe asked quietly. "What's the plan?"

"I still say we need to make it down to the Four Courts and join forces," Clarke insisted. Discussion of this idea had been going on for the last hour.

"I agree," Pearse said, straightening his shoulders a little. "I say we fight a final round."

"At least another round," Clarke added. "We could last longer than that." No one wanted to give up, least of all Clarke, who had promised his wife that he would never surrender under any circumstances.

Joe feared that they didn't have the time for much more than one last battle. The injury to Connolly's leg looked badly infected, and it seemed that it might kill him soon—if the British didn't. Of course he had refused to go to the hospital until it was all over, but he slipped in and out of consciousness. It looked like it might already be too late for him to recover, even with medical help.

Joe knew he must look awful as well, and he realized that the others were most likely thinking that he might not make it too much longer either. While it was true some thought he was dead on his feet, he couldn't pay attention to that. Now that he could rest for a while, he knew he would be fine. He would make it through the night, and in the morning he would be up and ready to fight again.

It was late by the time they had all settled in, but the tension relaxed in the stillness of the night. Joe could hear some quiet conversations coming from various corners, and it sounded like some Volunteers were reciting the Rosary in the next room. They spoke the familiar prayers together quietly, and he could feel the calming influence they were creating for the other men. The sound was comforting to him too, and although he wanted to join in, he didn't think he had the strength. He took his rosary out of his pocket nonetheless and held onto it as he listened to the hushed, chant-like prayers.

Joe leaned against the wall and closed his eyes. He longed to be with Grace and to hold her in his arms again, even if only for a couple of minutes. He wondered what she was doing at that moment. Was she in bed by now? Could she be thinking about him too? He thought about the flowered scent of her soft, dark-auburn hair and the touch of her hands. He could almost feel his lips against her soft skin as he imagined kissing her forehead, her mouth, her throat, down to her collarbone.

He must have fallen asleep for a time, because he was suddenly jolted awake by a huge explosion that shook the ground, causing everyone to jump to attention. Joe sat up quickly as well, reaching for his pistol with his right hand and automatically putting his other arm out to shield Connolly. Men were grabbing their rifles as pieces of the plaster ceiling fell to the floor.

After a moment they realized they were not under imminent attack and settled back down. It seemed that the fires from the GPO had finally reached the explosives and ammunition in the basement. Some of the men went to the windows to try to get a view of the newest inferno, but Joe retrieved his rosary from the floor, where it had landed when he grabbed his pistol. He removed his glasses and rubbed his eyes, then settled back against the wall. He had seen more than enough magnificent blazes to last a lifetime.

38

Upstairs in her sister's house on the south side of the city in Ranelagh, Grace heard the blast as well. It was about three in the morning, and she had been lying in bed, staring at the ceiling. This was what she did most nights, eventually—and just barely—sinking into a shallow and fitful sleep a couple of hours before dawn. Nonetheless, she continued to go to bed early night after night. When she did awake, early in the morning, she continued to lie there, hoping to drift away again for a little longer.

This was not just because she was so exhausted and pale, with the dark shadows under eyes growing more pronounced every day. She longed to sleep more so that she could slip into the temporary release of unconsciousness. The time she spent asleep was free from thoughts and worries. Sometimes she could even escape her dreams for a short time, blending into a comforting and wordless darkness.

It was the only time she could get away from the constant anxiety she felt. She had no way of knowing what was going on with Joe, and she worried about her sister Nellie, who was still out there somewhere fighting as well. These worries, along with thoughts about the rest of her friends and family, had begun to consume her with an apprehension so acute that she felt sick to her stomach and often had to remind herself to breathe.

The last couple of days at Muriel's had been agonizing for both women. On the surface Grace and Muriel tried to act like things were fine, chatting cheerfully and remaining optimistic—constantly, resolutely, and self-consciously optimistic. It was a strain, and there were times that Grace could hardly take it. She just wanted to break down and scream what was circling like insanity in her head.

"I'm so afraid that he's already dead!" She wanted to cry, and she wanted her big sister to hold her and reassure her. But she kept it to herself. She kept so much to herself. She had been having doubts about the rising—whether it was worth all of this anxiety and loss. She still loved Ireland as much as ever, and seeing so many shattered Dublin neighborhoods had made her appreciate her city more than she had before. But concepts like freedom and nationalism seemed to be drifting far away, pale wisps of their former selves, all but lost in the smoky air. These ideas had lost much of their color after a week of dead bodies and so much rubble.

She couldn't give voice to her doubts about the rising or her fears for Joe and the other fighters. Her sister's anguish was no doubt worse than her own, and she had no right to be so selfish. Muriel and Thomas had been together for years already, and they had a family. Grace couldn't imagine what her sister must be going through. She couldn't let herself get too emotional and become a burden.

Besides this, the children were always there, and they needed to believe that things were fine—that their father would be home soon, a big hero. So the women all smiled their pale, strained smiles, playing games and chatting about anything they could think of. Only when she reached the privacy of her own room could Grace behave honestly.

Her poise sometimes collapsed almost immediately. Barely making it upstairs to her room in time, she would lean back against the closed door and slide to the floor, crumbling into tears and feelings of total hopelessness and isolation. She felt that even fighting on the front lines would be better than all of this waiting and waiting, while each tense and ominous minute crept by.

After crying away some of the tension of the long day's strained pleasantries, she would pace or try to read awhile. Sometimes she recited her Rosary. Joe had taught her the prayers and the sequence and the mysteries. It made her feel closer to him. She had only been doing it for a few months now and just barely had some of the prayers memorized, so it didn't provide the same level of comfort it might have if it were habit she had developed as a child. On the other hand, concentrating on getting the words and the sequence correct was a welcome distraction.

Some of the verses meant more to her now than they had before. And in her present fear and uncertainty, she felt herself taken by strong surges of devotion, especially as she recited Hail Holy Queen through her tears:

Hail, holy Queen, mother of mercy,
our life, our sweetness and our hope.
To thee do we cry, poor banished children of Eve:
To thee do we send up our sighs,
mourning and weeping this valley of tears.
Turn then, most gracious advocate,
thine eyes of mercy toward us;
and after this, our exile,
show unto us the blessed fruit of your womb, Jesus.
O clement, O loving, O sweet Virgin Mary.

Grace wondered what it would feel like to have a mother who was her advocate—one who was merciful. Grace knew it was normal for mothers to hold their children when they cried with fear or grief, but she had never felt this comfort. It was a loss she could not understand because she had never known the feeling. Her older sisters had been sweet and patient with her, and now she had Joe to show her kindness and understanding. She didn't know what she would do if she lost him. She really had no idea how she would make it through all of this if it didn't end with his return to her.

When these thoughts persisted, she forced herself to return to the Rosary for the distraction if nothing else. During periods of heavy fighting, each explosion or crack of cannon fire made her lose her place in the beads or forget where she was in the prayer. At these times she often ended up feeling more upset than when she started instead of gaining any comfort at all.

She would have given many years from the end of her life if she could have Joe there to hold her for just a minute or two. If he was still alive. She had no way to know; they'd heard nothing for days. Rumors flew endlessly through the city, but no one really seemed to have any idea what was going on. She had been told that the GPO was now isolated more completely than any of the other positions. She knew there were cannons and fires in the city. Lots of fires.

When, in the middle of the night, she heard a huge explosion that sounded like it came from the direction of the GPO, she was terrified. No one could have lived through something like that. She went to the window and looked out at the glowing red-and-orange light in the distance. There was a massive bank of black smoke hovering above the Dublin cityscape for as far as she could see.

The dark mass had been there for days, so it told her nothing. At night the huge, permanent cloud was tinged with a dirty red light from the fires below. Each new explosion reflected against the bottom side of this vast wall of dense smoke, lighting it up like lightning and illuminating the depth and density of the heavy, shadowed mass above. It looked like everything was upside down and hell had risen into heaven. It was hard to imagine that this huge, dark bank of smoke would ever leave her city.

39

Saturday April 29, 1916. About noon.
Somewhere in Moore St.
My Darling Grace,

This is just a little note to say I love you and tell you that we will meet soon. Regarding the rising, I have no regrets. Whatever happens next, I have done my best, and I know that you, at least, will understand that. Give my love to my family and friends if I can't do so myself, and please know that I want more than anything just to be with you, my darling, darling Grace. Love me always as I love you. If you can promise me that, then you have my blessing in anything and everything you do. I wrote a will saying that you are to have all that belongs—or will belong—to me. My brother George was witness, and I've told some others. This is my last wish, so please accept it.

Love,
Joe

Joe tore the letter out of his field notebook, folded it, and then handed it to Connolly's secretary, Winifred Carney. He hoped that she might not be arrested when this was over and would be able to get to Grace right away.

ʚɞ

The Brits seemed to be shooting at anything they saw move, which included many civilians. This was extremely stressful for the Volunteers positioned at the windows facing the street, who could do nothing about it, and they went to the leadership in an outrage.

The new rebellion headquarters was at 16 Moore Street, a narrow butcher shop near the middle of the block. A family in a little house on the opposite side of the street had tried to leave after being trapped since the previous morning by the British forces, who fired almost continuously from their barricade at the top of the street. One of the Volunteer officers in the window saw the little group peering out a doorway across the street that morning with white flags waving. He feared what might happen if they tried to leave their building, and he called out an order to cease fire. Pearse and Joe went to the windows as well, and they all watched, filled with tense helplessness.

One woman, a little girl, and two elderly men hesitantly stepped out of the doorway. Joe could almost feel the other men at the windows holding their breath in fear for this little group. All was silent as they prepared to walk out into the street, which was littered with debris and dead bodies. The woman walked in front, waving a white flag above her head frantically, with the little girl following close behind and then the two men. Joe noticed that the little girl carried a rag doll of some sort, clinging to it like it might keep her safe. The woman carried a small package in one arm—probably a little food for the four of them—and waved the white flag in her other hand.

As soon as they closed the door behind them and had taken a few steps out into Moore Street, the British opened fire. They seemed to be aiming for the old men; both of them went down right away in a hail of machine gun fire. The little girl was hit as well and looked faint and terrified, although she did not cry out.

The woman screamed and dropped her package and flag. She picked up the little girl and ran over to one of the old men, who was lying totally still—Joe thought that he was probably the woman's grandfather. She started to bend down to check on him, but the firing continued, one bullet hitting the skirt of her dress. She had no choice but to run, holding the little girl in her arms. The old men lay in the street next to the package of food and the white flag, which looked to be a piece torn from a very white sheet tied to a broom handle.

Joe walked unsteadily back to Connolly's mattress and sat down heavily. He was too exhausted to maintain the feeling of rage he felt building inside him. If only he weren't so ill, he could lead another charge on the barricade. It wouldn't be smart—probably suicidal—but it felt like the only reaction that could equal what he had just witnessed. If only he weren't so damn feeble and useless right now! In his exhaustion he couldn't think of anything more frustrating than wanting to fight and being unable to.

Connolly was awake after the sound of the shooting, but he didn't ask what had happened. He couldn't move at all, and his wound was looking bad. The infection was traveling up his leg in an angry red line.

Pearse hadn't moved, and as he continued to stand, staring out the window, he seemed to wilt. He sighed once, deeply, and then announced that a Military Council meeting was required immediately.

The leaders gathered around Connolly's mattress and spoke for a while. Winifred Carney was there too, as well as Willie and the nurse, Elizabeth O'Farrell.

"I'm done," Pearse said simply. "Too many civilians are dying." Although the others did not want to give up, nobody could disagree with his reason. The deaths of so many Dublin citizens had weighed heavily on the leaders all week. This was their city, and these were the people they wanted to free. Although most of the deaths were due to accidents—which was bad enough—they had heard many stories of events that were similar to what they had just seen. They realized that, for whatever reason, Dublin citizens were being targeted purposefully by some within the British forces.

It was almost as if the government troops saw everyone in Dublin as a part of the rebellion, even though most of the city did not even support their cause. This seemed especially odd, since so many of the British soldiers were actually Irish, many of them from Dublin themselves. Whatever the reason, more fighting would mean more civilian deaths, and Pearse argued that this was not acceptable. He wanted to negotiate for surrender, offering up the lives of the leaders in hopes that the rest of the men and women involved would be spared.

"If they can execute those of us who signed the proclamation, it might be enough for them. Maybe they'll let the rest go," Pearse continued.

"No. We can't quit now. We can't surrender!" Tom Clarke argued. "If it's going to end, then let it end here, in battle. I won't die in prison. I won't die in their custody!"

"I don't know, Clarke," Sean MacDermott said. "I think Pearse might be right."

Willie nodded in agreement with MacDermott, too tired to argue or state his position.

"I'd stick it out to the end with you, Clarke," Connolly smiled up at him weakly, "but I'm afraid I wouldn't be much help."

The discussion continued as they gathered around Connolly's bed, making their arguments in intense but hushed voices. Besides the lives of citizens, there was another important benefit to surrendering. They had taken a stand this week, and they had made their point clear. This was the most potent military action the Irish had ever taken against the British Empire, and it would never be forgotten. If they ended it now, there was a good chance that many of the men who served under them would survive to fight again at the next opportunity. They felt sure that the momentum of their fight for freedom would not be lost after the effort they had made over the past several days.

Joe was almost too sick to go on, and he knew that Pearse had a point, but he didn't want to give up. Still, he knew that the surrender would be put to a vote, and he could see the way things were going. It didn't matter much either way what he decided. He had reached the end of his opportunity to fulfill his destiny, and although he had many conflicting emotions, they were becoming as weak and faint as echoes. He felt numb.

He finally agreed to the surrender—sullenly, like a disappointed child—and walked away to gather his thoughts. He could hear Tom Clarke crying in the next room. Clarke had lived through all the rebellion of a previous generation and fifteen years in prison, and Joe had never seen him show any sign of weakness. Not ever. Joe feared that this disappointment might be the one thing that would break this seemingly unbreakable man.

Joe knew that the others were probably right about the surrender. He was being foolish to stand in the corner, pouting about it. He closed his eyes, took a few deep breaths, and said a prayer to steady his nerves.

This is it, he prayed silently. *I have done what I could do, and I only hope it was enough. I wanted to be better—to be more—but I did the best that I could. Please, God, be with me through whatever comes next. I think it will be difficult, and I can only ask that you continue to make your presence felt. If I can feel you next to me, then I know I can get through anything. Thank you so much for getting me this far and please,* please, *God, let me see Grace one more time. If I can have that, then I will die a happy man.*

After a moment or two, he recovered his perspective, and he felt like himself again. The decision was made. It was time to move on to what needed to be done next. He wrote his letter to Grace and gave it to Winifred Carney then sat speaking with her and Connolly while someone found a white handkerchief and attached it to an old broom handle. Connolly was disappointed and complained a little, but he was his usual gruff self, which was reassuring. Joe wished that they had become friends sooner.

Nurse O'Farrell took the newly constructed white flag and made it safely to the barricades to speak with British officers. Apparently, the soldiers at the barricade to the north were happy enough with the prospect of the rebels' surrender that they were able to resist shooting at her and her white flag. After quite a while, she came back to report that there would be no negotiations. The leaders could make no demands or requests whatsoever, and any surrender would have to be unconditional. Eventually Pearse went back with her. He left with some British officers and was gone for long time. Nurse O'Farrell came back alone with the terms of surrender and read them aloud to the remaining leaders.

40

They had their terms of surrender. Connolly was to be handed over at once. After that, all the rest of the leaders and Volunteers were to proceed—with white flags raised—back the way they had come, down to Henry Street then out to Sackville Street. Then they would cross to the other side of the wide street, to within a hundred yards of the group of soldiers who would be gathered at the Parnell statue just north of the GPO. There they were each to advance five paces, lay down their arms, and return to formation.

Winifred Carney and some of the Volunteers helped Connolly to get ready. He shaved, they redressed his wounds, and after everything he had been through that week, they did their best to clean up his uniform. He was carried on a stretcher out the front door of 16 Moore Street by four Volunteers who had also been cleaned up for the occasion and looked surprisingly fresh after a week of fighting.

With Connolly gone it felt like things were truly over. Some of the men started to speak up violently against the surrender. Nothing could be said to calm them down, and it looked like the leaders might have a mutiny on their hands. Eventually Sean MacDermott was able to get through to the men with reason and patience. He listened to their arguments closely and with great concentration. He took his time, asking them questions and giving carefully reasoned answers. Just the act of discussion and communication calmed things down a bit before he had even started making his own arguments.

"So many civilians have already died," MacDermott said gently. "The innocent now litter the streets of Dublin." He continued as a few of the men looked at their feet, ashamed of their passion for the fight. "Right now we are surrounded by some of the very poorest neighborhoods in the city, and the British will have no problem at all with butchering the local residents right along with us." The men all had to admit that this was true, and there would be no way to get around it. It would take a lot of fighting just to get out the door and down the street, let alone all the way to the Four Courts.

But there was another reason for the fighting to stop that was even more convincing to the men who wanted, more than anything else, to continue fighting for the freedom of their country.

"All that matters now is that you survive—all of you who are left," MacDermott told them. "You've fought a good fight, but you could only lose by continuing it now. This job is not done, and we need you to all survive today. We, the leaders, will almost certainly be executed. But we can die satisfied only if we die knowing that there are still plenty of you to finish the job that we started." The men had no answer. It was clear that everyone had to start thinking ahead and move back into strategy mode. If they were going to surrender, then it would be done well—just like their fighting—always aware that history was watching.

It was time to go, and they were ready now, even if they weren't all completely resigned to it. Joe was ready too; he was proud of what they had accomplished that week and he felt ready to face up to whatever end was coming,

He walked alone out the front door of 16 Moore Street carrying the white flag. Soon everyone who was left would line up behind him and then march south, back toward the GPO. He walked slowly to the middle of the road and stood with his back to the British military barricade, which was packed with rowdy soldiers, all with their guns aimed at him. There was a sudden hush as everyone at the barricade stopped speaking. There were more soldiers milling around in Great Britain Street, and they wandered over to see what was going on, curious about the sudden change in mood.

They stared at this officer in formal uniform who had walked slowly out the door. He was pale, with purple shadows under his eyes. He turned away and stood alone with his back to their troops. His black hair was a little wild, and he wore large rings on three of his fingers. He appeared to be unconcerned with the soldiers—or with their rifles and machine guns pointed tensely at his back. His lack of regard seemed to be an act of defiance—daring them to kill him now—but still, no one fired or even spoke.

Joe simply had other things on his mind; he was already thinking ahead to what was to come next, and these soldiers simply didn't matter anymore. He stood tall, calm, and silent. He was alone, surrounded only by the dead bodies of Volunteers and civilians scattered up and down Moore Street.

The snipers were still firing sporadically. Apparently, no one had alerted them to the surrender—or maybe they didn't want to accept it either. Joe called to one of the Volunteers who stood in the doorway of 16 Moore Street, watching him. This was the same steady and intelligent man from the Kimmage Garrison who had been at the window when Connolly had sent away the civilian the previous day. It was the man who was not surprised when Connolly told the civilian to go home because the fight was already over. A lost cause.

Joe asked the Kimmage man to go tell the British that he could not have the others come out into the street—or let them bring out the wounded—until they had reined in their snipers entirely. The Kimmage man walked up to speak to the officers at the barricade, and eventually the firing stopped. Joe gave the order, and the wounded were carried out and readied to be taken away to the hospitals.

Willie Pearse came out with another white flag and joined Joe in the middle of the street. The other men filed out and lined up behind them, four across, with the remaining officers taking up the rear, including Clarke and MacDermott. Once they were lined up, one of them read aloud the last order from Pearse regarding the surrender. Joe couldn't see who was reading, but it sounded like MacDermott.

> *In order to prevent the further slaughter of Dublin citizens, and in hope of saving the lives of our followers now surrounded and hopelessly outnumbered, the members of the Provisional Government present at Headquarters have agreed to an unconditional surrender, and the commandants of the various districts in the city and country will order their commands to lay down arms. P.H. Pearse, 29th of April, 1916, 3:45 p.m.*

There was a short addition that had been written by Connolly adding his agreement to the surrender on behalf of his Citizen Army, and it was done.

Willie gave a call, and they all began their march down Moore Street, turning left on Henry Place and moving past the little white house. They turned right and then left again to march on Henry Street along the north side of the GPO. It was in ruins—a smoking, blackened shell—and they could feel the great heat still emanating from the whole building. Joe saw that atop the pediment, the three statues of Mercury, Hibernia, and Fidelity were still intact. Hibernia, looking as proud and defiant as ever, gazed out over the wide boulevard, calmly observing the end of his battle. The Republic's Tricolor flag still flew, blowing in the breeze against the blue sky.

Sackville Street was swarming with British soldiers, and Joe guessed that there were at least a thousand in the area. As he and the others laid down their arms one by one, there were many shocked comments from government soldiers about the fact that so few men had defended Sackville Street the whole week. After the surprise wore off, the Volunteers and leaders faced a barrage of taunts and jeers from the British soldiers and officers alike about their primitive and inferior weapons. The abuse continued as names and ranks were taken down, but the officers ignored it all.

Joe was speaking to Willie and the other men around him about the future of the movement and international support for their cause when he was suddenly drawn out from the crowd and searched thoroughly by an officer. The officer found the will that Joe had written to Grace and kept in his pocket throughout the week. He taunted Joe about the will, making condescending remarks about his lack of confidence in the rebel troops. The officer spoke sarcastically at length, but Joe paid no attention to him.

He understood that, although this man was being cruel and unprofessional, he was just caught up in his role and his anger. He was a nonentity to Joe at the moment. It wasn't personal, and there were more important things to think about. When the officer had satisfied himself with his attempts to humiliate a rebel officer, Joe stepped back into place and continued his conversation with Willie about the future of the movement.

Nurse O'Farrell had started making the rounds to the other garrisons throughout the city with copies of the surrender order, and soon Ned Daly's men from the Four Courts joined Joe and his men. They were smoking and joking loudly as they marched up in perfect formation. They ignored the shouted orders from the British officers to stop smoking and seemed to be taking the whole situation as a game, mocking the Brits' accents with open scorn and laughing at the offense they caused. Joe was glad Ned Daly and his men were there. He and the others from the GPO had become far too serious and tragic, and the new additions cheered them all considerably.

They spent that night crammed tightly together on the little patch of grass in front of the Rotunda Hospital. No one was given any food or water, and it was all but impossible to sleep because everyone was in each other's space. There was no room to lie down comfortably. They were completely surrounded by armed soldiers and told that anyone who moved without permission would be shot. If any of them accidently put even a foot out onto the sidewalk, they were hit with the butt of a rifle and threatened with a bayonet.

The next morning they began the two-mile walk to Richmond Barracks. Each Volunteer had his own personal armed soldier who marched close behind, holding a bayonet to his back. The whole group was surrounded by more British soldiers. The prisoners were threatened and shoved violently if they got out of step or stumbled due to lack of sleep, food, and water. Just as they reached the bottom of Sackville Street and were about to cross the river, Joe heard a lone voice cry out, "God bless you, boys!"

But those would be the last words of approval they would hear. As they marched down Dame Street, the wide thoroughfare on the south side of the river, groups of angry women from the tenements ran out from the side streets hurling insults and old vegetables. They tried getting to the Volunteers, reaching and grasping at them past the loaded rifles of the British soldiers. If it hadn't been for their armed guards, the rebels would have most likely been attacked violently all along the way.

As they passed by St. Audoen's church, Joe was again thinking of Grace. This was the church she told him about—her favorite church to attend when she snuck out alone to go to Mass. At that point in the march, they were overtaken by another mob that screamed and chanted, over and over again, "Bayonet them! Bayonet them!" Joe realized the British soldiers were protecting them as well as imprisoning them.

They headed south and seemed to walk endlessly. It had been at least twenty hours since any of them had any water, and Joe felt dizzy. He blinked and shook his head a little to stay conscious but often slowed or stumbled. When he did, the soldier with a bayonet at his back would turn his gun around and shove him roughly in the back with the rifle butt.

Finally, they reached Richmond Barracks and were lined up outside on the square, where they stood for at least two more hours in the direct sun. Still no water was offered. There were several hundred soldiers in the square in addition to the guards surrounding them. He saw a great number of women and children milling around as well, looking apprehensively at him and the others. He realized that they were probably friends and family of the local men in the British Army and had come out of curiosity to see the rebels who had caused such trouble in their city. Some families walked around them in a big circle, just behind the guards, leering at the prisoners like they were zoo animals.

Finally, they were marched one by one toward the arched gate for processing. Joe heard someone asking him if he was all right. He turned and started to say, "Fine. Never better," just as that crushing exhaustion that had plagued him for days began to push in against him from all sides. The archway started to spin as he felt a nauseating, full-body spasm of weakness. The heaviness pulled at him as the ground rushed upward and everything went black.

Part Three

41

Joe opened his eyes to the fierce and painful sun and tried to remember where he was. Once he was able to focus, he saw a man looking at him from about a foot away, saying something he couldn't quite comprehend at first. When he looked down and saw that the man was wearing the uniform of a British officer, things came back quickly. He glanced around in alarm and saw that he had been taken inside the arched gate to Richmond Barracks and was lying in the dirt on a footpath. There were several men around him who were still unconscious, and some of them were being searched as they lay there, soldiers going through their pockets and packs.

He looked back at the British officer before him, who was still speaking. The man had a white mustache and kind, pale-blue eyes. He looked tired and concerned, and Joe realized that the officer was offering him water from a bucket and dipper he was holding. Joe managed to get out some sounds of gratitude and propped himself clumsily into a seated position. He drank his first water in as long as he could remember. It was sweet and cool, and he felt it moving through him, bringing him back to life.

"Slowly now, not too much at first, son," the British officer was telling him. Joe tried to listen, but he didn't want to stop drinking. Finally the man took the dipper away and asked if Joe thought he could walk.

"I think so … just a minute." Joe reached for his pack, which had been placed next to him on the ground, and made it slowly to his feet.

"There you are, young man, much better. Now, if you don't feel up to standing over there with the others, perhaps you could go over and sit by the wall."

Joe looked in the direction the British officer was pointing and saw a few men sitting against the wall near the entrance. "No … no, I can stand with the others. Thank you for the water, sir." The British officer with the white mustache patted him on the back and smiled so kindly that Joe felt like crying for a moment. He was just so tired.

He went to stand with the others from the GPO and the Four Courts who were gathered nearby, surrounded by soldiers with bayonets. He looked around for Thomas MacDonagh, but didn't see him anywhere. He hoped Tom was okay. He hadn't seen his friend since Easter Sunday, and he wondered now if he would ever see him again.

None of the men from the other garrisons were there at the barracks yet, and Joe was worried that some might not be willing to back down when they received news of the surrender. They had been so isolated in the GPO for days that he really had no idea how things were going across the city. If any of the other positions had been holding up well, they would not be at all pleased with the idea of surrender.

Joe looked around at the men guarding them now and listened to the accents. They were from England, and they seemed to be treating everyone politely enough in an impersonal way—especially in comparison to some of the other soldiers Joe had encountered throughout the morning. When he and the others from the GPO and Four Courts had first walked up to the barracks and were waiting to be processed, a large group of soldiers had rushed at them and looked like they might have attacked if it hadn't been for the armed guards. These very angry soldiers stood around yelling and taunting them for quite a while.

Judging from their uniforms and accents, Joe determined the men were from the Royal Irish Regiment in Belfast. Joe didn't think that any of his men were particularly scared of the angry soldiers—everyone had already faced so much during the long week, and they now seemed to be concerned only with what would happen in the end. They were worried about executioners, not bullies.

But none of them were prepared to handle this gang of Belfast soldiers rushing at them at first sight, out for blood, their faces twisted with rage. And that wasn't the only danger of the day. As impatient and abusive as some of the guards had been on the march over from the GPO, he was almost thankful for them now. It seemed a ridiculous thought, but he and the others might not have made it through the city alive with all of the angry Dubliners trying to get at them.

Now that he was inside the yard, most of the guards surrounding them seemed to be from England and Wales. There was not much shoving or abusive language for the time being, and most of these soldiers behaved as if it were all just a part of their day's work. Some of the soldiers they encountered throughout the day were from the south of Ireland, and some of them even had Dublin accents. For the most part, these men had employed the same professional and impersonal attitude toward their prisoners, but it didn't look like an easy day for them.

Many of the Dublin men wouldn't look their prisoners in the eye and seemed embarrassed to be corralling their fellow countrymen for the Empire. There weren't many jobs in Dublin, and the British service paid better than the few there were. Joe knew that some of these men might even have nationalist leanings themselves but simply needed work.

Nationalist or not, now they were playing a part in crushing the dream of Irish independence—a dream some of these men might even share. There were certainly men from nationalist families serving with the British military, and this situation had forced the conflict into a harsh light. Even more difficult, many friends and family members found themselves on opposite sides of the issue of England's rule in Ireland.

Joe found himself thinking about his childhood friend Kenneth O'Morchoe, from the time he and his family spent at their country home in Kilternan. He knew that Kenneth and his brothers were in the British Army now, and he wondered if any of them were here. They were likely all fighting in France.

At various points throughout the day, officers or detectives made their way down the line of prisoners, gathering information. As one British officer stopped to question each of them in turn, making out his list of names and ranks, he came to a young Volunteer and stopped before him. Without saying a word, the officer wrote something in his notebook and moved on to the next man in line.

"Why didn't he ask your name?" The young Volunteer's friend asked him.

"He's my brother," the Volunteer answered simply.

Joe glanced over at the young Volunteer, who betrayed no emotion at all, remaining strictly at attention staring straight ahead. For a moment Joe had a flash of concern about who might show up on his firing squad. Of course, if he was executed, he knew he'd be lucky to be shot, no matter who it was doing the shooting. The way things were going, he half expected to be hung like a criminal. For the time being, he would continue to hope for exile or imprisonment, which would be hard enough.

But soon more immediate concerns of water and rest replaced these thoughts of the future. And food! How long had it been since any of them had eaten? He couldn't say for sure. It seemed like there had been a roll and some tepid tea the previous day in Moore Street.

No one had offered the group any water, and Joe was thankful for the relative kindness of the officer with the white mustache. From time to time, he saw the same officer walk over to another man who had collapsed. He would crouch down, speak a few quiet words, and offer water. Eventually another man with a water bucket came around, but he would only give each desperately thirsty prisoner a cup of water if they had something to give him in trade. Some Volunteers were handing him watches, coins, even wedding rings and rosary beads—anything of value they still had—just for a small drink. Besides the fact that they had gone almost twenty-four very difficult hours without a drop of water, many of the men probably thought they would be shot soon anyway and wouldn't need their valuables.

Joe saw a group of British officers and some detectives from the Castle speaking nearby. They were comparing notebooks and pointing at various individuals within the ranks of the rebels. A couple of them began moving through the lines of prisoners, and eventually Joe, the other officers, and some others, including his little brothers George and Jack, were separated from the rest and directed into the gymnasium.

Just before he went inside to face whatever was coming next, Joe glanced back at the yard and saw another large group of men coming through the arched entrance, each one with a bayonet at his back. He didn't have time to see who the men were, but he thought again about Thomas MacDonagh and wondered if it might be the battalion from Jacob's Factory, where his friend had been stationed all week.

Once inside, Joe and the others were allowed to sit down on the floor of the gymnasium, which looked filthy and uninviting even after the week they had just been through. The flooring looked like it had once been close to white, but it was now gray with lots of brown and black smudges and stains and covered with thick, greasy dust. Joe sat with Jack.

"You know, I don't feel half as bad as I should," Joe told his brother. Despite the surgery and week without much sleep or food, he was starting to feel a lot better since coming to in the yard and getting a small drink of water. He wondered now how long he had been unconscious. In actuality, he suspected, he wasn't really doing any better now than before. There was just so much going on that it was easy to ignore his body's terrible condition. Still, he had started to feel optimistic again about at least living long enough to face his sentence. That thought made him smile and shake his head, thinking about how strange it was that he was thankful for the possibility that he might still be alive for the British to shoot.

"I don't see what's so funny about this," Jack was saying. "All this trouble for nothing, and now we'll probably all be killed. If I had to die, I wanted it to be out there on my own terms, fighting, not locked up like an animal."

"They won't kill you, Jack. They'll probably shoot the seven of us—we signed the proclamation, so there's no getting out if it, I'm afraid. But I bet they'll just send the rest of you to prison for a while. And you'll be together, so it shouldn't be too bad."

"You really think they'll shoot you? What about exile? Maybe they'll just send you to the colonies."

"Yeah, well, if they're smart they will. Otherwise, I think they'll bring a lot more people over to our side. But did you see what they did to the whole area around the GPO? It's completely destroyed. The Brits are angry, and I don't think they're making the most practical choices. They see this city as their own property, and they destroyed it just to get to us. No, I'm guessing they'll keep thinking angry and kill us fast." Joe paused, then asked hopefully, "Did you see whose garrison was coming in after us? Was it Jacob's Factory? I need to find out if Tom made it."

"No. Sorry, but I couldn't tell either. Just seen our guys around and those from the Four Courts."

Jack was summoned for questioning by the group of Castle detectives. Next it was Joe's turn, and he got slowly to his feet, stiff from his short rest. As he was taken over for questioning, he saw a small group of officers from St. Stephen's Green come into the gymnasium.

After asking Joe a few questions about his rank and his part in the uprising, the detectives directed him to sit against the wall, separated from most of the others. Clarke and MacDermott were already there. Over the next couple of hours, more small groups were brought in and sorted. After a while Joe laid down, resting his head on his forearm on the dirty floor. MacDermott roused him at one point.

"Here, take it," he said, holding out a small quilt.

"What? Where'd it come from? Don't you want it?"

"No, just take it, Joe. Try to get some rest."

Joe thanked him profusely and tucked the quilt under his head. He was just starting to feel guilty about the fact that no one else had a blanket when he fell asleep.

Joe awoke then sat up slowly, leaning his back against the wall of the gymnasium. There were several men sitting with him now, mostly the leaders from some of the other rebel garrisons throughout the city. In the center of the room were about two hundred more men. It looked like most of the battalions were represented, so he guessed there must be several hundred more men outside by now. Clarke and MacDermott sat nearby, speaking quietly together.

Ceannt was the only one not sitting down. He was pacing back and forth in front of the small group with his arms crossed tightly. He muttered under his breath, and he looked very pale. Joe wondered absently if Ceannt was angry at the British soldiers or at the GPO leaders who had decided to surrender.

Most of the Military Council was sitting with him in the small group near the wall, and there were several other officers mixed in. Willie Pearse was seated nearby with Patrick, but they weren't speaking. Connolly would still be at the hospital, and Joe didn't see Thomas MacDonagh or anyone else from the Jacob's Factory garrison. Eventually everyone was issued one small blanket each and escorted from the gymnasium in small groups.

42

Almost nothing at all happened on Monday or Tuesday, as far as Joe could tell. He and a group of twenty or so men were locked away in a tiny dark room where they remained most of the time. It should have been a welcome rest, but there was no room for everyone to sit or lie down at the same time, so the men had to take turns. Several would stand pressed against the wall while the others took the opportunity to rest or try to sleep.

There was a single bucket for a toilet, which was rarely emptied, and all they were given to eat was a hard roll and a half can of cured beef each. They were given a bucket of warm tea with a mug coated in red paint. The paint melted in the mild heat of the tea when they dipped it in the bucket, sending out little red veins, but everyone was too thirsty to refrain from drinking it.

Some of the guards treated the men well, occasionally sneaking them cigarettes or extra rolls. Others remained openly hostile and attempted to engage in psychological torture.

"Here you go, boys. Hope you enjoy your last meal on earth," a pale, skinny guard said as he tossed in their hard rolls and cans of meat.

"I sure am getting sick of all this babysitting," another guard said loudly, for the benefit of the prisoners. He was heavy and had a red face. "I'm looking to get some work on a firing squad and digging graves!" He laughed at his own cleverness, adding, "You know they're startin' the executions in the morning over at Kilmainham Gaol. Think they've got three planned." He trudged away down the corridor.

The prisoners were cheerful, given their pathetic circumstances, even if the cheer was often forced. After a week of violence and constant tension, they were hard to rattle. They had no respect for the authorities that held them captive but also felt no need to make a show of their contempt with any further attempts at revolt.

They had made their point well and, for the most part, felt proud and satisfied. Early on the prisoners realized that their casual and happily dismissive attitude bewildered and angered the worst of the guards, so being cheerful and watching the reactions had become a form of entertainment. While the sympathetic jailers got the joke and became even more solicitous, the angry and abusive guards were perplexed and infuriated by the polite and good-natured response of their prisoners in the face of mistreatment.

The nights were long and cold and unpleasant. With each dawn came hope that they would be moved somewhere with more room to move or lie down, but they were kept in the same pathetic room throughout their time at Richmond Barracks.

From time to time, the inmates were taken away for interrogations. Joe had been separated from the other leaders, so he was called out for questioning more than any of the others in his cell. He welcomed the frequent breaks from their dark, dank little cave, even if it was only to be placed in a room full of military men who took turns yelling questions at him.

The interrogations didn't trouble him, because he had nothing to hide and there was nothing they could do to him that would be worse than what he was already expecting.

While stony-faced detectives scribbled notes and various red-faced officers yelled in his face, he often let his mind wander to his worries about Thomas MacDonagh and Grace. He had heard from some of the other Volunteers that Tom had made it through the rebellion alive and was seen at the barracks at some point, but he wasn't sure where his friend was now.

Joe wanted to speak with Thomas and share stories about the week. They really should have been fighting together. He missed Grace even more. He hoped that she got the letter he had given to Winifred Carney to deliver. It was very likely, however, that Winifred was imprisoned as well, and in that case, Grace might not even know he was alive. He would need to find a way of getting another message out to her soon.

The yelling had ceased for a moment. Apparently, the military interrogators had asked him another question.

"Sorry, could you repeat that?" Joe asked.

"What can you possibly have to say to defend yourself after such rank treason against the Empire?" a tall, bony officer demanded. The man's skin was waxy and yellowed, but his cheeks were flushed, probably from all the yelling. He really seemed to be angry about all of this. But his question seemed rhetorical to Joe, who could think of no answer that would satisfy the man.

"There was no act of treason, sir," Joe said, purposefully keeping the contempt he felt out of his tone."I do not recognize the authority of the British Empire, and I was attempting to defend my own country from an occupying enemy force."

The man looked like he wanted to punch Joe hard in the face. Resisting his urge made his yellow skin even paler than before and his flushed cheeks burn a brighter shade of red. Joe was almost worried about the officer and began to hope that, simply for the sake of the man's health, he would let someone else take over for a bit.

He did. When the bony, yellow man sat down, the emotional temperature in the room decreased considerably, and the other detectives and officers continued along a more routine line of questioning. They wanted to know who had done what, when certain tasks had been accomplished, and what his particular role had been throughout the planning and execution of the rebellion. Joe told them about his role in strategic planning. As often as possible, he added that only a very small group was involved—only the Military Council. No one else had any idea of what was about to occur, and they should not be held responsible.

No matter how many times he explained all of this, these men did not seem to hear him. It took him a long time just to explain that Sinn Fein was not involved—that they were simply a political organization that had played no part in the planning of the insurrection. To these detectives and military men, any Irish rebel was a Sinn Feiner; they knew nothing about the IRB. Once Joe had clarified this for them, they began blaming the Irish Volunteers for the plot, and Joe had to begin all over again.

"No, the Irish Volunteers had no knowledge of what was going on. MacNeill leads the Volunteers, and did all he could to stop us. The Volunteers themselves showed up that day simply to practice maneuvers." This was the second time he had explained this, and not one of the detectives looked like they understood him. "The only people who should be blamed for this are the seven of us that signed the proclamation," Joe said again. "No one else knew what was going to happen."

"So it was this so-called... uh... IRB—this... uh..." A stocky detective with a Dublin accent looked at his notes.

"This… Irish Republican Brotherhood, that planned the whole thing?"

"No, the IRB didn't know either." Joe's patience began to strain as he started all over again, giving the same explanation he had given before. "It was just the seven who signed the proclamation. We kept it from everyone—the Volunteers, the IRB, everyone. No one else knew anything about what was going to happen."

All of this interrogation was almost a pleasure compared to standing in the dark, pressed against the cell wall, with twenty men who had little to think about besides the fact that they might soon be killed with no chance to even say goodbye to their families. Joe wanted all of them to make it through this thing alive, and he was doing his best to make that happen by trying to get the government to understand who had actually been in charge.

On his way out, Joe found his brother Jack waiting for his turn. Jack looked despondent and sullen and began talking again about what a waste of time the whole thing had been. Apparently some of the men in his cell were saying that, because of the surrender, there was no hope for Irish independence for another two hundred years. He felt like a failure and wished more than ever that he'd been killed in battle.

"You're wrong, Jack, believe me. What we did last week set the stage for what is to come. If we'd all fought to the death, there would be no one to continue." A nearby guard told them to keep quiet, so Joe continued in a hushed voice. "If we had kept fighting and everyone died, then it would have taken another two hundred years to rise again, but now it will be soon. I promise you. Ireland will be free, and you'll be there to see it."

Back in the cell, he gave the other men what little new information he had. He then managed to get a hold of a small pencil from one of them. He took out the will he had written out to Grace more than a week earlier and wrote her a note on the back. The piece of paper was very small—not even a quarter of a full page—so his note was short. He said nothing about the possibility (probability?) of executions. This was not certain, and until or unless it became certain, he saw no reason to alarm her.

Richmond Barracks
Tuesday, May 2, 1916
My Darling Child,

This is my first chance of getting a message to you since we were taken. I really don't have any idea of what they intend to do with us, but I have heard rumors about exile, among other possibilities. So it seems possible that I could to be sent to England. I'm happy with everything—all we did—except for the fact that I'm not with you. George and Jack are both here and are both doing well. I've also heard that Thomas was brought here to the barracks yesterday, but I haven't been able to see him. If you have a chance of getting in to see me, please try. I will see if it's possible for us to be married while I'm in custody, just in case we're unable to do so later. I hope you know how much I love you, Grace. I have to go, but I need you to know that. Even though it seems like ages since I've seen you, I know you love me, and because of that, I am happy.

Yours very truly,
Joe

43

Joe was lying on the filthy floor of the gymnasium again, and someone was shaking him by the shoulder to wake him. For some reason he no longer felt ill at all. His chills were gone, and he had no pain in his neck or throat. He sat up without effort and turned to see his best friend, Thomas MacDonagh, sitting right next to him, smiling with his usual warm, cheerful eyes.

"Well, good morning, Joe!" Thomas said.

"You should have been with us at the GPO." It was the first thing to jump out of Joe's mouth when he saw his best friend alive and well. It was a stupid thing to say, but all week long he had been wishing they were fighting together. He was just so relieved to see Thomas again. He smiled back at his friend and added, "I'm just so glad you made it."

Joe awoke with a sudden, brutal feeling of alarm that left him breathless, his heart pounding against his ribs, his pulse audible in his own ears. He had just been dreaming. It made him miss his friend terribly. It was well before dawn, but the dismal gray glow through the windows showed that it was early Wednesday morning. The cold dampness in the air completed the loneliness he felt, despite the fact that he was packed into the small cell with many others. New feelings of loss and dread welled up into his chest and took on a weight that felt too heavy to bear.

The stone floor of the cell had become painful after his couple hours of sleep, and he felt like crying, but he wasn't sure why. He blinked hard and held back any tears, but he was afraid to go to sleep again and face the possibility of dreaming about Thomas or Grace—or maybe even his father. He just didn't know if he could take it at that point. It was best not to dwell on this sadness. He knew he would feel better once the sun was up and the day's activities could distract him.

He had heard that his court-martial proceeding might be later that same day. That would give him plenty to think about, keeping him from thinking about his illness and the heavy, sad feeling in his chest. He stood up stiffly and took a spot against the stone wall so one of the other men could start his resting time early.

Joe watched as the gray glow through the small iron-barred window turned to a full, sunny dawn. It felt like a gift. He wondered how many more sunrises he would see in this lifetime and marveled at how this warm, rosy, and reassuring light continued to reach into even the darkest and most hopeless corners of the world. He prayed that God would help him to die in a courageous manner that would not detract in any way from what they had accomplished by facing up to the British Empire. Dying well wasn't his first choice, but it might be the only thing left to do for Ireland.

So many of the Irish stories he had heard time and again as a child portrayed the heroic and valiant side of defeat. The volumes of ancient mythology were full of stories about the great deaths of the greatest warriors.

Joe's favorite story was about the death of Cú Chulainn, an ancient Irish hero who was said to be the son of a god and a human princess. He was known to be a supernaturally fierce fighter who was able to enter into the famed warp spasm. When in this altered, frenzied state, Cú Chulainn was transformed into a terrifying and unrecognizable monster warrior.

After being mortally wounded during his final battle, Cú Chulainn continued to fight ferociously. When his strength was drained and he realized that he was near death, he tied himself upright to a standing stone so that he could continue to fight. After he could hold onto life no longer and died, his foes were so scared of him that they remained at a distance, believing he was still alive and afraid to even approach him. It was only when a raven landed on Cú Chulainn's shoulder that they finally realized he might be dead. Some believe that the raven was actually An Morrígan, the goddess of battle, in one of her altered forms.

After Cú Chulainn's foes saw the raven on his shoulder, they carefully approached him. His longtime enemy Lugaid stepped forward in victory and cut off Cú Chulainn's head. It is said that Cú Chulainn's body then began to glow with a mysterious light. His sword fell from his lifeless grasp and cut off Lugaid's hand.

The last several hundred years of Irish history seemed fraught with one loss to the English after another, and as a little boy Joe wondered what there was to celebrate in these stories. Why were there so many proud songs of defeat? As he matured he learned that dying well was not about death or defeat. It was all about making the ultimate sacrifice to a destiny greater than the self and living on in history.

If he and Grace could be married, then he would have no regrets at all. Having had the chance to fulfill his destiny by standing up for Ireland, dying the husband of the woman he loved was all he wanted. He needed to say goodbye to his father, his brothers, and Thomas MacDonagh as well. Surely there would be enough time for all of this.

ⵚ

The group of men who were sorted out in the gymnasium for the courts-martial on Sunday was big—Joe heard that the list was up to two hundred. All of those trials would probably take weeks, if not months, even if the authorities rushed things appallingly and offered no defense or due process at all. After that there would be appeals, and then, most likely, the executions would begin.

He had written to Grace that he might be sent overseas because he didn't want to scare her, but he didn't really see much chance of that. While there were rumors running through the barracks about all sorts of things, including sentences of exile and foreign imprisonment, it was probably better to prepare for death.

Along with Wednesday's dawn came the guards with their rations of hard rolls and tepid tea. Soon Joe was taken out of the packed cell and brought down to a little grassy courtyard to wait for his court-martial. Many of the other leaders and officers from the GPO and other garrisons were waiting there, and they were told that twenty-two men would be on trial that very day. Twenty-two courts-martial on one day?

Apparently many more courts-martial had already been completed on the previous day, and Joe received a little information on how they had gone. It had been determined that the names at the bottom of the proclamation could not be used as evidence against the seven signatories because no one could find the original document.

This was good news, Joe supposed, but Willie Pearse reported that there were rumors going around that Patrick Pearse, Tom Clarke, and Thomas MacDonagh had already been sentenced to death after the previous day's courts-martial.

He had even heard from one of the guards that all three men had already been executed early that morning at Kilmainham Gaol on the west side of town.

Joe didn't want to believe that, and he decided not to. He had heard so many wild rumors in the last week that there was no reason to take this one seriously when it was just about the worst thing imaginable to him. But he felt his chest tighten as he remembered his dream from earlier that morning, just before dawn. Whether or not they had started the executions, it was clear that these so-called courts-martial were not going to be legitimate trials. They were clearly just brief shows of formality so that there would be something on paper to justify rushed executions.

At one point a guard walked up to Willie Pearse, who was standing next to Joe.

"Excuse me, but are you the brother of Patrick Pearse?" The guard asked formally. He had a British accent.

"Yes, I am," Willie said. "Do you have some... information about my brother?"

"I just needed to tell you that..." The guard paused. He looked like he was second-guessing his decision to come over. "Well, I was there for your brother's court-martial. You should know that he handled it all with such courage. I've never seen anything like it."

"What do you mean?" Willie looked pale, afraid to ask, his eyes filling with tears.

"He had his say—and spoke powerfully but with respect. The judges seemed impressed. I heard some discussion among them after he left. They were saying that having to punish such a man simply for doing what he so obviously saw was his duty in defense of his country seemed like a tragedy."

Apparently, Pearse had taken full responsibility for his

role in the rebellion and asked the judges many times during his statement to hold only the leaders responsible and to let all of their followers go free. He told them that he had sworn as a child to spend his life fighting for Ireland's freedom.

"They said that you," the guard continued with a glance at Joe, "all of you are … not what they expected. They seemed to be unhappy that they've been so rushed to hand out the sentences."

"Thank you for coming to me," Willie said, then hesitated and dropped his eyes, adding, "Is it true that the … executions have … already begun?"

"I've, uh, been stationed here the whole time," the guard told him, looking at the ground now as well, "so … I'm not really sure what they're doing over at Kilmainham." The guard walked back to his post and didn't look over at Joe and Willie anymore, instead staring straight ahead, looking very official.

After an hour or so of general conversation and speculation with the others, Joe sat by himself. He was lost in thought as he waited, sitting in the cool grass, the bright morning sun warm on his back. He tried not to think about the fate of his best friend—it couldn't be true that Thomas was already gone. He focused instead on enjoying the relative beauty of the grassy barracks square after two days in the packed, dark cell.

Finally, Joe was called by the guards and taken into the large building opposite the little sunny patch of grass. He was led inside to a room that had been set up to resemble a courtroom, with a long table at the head and two smaller tables set up facing it. Three British officers—the judges—sat at the larger table, dripping with medals and importance. Joe was led to one of the smaller tables and stood there facing the officers. There were two guards at his back with bayonets fixed and two more guards at the door.

Two of the three judges looked sad and exhausted, as if the two days of presiding over the courts-martial was work in which they took no pleasure whatsoever. Joe was perplexed by the concern in their eyes as they looked at him with what seemed to be regret. The third judge looked like he was doing just fine as he primly organized his paperwork. Joe almost expected him to start humming to himself.

After formal introductions were made, it became clear that Joe would receive assistance from no lawyer. He was surprised when they told him that he was allowed to call witnesses if he wanted to. But this was the first he had heard of it, and the proceedings would not be delayed. Since he had not had the opportunity to prepare for calling any witnesses, the offer meant nothing. Joe now had little hope at all that he would receive anything close to a fair trial. He took a deep breath and tried not to think about the fact that he seemed to be one step closer to execution.

44

Joe now knew for sure that he would have no opportunity to mount a defense. *Perfect,* he thought. *A complete farce, as expected.*

This final confirmation decreased the pressure he was feeling. Since the courts-martial were clearly all for show, he relaxed, ready to simply observe the theater. The charges were read aloud by a court assistant of some sort who sat next to the large table full of decorated judges. He stood, cleared his throat, stated Joe's name and prisoner number—thirty-three—and then read the charges word for word in an automatic, unpunctuated, and neutral monotone, as if he had already read the same thing many times and was no longer extracting any meaning from the text.

"The defendant did take part in an armed rebellion and engaged in waging of war against His Majesty the King, such act being of such a nature as to be calculated to be prejudicial to the Defense of the Realm and being done with the intention and for the purpose of assisting the enemy." This made little sense to Joe, especially the part that claimed he was assisting the enemy, but he got the point of the charges in general. He assumed that the enemy they claimed he was assisting was Germany. One of the judges asked Joe for his plea.

"Not guilty."

The first witness against Joe was sworn in. He was Major Philip Holmes, a short, stocky young Irishman who stood at the other little table. He seemed to be carefully avoiding looking in Joe's direction, instead keeping his very pale blue eyes forward as he spoke to the judges.

"Yes I, uh ... identify the prisoner as one of a large company of Sinn Feiners who surrendered on the evening of the ..." He paused here to look at some notes in front of him on the table, then continued. "The evening of the 29th of April, 1916. The company surrendered at the northern end of Sackville Street. This was after several days ... the Sinn Feiners had occupied the GPO ... uh, the General Post Office, for several days. But they were burnt out. Or ... they were forced to leave after we burned the post office."

Joe thought about the time he had spent during his interrogations attempting to educate the officers and detectives regarding the fact that Sinn Fein was not involved in the rebellion, and he wondered idly how many of the others had corrected them on this same point. And yet they still continued to repeat the same inaccurate intelligence. It only served to underscore the uselessness of the proceeding. He knew he could have been angry about all of it, but given the fact that the end result would probably not be any different even if they had been listening to him during the interrogation, he decided that it was more comical than infuriating.

"He and the other Sinn Feiners in the post office had been firing on us ... on government troops for several days. They wounded and killed many of our men," continued Major Holmes. Then, motioning with his arm toward Joe but still keeping his eyes straight ahead on the judges, he added, "At the time of the surrender, he was dressed in the same uniform he is wearing at this time ... with the captain's rank badge on his sleeves. He was leading the company and, uh ... they were armed at the time of surrender."

"Does the prisoner have any questions for the witness?" asked one of the judges.

"The prisoner does not," Joe answered, nearly losing his struggle to address the court with respect. Holmes had basically got it all right. Joe didn't remember seeing Holmes during the surrender, but there had been at least a thousand British officers and soldiers milling around at the time versus just a hundred and fifty or so on the rebel side.

The second witness was Sergeant John Bruton, a local man from the Dublin Metropolitan Police. Joe easily recognized Sergeant Bruton as one of the many officers and detectives who used to stand around outside of Volunteer headquarters and meetings. They had tried to blend in and look casual as they watched the street like hawks, writing in their little notebooks. After he was sworn in, Sergeant Bruton identified Joe and then went on to describe how he knew him.

"I frequently patrolled the headquarters of the Irish Volunteer movement. The address of this office is Number 2 Dawson Street," he explained. Then, motioning toward Joe's table, he went on. "I have seen the prisoner at this address several times. On at least two of these occasions, he was dressed in an Irish Volunteers uniform. Judging from my experience and research regarding the Irish Volunteer organization, the prisoner had badges indicating the rank of captain."

Bruton seemed to be enjoying his testimony, playing the expert, and relishing his rare moment of power. "In addition to this, the prisoner's name appears on the proclamation that was issued by the Irish Volunteers, and we have information suggesting that he was a member of the executive council of this organization."

Bruton was bringing up the signatures on the proclamation, which was supposed to be inadmissible, but Joe didn't see the point in objecting, since he had signed it and was proud of that fact. He did not want the Irish Volunteers to be blamed for anything, however, so when asked if he would like to cross-examine the witnesses, he told them he had just one question.

"Why do you say that the proclamation was issued by the Irish Volunteers? What do you have to back up this statement?"

"I know that the men who signed at the bottom of the proclamation are … connected with the Irish Volunteers," Bruton answered. "They include Patrick Pearse, Eamonn Ceannt, Thomas MacDonagh, Sean MacDermott, and yourself and … others … who are members of the Irish Volunteers. We have reason to believe that all of the men who signed the proclamation were on the executive council of the Irish Volunteers and constantly attended meetings at Irish Volunteer headquarters."

Joe wasn't allowed to testify at this point, but he could correct the record later. The third witness didn't have much to say. Lieutenant Colonel H.S. Hodgkin was the first witness from England, and after he was sworn in, he stood there stiffly at attention, giving his short testimony in two clipped and explosive bursts.

"The prisoner was among those who surrendered on the 29th of April, and I saw him there at Sackville Street. He was armed at the time with a sword and at least one pistol." True enough. Joe had no questions for Hodgkin.

Joe was next invited to state his defense. He had none but decided to try once again to clear things up for the record. "I have nothing to say in my own defense. I fought at the GPO. I held the rank of captain. I do, however, want to point out, once again, that the proclamation referred to by Sergeant Bruton was not issued by the Irish Volunteers organization. They had no knowledge of our plans and were taken completely by surprise. Only those of us who signed the proclamation should be held responsible."

Notes were taken and stacks of documents shuffled about, then Joe was taken away. As the guards led him out of the room, he heard one of the judges at the big table sigh deeply then speak grimly to the others: "There must be something very wrong with the state of things if it turns men like these into rebels."

The whole trial couldn't have lasted more than fifteen minutes. No wonder they were getting through so many in a day. Thankfully, Joe was allowed to wait in the grassy barracks square once again instead of going back to his cell.

Soon he was called back inside. The judges gave him his guilty verdict and announced that his sentence was death, to be carried out as soon as possible at Kilmainham Gaol. He was taken back out to the square to await his transfer, where he stood feeling a little stunned. He had known what was coming, but things were happening much more quickly than he had expected. He had thought he would get a chance to see Grace again before being executed, but how was that going to happen? How long did he have?

He thought about his father, who had tried to come fight at his side at the GPO on the first day. He knew it was too dangerous for his father to stay for the fight, but now Joe wished he had not sent him home after all. They would have had more time together. He had heard that both of his parents had been arrested anyway because they had turned the family estate into the Kimmage Garrison, so his dad might as well have stayed and fought.

At that moment Joe felt someone watching him. He looked up at the windows of the guardroom and saw his father looking down at him. Joe knew this might be the last time he would ever see anyone from his family, and he wished they could speak, even if just for a minute or two. His confidence drained from him upon seeing his favorite parent, and he felt small and alone, like a little boy again. He found himself longing for his father to somehow fix the whole situation and assure him that everything would be okay. But the Count was a prisoner as well and wouldn't be fixing anything.

Joe hated to imagine what his father was thinking as he looked down at him in the square. He couldn't have heard about the death sentence already, but surely he knew what would happen. They stood still and quiet, looking at each other through the window for what felt like a long time. Eventually two guards came to take Joe to Kilmainham Gaol. As they prepared him for transfer, he took one last look at his father. Joe didn't want him to worry, so he tried his best to look cheerful and fearless as they led him away.

45

Grace had been busy nonstop since early Tuesday morning. There was so much to arrange. She woke up filled with a heavy dread that grew steadily in her body like nausea then pulled and tugged at her mind with incessant whispered messages. The whispers warned her that time was running out. She began to feel strongly that Joe might be gone soon. After a week of pacing and fretting, she could not sit by any longer, waiting to be summoned for a visit, when there was no guarantee of what was going to happen. More than anything else, she needed to see him. She didn't know how she could go on if she couldn't say goodbye—couldn't hold him again.

She needed to marry Joe as soon as she could in case he was imprisoned or exiled. If they were married, she assumed that she would have more access to him in either case. If he was to be executed, then it was even more important that they marry immediately—it would truly be their only chance. She had been thinking about these things all week, but she had begun to feel that today was the only chance the two of them would have. This made her feel sick and a little breathless. She tried to relax and be patient, telling herself that her anxiety was simply going out of control because of the severity of the situation, but she could not get the whispered warnings out of her mind.

At breakfast a messenger arrived with a letter that Joe had sent to her from the Richmond Barracks. The woman who brought the message worked for Grace's mother in the family's kitchen. She reported that a British soldier had delivered it to the family's address in Rathmines the previous night. *Why had the message come from a British soldier*? Grace thought that couldn't be good news. She felt faint as she unfolded the small scrap of paper quickly, fearing the worst.

It was not bad news after all. Joe had written that he, his brothers, and Thomas MacDonagh were still alive and well, and were being held at Richmond Barracks. She sat down quickly so that she wouldn't fall as relief took the strength from her legs. The piece of paper was nothing but a scrap a few inches wide and she guessed that Joe must have been unable to get any paper in jail. He must have sneaked it out with that British soldier, and she was thankful that the man had delivered it to her family at all.

Because of the size of the paper, Joe's handwriting was small and cramped. This was so different from his usual intense, careless scrawl, but she knew the words were from him. The connection brought on tears of relief and gratitude after so many days of worry.

Joe brought up marriage again—a prison wedding this time—and he wrote that he might be sent to England. She supposed he knew more about what was happening than she could possibly know and told herself that he might live after all. On the back of the message was a will he had written out over a week before, leaving her everything. She thought about the fact that this little piece of paper had been with him, in his pocket, pressed up against him for the entire week of rebellion—through all the flames and shooting and explosions. Even more than before, she longed to see him and hold him close.

Forcing back her tears, she held the little note close as she walked back to the breakfast table. But that feeling of dread persisted, and every minute that passed felt like a missed opportunity. As she tried to make polite conversation with her sister and the children, her mind was miles away at Richmond Barracks.

Soon a message arrived for Muriel, who brought it back to the table before opening it. She became unnaturally pale as she read the message silently then sat very still for a moment, saying nothing at all. Suddenly she dropped the note on the table and ran from the room, leaving Grace with the children and Eamonn Ceannt's wife. Grace picked up the note and read it herself. Thomas had been executed early that morning. He was already gone.

They had received word the previous day that the execution was likely to happen soon, and Muriel had been instructed on how to go see him a final time at Kilmainham Gaol. She had gone to the prison the previous evening as instructed, but once she got out there, she was told that she lacked a required pass. They wouldn't let her in no matter how she begged.

After speaking with numerous military personnel, Muriel had been sent home with assurances that the executions would most likely be postponed, since the courts-martial had only begun. Now Thomas was gone and it was too late. The phones had been back on for days, so Grace called home, telling them to immediately send over anyone who could come because Thomas was dead. She then ran upstairs to find Muriel.

As soon as Isabella showed up to look after Muriel, Grace left the house with a long list of things that needed to be done. She went back and forth across the city for hours, first to Richmond Barracks, where she was told that Joe was to be transferred to Kilmainham Gaol at any time. She found that he had already begun trying to arrange for them to be married at the jail, something that had never occurred there before. She went to see her priest, who promised to speak with the Kilmainham chaplain immediately about having the wedding in the prison chapel. The chaplain, in turn, would need to get approval from the jail superintendent.

By the time everything had been arranged, it was early evening, and Grace decided that she would try to get herself a wedding ring. Of course, Joe should be the one to buy her ring, but under the circumstances, this would be the only way. He already had the family ring she had given to him when he asked her to marry him.

She thought for a moment of that day when they sat huddled together in the cold on a bench in St. Stephen's Green. She had believed at the time that they would have many years together for their long talks; she had been so happy. They had really only started to get to know each other, and it felt like the beginning of the happiest time of her life. Now she realized that it might be over.

She arrived at Mr. Stoker's jewelry shop in Grafton Street just as he was closing his shop. He let her come in despite the time, and seeing that she had been crying and was clearly on the verge of starting up again at any moment, he asked her what was wrong. He had such a kind and concerned look that she found herself telling him about Joe, the jail wedding, and the executions.

Mr. Stoker blinked a couple of times and said nothing at first. It was a lot to take in.

"But it's been only a few days since the surrender," he said. "Surely they can't have started the executions already."

"But they have," Grace cried out. "They already killed my brother-in-law and two others."

"That's outrageous! We've heard nothing about it. I ... I'll call the papers now, dear. Maybe if the people know what's going on ... certainly the city's in an uproar, but Ireland is a civilized country. The people will want justice in the proper way."

Grace went home and quickly changed. She made it out to Kilmainham Gaol at about six in the evening, as she had been instructed. Before she walked hesitantly through the entryway, she looked up at the huge doorframe with its intricate, three-dimensional design of five intertwined demon-like serpents of stone that twisted and writhed. They snarled, flashing huge fangs, their soulless eyes staring vacantly at the world as they strained against the heavy chains around their necks. Grace wished more than anything that she and Joe were somewhere else—anywhere else in the world. She found some soldiers just inside the front door and explained that she was there for her wedding.

"Everything has been approved. They told me to be here at six."

"Absolutely not. We've been told nothing about this," a British officer informed her with a brief glance. He then looked back to his notebook, implying that she was dismissed. He seemed to be the one in charge. No one questioned him.

She insisted that things had been arranged. After much explanation, and after she listed the names of everyone who had approved the plan, the officer with the notebook begrudgingly asked one of the other men standing around to go ask about her story. It was almost completely dark, with just a few candles placed around the room. The gas was out in the whole neighborhood; she guessed it had something to do with the rising. She waited for over an hour before the soldier came back and confirmed what she had told them. The soldier with the notebook looked annoyed.

"Well, I guess you can wait here until they come down to get you," he said without looking at her.

Grace sat in a dark corner, worried that she would be in the way, giving them an excuse to make her leave. After a couple more hours, the soldier with the notebook left, and she felt more at ease. She began to pace around the small entry room to try to stay warm. One of the other soldiers even offered her some tea. Grace thought about how close she was to Joe. She felt tormented by the thought that he could be within a hundred feet of her right now, and she longed to spend this time speaking with him. It was already getting late, and she wondered if they would get much time together after they were married.

Surely she would be allowed some time to sit alone with him and talk to him then, but she wondered why she couldn't speak with him now instead of sitting alone for hours. She had never been so frustrated in her life, but she was afraid to complain because she felt that this one chance to see Joe could be taken from her at the slightest provocation. She had so many things to tell him—a lifetime of things that she needed to say—and her mind raced through it all.

She was so scared of this place, and she hated to think that Joe was here, especially when he must be terribly ill after the surgery and a week of fighting. He had barely been able to stand when she went to meet with him at the nursing home the previous week. Intermingled with her fear and worry was also joyful anticipation of seeing him again. It made her stomach feel fluttery and jumpy, like the candle flame across the small, drafty room. She could hardly contain her excitement despite the cold, damp air and the dark stone walls.

46

Two more hours went by. Grace was beginning to feel she could stand it no longer. She sat alone, shivering on a stone bench in the corner of the jail's entryway, thinking she wouldn't be allowed to see Joe after all. Finally, at eleven o'clock that night, Officer Kenneth O'Morchoe, a Dublin man about her own age, came downstairs to meet her. He told her that he was the officer in charge and that he would be bringing her up to the chapel. His eyes were filled with concern, but he chatted pleasantly as he led her by candlelight through the dark stone maze with its uneven, cold stone floors. There was a wet and lifeless chill in the air that she felt down to her bones.

"You know, Joe and I were good friends when we were young," he told her as they walked, looking ahead into the dark corridor. "Joe's dad bought the property next to our family's estate. We used to roam the countryside together—the whole bunch of us. We invented all kinds of complicated games and stayed out from morning 'til night in the summers." Kenneth smiled a little at the memory, then stopped speaking. He paused and turned to Grace. "I don't know how it all came to this. I … I hate the fact that he's here at the jail, with the … executions and … listen, I don't think you should be too worried about … an execution. I've heard talk about a possible last-minute reprieve because … you know, because of his illness."

"Thank you, Mr. O'Morchoe—Officer O'Morchoe. I hope you're right." Grace didn't know what to say. The possibility of a reprieve was better news than she could have expected, but she was afraid to hope.

"Please, call me Kenneth," he insisted. "And I'm so sorry they kept you waiting downstairs all night. That's unacceptable. I only just now learned you were there. Here we are now."

They finally arrived at the door to the chapel, but it was pitch dark inside. Kenneth O'Morchoe held out his candle as Grace felt her way carefully down the flight of wooden stairs that led to the altar at the front of the room. To her left were the rows of wooden benches where she assumed the prisoners sat during services. When they got to the altar, Officer O'Morchoe walked through a door at the other end of the room with his candle to see about having Joe brought down. Grace was left standing alone in complete darkness.

She waited for what seemed like ages, listening to muffled, distant voices, slamming metal doors, and what sounded like heavy chains dragging across stone floors. She thought again about the stone serpents over the entryway and shuddered. Joe and his friends didn't belong here. She guessed she would definitely be given some time alone with Joe, given the circumstances—when they knew she had been waiting for so long. And maybe Kenneth was right about the reprieve after all. If Joe were set free, she was sure she could nurse him back to health.

Finally she heard people speaking nearby and the sound of footsteps and chains at the door of the chapel. First came the priest and Kenneth O'Morchoe; he was still carrying the candle. Next came three soldiers followed by Joe, and then three more soldiers at his back. All six of the soldiers surrounding Joe had their large rifles ready, with bayonets fixed.

At the first glance of Joe coming through the door, Grace felt a jolt in her chest that radiated upward, bringing tears to her eyes. She wanted more than anything to be cheerful and optimistic for him, but she just felt so sad and scared. Joe was in handcuffs and leg shackles despite the numerous armed guards surrounding him, and the chains at his feet scraped and banged with hollow resonance along the wooden floor of the chapel. When she could finally see his face in the light of the single candle, her fear melted away; all she felt was the strongest urge to just hold him tightly. After such a week, she could hardly believe he was standing there right in front of her.

Despite the circumstances surrounding them, Joe smiled radiantly as the soldiers removed his handcuffs for the service. The serene elation of his bearing seemed so incongruous with the situation that she began to wonder if he had just received news that he was to be pardoned. That seemed unlikely, judging from the level of security. As she looked up into his shining dark eyes, all of these thoughts dissipated. She began to feel more at ease, even smiling back at him a little.

Once the cuffs were removed, Joe rushed to put his arms around her. She moved forward as well, with a desperate longing to feel his arms around her again, perhaps for the last time. It meant everything in the world to her at that moment. She felt that she might endure everything just to hold onto the memory of one final embrace.

But the second Joe put out his arms toward her, all six of the soldiers who were bunched around him jumped to alert, two grabbing his arms and the rest taking a step back and raising their guns. Grace stepped back in alarm. Disappointment and frustration welled up inside her. She covered her face with her hands for a moment to keep from crying.

"Gentlemen," the priest spoke quietly and raised his hand to put the soldiers at ease. "Stand down. The prisoner shows no signs of escape or attack." He turned to Joe and Grace, telling them, "Young man, young lady, I'm afraid that you will not be allowed to touch … except perhaps to hold hands—if Officer O'Morchoe will allow it." He looked sternly at Kenneth.

"Of course I … of course they can hold hands," Kenneth answered, clumsily walking the line between officer in charge and childhood friend. "Rules for visitors say that there must be space between their bodies at all times. I'm sorry. Anything else is … fine."

Grace recovered herself and took a deep breath. She held out her hands, and Joe took them both in his own. He held on tightly, looking into her eyes, and she felt safe and warm for the first time in over a week. This is how she wanted to feel for the rest of her life.

The service was the shortest possible, not more than a couple of minutes long. Joe's hands were warm in the chilled, heavy air, and his eyes never left hers as the priest read some short passages and spoke briefly. Letting go of Joe's hand reluctantly, Grace brought out the ring she had bought for herself that day and handed it to him. Following the priest's instructions, he placed it on her finger. Joe took off her family ring she had given to him upon their engagement. He gave it to her, and she placed it back on his finger, then immediately took both of his hands in hers tightly—holding onto him as desperately as if she were drowning.

Once the priest finished the ceremony, there was paperwork brought out. She had to let go again so that she and Joe could sign where they were told to. Two of the soldiers signed as witnesses, clumsily shifting their guns from arm to arm to take the pen. Then it was over.

Grace wondered what would happen next. Where would they be allowed to sit and talk now that they were married? Would they be left alone for a few moments to speak in private? She knew that some of the condemned men had been allowed to spend hours with their friends and family members in their prison cells, so now that she was Joe's wife . . .

I am Joe's wife. I am married now—a married woman. It was hard to comprehend, and although it did give her some satisfaction, she felt more excited about having some time alone with him now—her new husband.

But the soldiers were ordering Joe to let go of her hands. He wouldn't do it until they gave the order a second time, and then they were replacing the cuffs. After the cuffs were back on his wrists, she grabbed his hands, terrified that they might take him away again for the last time.

"Joe?" She looked up at him desperately, but they were already starting to lead him away. Her hands were torn from his.

"Don't worry, Grace. It'll all be fine," is all Joe had a chance to say in response as they took him away through the same door he had entered just moments before. He looked back at her until his face disappeared into the darkness of the room. Kenneth O'Morchoe told her that he would be back soon to take her out, then rushed to get ahead of the others with his candle to light their path down the maze of stone hallways. Grace stood there alone in the darkness once again, listening to the sounds of the prison.

47

Joe was alone in his cell, a married man. His prayers moved quickly between expressing his gratitude for the wedding and asking for the courage to face what would come next. But he didn't really need to pray anymore because he was prepared—already with God, in a way. When he closed his eyes, his cell seemed filled with the delicate, iridescent filigree of angels' wings. He could almost see around him the compassionate faces of Saint John of the Cross and Teresa of Avila. He felt joyful and bright, without much concern for his situation or his surroundings.

Sitting on the little wobbly wooden bench, there was just enough light from a single candle in the corridor for him to make out the shapes around him in his cell at Kilmainham Gaol. He had the place to himself this time because he was being kept in the wing where they put men due for execution; it was closer to the Stonebreakers' Yard, where they set up the firing squads. There was his single blanket lying on top of the raised planks that served as his bed. On the planks as well was a metal bowl filled with some kind of cold, pasty substance they had given him to eat with no spoon. He had to keep it on the bed because when it was placed on the floor, he heard scratching claw sounds in the dark corners of the cell and feared that the unknown substance in his bowl was bringing in uninvited guests.

But Joe felt no hunger—no discomfort of any kind. The

only thing tugging at the edges of his consciousness was a need to see more of Grace—to hold her and say something that might bring her comfort in the coming days and years. There was a selfish, childish part of him that wanted her to love him always, to never find another man that could live up to his memory or make her feel quite so loved and understood as he hoped he had.

But he knew this was wrong. In truth he knew he must hope for her to forget her love for him as soon as possible so that she could be happy and love again. Now that he had everything he could have asked for in life, he would pray for her to forget him and be happy for as long as she lived. After that? Well, he would be waiting for her.

She deserved to have a wonderful life, and as he thought about the sadness in her dark eyes when they stood in the chapel, he was aware of the fact that all her misery was of his own making. He had known from the start that it was wrong for him to tell her how he felt when he was likely to be gone so soon. If she felt anything at all for him, he was bound to make her miserable.

But he hadn't been able to keep himself from sharing his feelings for her, and he knew that he had done all he could to win her love and make her need him. As wrong as that was, the last few months with her had been better than any other time in his life, and he knew he had made her happy as well. He only hoped that she didn't now regret having known him at all.

For himself, he had no regrets. He had fulfilled his purpose and put up a good fight for his country and his generation. On top of that he had known true love. What else mattered?

He needed to be sure that Grace knew how happy he was, that she had no need to worry about him, but he had been unable to speak to her at all at their short marriage ceremony. The whole thing couldn't have been much longer than five minutes. Ever since they led him away from the chapel, he had been campaigning for just a few minutes more with her. He argued his case all the way back to his cell and asked any passing guard if a decision had been made. Would they let him see his wife just one more time before they killed him?

The executions were scheduled to start in just a couple of hours. He sat thinking of Grace and praying for her. He thought of her face in the chapel candlelight looking up at him. She had been wearing a light cotton dress and a lacy little hat that looked like springtime—so sweet and out of place in the dismal surroundings of the prison. Thinking of her now, he felt overwhelmed with gratitude that he had been able to find her and love her before dying. But he needed to tell her all of this.

"They're bringing her back," a voice interrupted his thoughts. It was one of the guards who had been in the chapel.

"Here? They're bringing her here to my cell?" Joe asked.

"Yeah. She's coming now, but you'll only have a short time."

Joe thought about how scared Grace had looked in the chapel after having been led through the cold stone passageways, and he was concerned. This cell was so much worse than anything she had seen there, and he hated for her to have to meet with him in such an awful place. But she was coming, and that was all that mattered.

Perhaps they would even have a few minutes alone this time so that they could really speak. He got to his feet as he heard a large group walking closer, and soon he could hear them coming up the long, metal stairs. He looked out the little hole in his cell door, his empty stomach tied into knots of excitement at the prospect of seeing her again.

He needed to somehow reassure Grace that he was not afraid. If she felt even half as strongly for him as he felt for her, then their next few minutes together could affect the rest of her life. How could he assure her that he was now resigned to the fact that he would die at the hands of this corrupt, invading force—that this was just the next necessary step toward Ireland's independence? She also needed her to know that nothing they could do to him would ever take him away from her side. Even after death he would be with her.

He could see the bobbing, flickering light from another candle as it reached the top of the stairs, just feet from his cell, and there was fumbling with chains and the lock on the heavy door. It swung open slowly with a painful creaking, and then she was there. She looked small and out of place surrounded by at least a dozen armed British soldiers. They all filed in with her, packing themselves into his small cell. They watched Joe warily, as if he might be capable of escape by somehow levitating and flying out of the tiny, barred window.

Grace's dark eyes were shadowed and edged in pink from long hours of crying, and they darted between the faces and rifles surrounding her at such close quarters. Joe realized with a wave of guilt what this week of rebellion had done to her. She looked exhausted, and he began to worry that she might faint. He had her sit down on the little wobbly bench and knelt on the cold stone floor beside her. The lieutenant took out a pocket watch and looked at it carefully.

"You've got ten minutes," he said without raising his eyes.

Joe took Grace into his arms, and they held each other tightly. The smell of her hair, the feel of his hands on her back and her soft face against his chest—he could hardly take it.

When they finally let go, he took both of her hands in his and looked carefully into her eyes. She was silent and pale, staring back at him with heavy, exhausted eyes.

He started talking about how hard everyone had fought at the GPO and the other garrisons—how brave they had been. He spoke of Connolly and The O'Rahilly and the other leaders. He told her how proud he was to have fought at their side. He assured her that none of their lives would be lost in vain because soon the people of Ireland would see that they were right and overthrow England's rule once and for all.

Grace didn't seem able to speak at all in front of all of the soldiers towering around them with their guns and bayonets, so Joe kept talking about the week of fighting. At one point he heard himself then, remembering the time, stopped abruptly. He meant everything he was saying, there was no doubt of that, but why was he saying it now? Why was he saying it to her in their last few moments together in this lifetime? Maybe he was speaking in defiance, trying to get a message to the armed soldiers surrounding him. Was that really how he wanted to spend his last few minutes on earth with Grace?

He took a deep breath and focused once again on her eyes. They appeared larger and darker than ever after her long night. Her skin looked like porcelain in the candlelight.

"I'm so sorry, Grace. I'm so sorry to do this to you—to leave you now, before we even had a chance to begin our life together."

She took a sudden, deep breath, as if restraining a sob, but still said nothing.

"Please understand that they can never take me away from you," he continued. "No matter what they do to me, no one can ever take me from your side. I will always be with you for as long as you want me there—maybe even longer."

Joe smiled at her, but she still sat totally still, her eyes glued to his, with silent tears streaming down her face. She usually had so much to say—so many strong opinions and viewpoints. They never seemed to have enough time to say all that they wanted to say to each other. But now, just before his death and surrounded by these strangers, she could say nothing.

"Grace, I want you to understand that I am not afraid to die. I'm ready. This might sound crazy to you, but I feel proud and honored that I have had a chance to stand up for Ireland. You know that's what I've always wanted. My only regret is that I am making you sad. I am so sorry that I dragged you into this. I had no right at all when there was always reason to believe it could end like this. I'm so sorry, Grace, and I wonder if you might possibly forgive me someday."

She took in another sudden and involuntary breath. Joe knew she was trying not to cry any harder. She leaned forward and took him in her arms again, giving up the battle against tears and sobbing against his shoulder.

"Of course, Joe, of course I forgive you," she whispered.

He pulled away from her and held onto her arms, looking directly into her eyes. "Then please know that you will never face any hardship on your own for the rest of your life. I will always be there with you. There is nothing for me in the afterlife that could compare with being at your side, and I have no reason to leave you. I will wait for you, Grace. But please make me wait a long, long time, okay? Live a good, long life." He smiled at her again and thought she almost smiled back, but then there were more tears.

"If you'll promise me now that you'll be happy, then I can die without any worries at all. Will you try? Can you promise me that you will do anything you can to move on and be happy again?" He was so scared to ask her for anything.

She nodded almost imperceptibly. "Yes, Joe, I promise. I promise I'll try," she whispered. But the look on her face made the words seem impossible.

He took her in his arms and held her tightly. "Thank you. Thank you. I love you so much."

"I love you too, Joe," she sobbed against his shoulder. "I've wanted so much to tell you all—"

"Your time is up," the lieutenant interrupted.

For a moment Grace looked like she had been slapped but she rallied quickly. She had brought a small pair of scissors in her bag, and she asked to take a lock of Joe's hair. The lieutenant agreed to wait another moment, and Grace got her scissors. Joe longed to hold her as he felt her fingers lightly touching the back of his head. He gave her his house keys and then started to take off his wedding ring. But she stopped him.

"No. No, I want you wearing it when…" She took a deep, shuddering breath. "I want you to wear it."

He took her in his arms again and held her until the lieutenant gave the order to take her away. He kept holding her until one of the armed soldiers put a firm hand on his shoulder.

When she was gone, he stood and looked through the little hole in the cell door, listening to the group's footsteps and watching as the light from the candle moved down the stairwell and disappeared.

48

Officer Kenneth O'Morchoe hadn't been able to sleep at all. After the wedding in the chapel, he had been granted a few hours off so that he could rest before the executions began in the morning. That was what was really getting to Kenneth, and it was the reason he knew he would not be getting any sleep during his break. In just a couple of hours, he was expected to command firing squads in the executions of four more prisoners. One of these men was once a good friend.

He thought of the sweet and pathetic candlelit wedding ceremony he had just seen between Joe and his fiancée. If that made it into the papers, he knew it would cause some sympathy among the people of Dublin—especially after the bridegroom's execution.

Joe was so ill anyway. Kenneth couldn't imagine that he would be ordered to go through with the execution. Surely the authorities would grant a reprieve, and this was Kenneth's only chance. The executions were scheduled to begin at three thirty in the morning, which was just a couple of hours away. Just to be safe, he had scheduled Joe's execution last.

A short time later, Kenneth was called to ready himself for service. He looked out the window as he dressed and saw that it was raining for the first time in many days. The air was so thick with moisture that everything appeared to be gray, and there was no visual separation at the horizon between the land and the sky. As he descended the stairs and walked through the stone maze of corridors, he prayed that God would see what was happening and intervene. He was greeted and saluted by men whom he didn't see and wouldn't remember passing. All of his mind was focused on getting this morning over with.

Stepping out into the clammy chill of the exercise yard, he was advised that the first of the condemned, Edward Daly, was ready and that the other three were with the priests. His heart suddenly felt too heavy to beat.

"So there will be four, as originally scheduled?"

"Yes, sir."

Standing inside the high stone walls of the yard in the pale, predawn light, it felt like all of the world must be just as gray. The yard was crowded because there were four separate firing squads—one for each execution that day—as well as many others who were assisting in the preparation.

Kenneth saw the twelve men who would serve in the second squad of the day being prepared for their turn. As an officer explained procedure, other men sat across the yard, loading guns for them. As Kenneth walked by, he heard the men on the squad being told that one of their rifles would be loaded with a blank cartridge. This way each of them could hope that he had not been the one to kill an unarmed man standing before him, bound and blindfolded. Kenneth thought absently that this might help them sleep better than he could.

He walked through an opening in the stone walls and entered the Stonebreakers' Yard, where the executions would commence, and found that everything was ready. After a few words with some of the other officers, he made the announcement that it was time to begin. The twelve men on the first squad were already there, and they moved into position, six kneeling on the cold stone and six more standing behind them. After a moment Edward Daly came into view, blindfolded, with his hands bound behind him. He was led by one of the priests and followed by two armed guards.

49

Joe stood inside with Father Sebastian, waiting for his turn to die. He was weak and heavy with exhaustion but felt no discomfort from his illness and no fear of what was to come.

The sudden burst of fire from twelve rifles at a time had given him a jolt; it was so loud and came completely without warning. But he was a little surprised that it did not scare him more profoundly. He was relieved at his lack of last-minute panic; the one thing that was left for him to do was to die with dignity. Word was getting around about the court-martial process—that all of the others had been brave and honorable. He had heard the same thing about Pearse, MacDonagh, and Clarke during their executions the previous morning.

He felt a pang of distress thinking of his best friend and the two men he so admired. He started to think about the families they were leaving behind but cut his thoughts short and took a breath, forcing himself to concentrate on the present. This moment was all he had. If he let himself focus on sadness and loss, he would soon be thinking about Grace, and that wouldn't help. That was all over for now, and he needed to focus on what was coming next. He would see Thomas soon, and he would be with Grace again someday. He was losing nothing, and within a few moments, his opportunity to represent Ireland in history would be complete.

He had done his part, and that's what mattered. He had lived through the rising and the days since the surrender.

There would be no rotting away in a cell for him, and this gave him satisfaction. He was forcing the British military to kill him outright, along with the other leaders. They thought they were punishing the rebels, but what they were really doing was assuring him a place in history. Other than having actually won the revolution, Joe couldn't think of a better ending.

In addition to this, he would soon have information that no living person could know. A philosopher and researcher, he actually found this to be exciting. He had spent so many years wanting to be closer to God and wondering what came after life on earth that he felt almost anxious to get all of this sad procedure out of the way and move on so that he could see what came next.

Everyone was so tense and exhausted. The guards had even seemed apologetic as they brought him downstairs, saying very polite things and refusing to make eye contact. Even Father Sebastian looked so sad, his eyes heavily shadowed from sleepless nights. His face was so filled with concern that it was almost as if he didn't quite believe the reassuring words he spoke so kindly. Joe caught the priest's eye and interrupted.

"Don't worry, Father. I want you to know that I am very happy. I'm dying for the glory of God and the honor of Ireland."

Just then they were told that it was time. Joe was brought into another room, closer to the yard. He took off his glasses and handed them to Father Sebastian.

"I guess I won't be needing these any longer. Could you please give them to my mother? And my wedding ring. Would you mind getting this to my wife, Grace?" He liked saying, "my wife, Grace."

He took his rosary from his pocket and hung it around his neck, holding it a final second before the guards tied his hands behind him and placed a blindfold over his eyes. The dark made him a little dizzy—unsteady on his feet—and he hoped he could make it out to the Stonebreakers' Yard. He thought for a moment of Cú Chulainn, tied to the standing stone to remain upright so his enemies wouldn't know he was dying. Joe knew he didn't have much further to go and he was determined to stay strong. The raven hadn't landed on his shoulder yet.

He felt them pinning the little piece of white cloth over his heart—the target for the firing squad. Father Sebastian took his arm to lead him.

"Thank you, Father," Joe said, stepping out into the cold rain.

50

Officer Kenneth O'Morchoe was beginning to feel a little desperate. Time was running out, and he had received no word of a reprieve for Joe. Even without his friend's execution, the last half an hour had been the worst time of his life by far. He had already led the executions of Edward Daly, Michael O'Hanrahan, and Willie Pearse, each within several minutes of each other. They had all faced death so bravely that the whole thing felt wrong and unnecessary.

When Joe walked into view, Kenneth felt like he might be sick. Straining to maintain his balance against the dizzying waves that began to heave inside his head, he came to attention and saluted his friend, drawing confused looks from the firing squad. Despite his blindfold and his bound hands, Joe walked with a pleasant ease, bringing a feeling of serenity with him across the yard. Once he was in place, standing on the same patch of stone where several of his colleagues had already died, he took a deep breath and then simply waited. He wasn't shaking or tense, and Kenneth thought he even saw a slight smile.

The squad was ready, about fifty feet from their target, six kneeling and six standing. Some of their barrels had begun to sway slightly from nerves. Even they seemed to feel that things weren't going the way they should.

Damn it, Kenneth thought. *This is it. There will be no reprieve.* He looked up to the gray sky and tried to remember to breathe. He stalled, checking the paperwork—yes, all the signatures were there. Everything was in order. He was trying to think of a way out. The situation was impossible.

"I'm sorry, but I have to go. This one's up to you," he said quietly to the officer standing near him who was the next in the chain of command.

"What? What are you talking about? You have to remain in command, or there'll be a court-martial. You could be dishonorably discharged," the other officer hissed back, trying to keep his voice very low despite his alarm.

"I'm sorry, but I can't do it. I can't kill a friend." Officer Kenneth O'Morchoe took one long last look at Joe standing calmly in front of all of those rifle barrels and then walked briskly from the yard.

51

Grace was cold and wet, but she could not bring herself to leave until she knew for certain. Officer O'Morchoe had assured her many times on their way to the chapel that there would be a reprieve for Joe. She had received no such news and did not want to let herself hope for it too badly. Standing in the courtyard at the entrance to the prison, she was directly on the other side of the high stone walls of the Stonebreakers' Yard, where the executions were taking place.

So far there had already been three sudden bursts of gunfire. They seemed to come from nowhere—there was no shouted order—and all of those guns firing at once made a terrible sound. Each thunderous volley brought astonished cries and renewed torrents of weeping from the small groups of friends, family, and supporters that huddled together in the rain.

There were four executions scheduled that morning. While it was possible that Joe was already gone, if a fourth volley sounded, then she would know for sure. If there were no more shooting, then it was possible that she and Joe would be able to start their lives together after all. She didn't want to hope that the three already killed that morning were the loved ones of the other people standing with her in the rainy stone courtyard. All the same, she couldn't help praying harder than she had ever prayed before that Joe was still alive.

Each time the guns fired, it made her jump with alarm

and then feel very faint. She wasn't sure how much longer she could stand there, and she leaned back against the cold stone wall. She knew that she was as close as she could get to where she feared Joe might be standing at that very moment.

She had no idea who had already been killed, and she had no logical reason to think that Joe was still alive. But she felt him there, just feet away from her, on the other side of the wall. He was still alive. She reached out to him in her heart, wanting him to feel her love and support at such a terrifying moment.

It seemed that it had been quite a while since the last execution, and she began to hope that perhaps the delay was due to a last-minute reprieve. She imagined a young soldier running through the rain with a letter. She pictured him out of breath and red-cheeked as he handed it to the officer in command.

Her restricted lungs allowed her a single deep breath as she leaned more heavily against the wall for support. She felt fevered and turned her face to the side, placing her cheek against the cold, wet stone. He was right there—just a few feet away—and he was still alive.

Just as she began another prayer for Joe, the fourth explosion thundered dully in the gray, predawn light.

Epilogue

The executions at Kilmainham Gaol continued for more than a week. Overall, fifteen rebels were shot and killed, including all seven who signed the proclamation. While much of Dublin's populace resented the chaos and bloodshed caused by the rising, most admired the rebels' courage in standing up against the British Empire.

While the leaders of the rising lost this battle, it can be said that they won the war. After the Irish public found out about England's rush through the courts-martial and executions, many who were initially opposed to violent insurrection began to radicalize, as they now resented British rule more than ever. They changed their views and joined the movement in support of the rebels.

In 1917 the nationalist political party Sinn Fein was established, and the independence movement intensified. When England enacted conscription in Ireland in 1918, support for Irish independence continued to grow and the Sinn Fein party won landslide victories throughout Ireland. The following year they declared their independence from the British Empire, which led to the War of Independence. In 1922 all but the six northernmost Irish states were declared a self-governing free state as a part of the controversial Anglo–Irish Treaty.

Grace Gifford was widowed just hours after her marriage to Joe Plunkett. She remained active in the nationalist movement and fought for Irish independence for the rest of her life. Joe's family refused to honor the will he wrote during the Rising that left everything to Grace, and she had very little money. Although she had many admirers, Grace never married again.

Made in the USA
San Bernardino, CA
24 April 2015